I0658594

# THE SURVIVALIST

## #25

## WAR MOUNTAIN

Books by Jerry Ahern

## The Survivalist Series

| | |
|---|---|
| #1: Total War | Mid-Wake |
| #2: The Nightmare Begins | #16: The Arsenal |
| #3: The Quest | #17: The Ordeal |
| #4: The Doomsayer | #18: The Struggle |
| #5: The Web | #19: Final Rain |
| #6: The Savage Horde | #20: Firestorm |
| #7: The Prophet | #21: To End All War |
| #8: The End is Coming | The Legend |
| #9: Earth Fire | #22: Brutal Conquest |
| #10: The Awakening | #23: Call To Battle |
| #11: The Reprisal | #24: Blood Assassins |
| #12: The Rebellion | #25: War Mountain |
| #13: Pursuit | #26: Countdown |
| #14: The Terror | #27: Death Watch |
| #15: Overlord | |

## The Defender Series

| | |
|---|---|
| #1: The Battle Begins | #7: Vengeance |
| #2: The Killing Wedge | #8: Justice Denied |
| #3: Out of Control | #9: Deathgrip |
| #4: Decision Time | #10: The Good Fight |
| #5: Entrapment | #11: The Challenge |
| #6: Escape | #12: No Survivors |

## They Call Me the Mercenary Series

| | |
|---|---|
| #1: The Killer Genesis | #10: Bush Warfare |
| #2: The Slaughter Run | #11: Death Lust! |
| #3: Fourth Reich Death Squad | #12: Headshot! |
| #4: The Opium Hunter | #13: Naked Blade, Naked Gun |
| #5: Canadian Killing Ground | #14: The Siberian Alternative |
| #6: Vengeance Army | #15: The Afghanistan Penetration |
| #7: Slave of the Warmonger | #16: China Bloodhunt |
| #8: Assassin's Express | #17: Buckingham Blowout |
| #9: The Terror Contract | |

# THE SURVIVALIST

## #25

## WAR MOUNTAIN

JERRY AHERN

SPEAKING VOLUMES, LLC
NAPLES, FLORIDA
2013

THE SURVIVALIST
#25 WAR MOUNTAIN

Copyright © 1993 by Jerry Ahern

All rights reserved. No part of this book may be reproduced
or transmitted in any form or by any means without written
permission of the author.

ISBN 978-1-61232-287-2

This is a work of fiction. All the characters and events
portrayed in this book are fictional, and any resemblance to
real people or incidents is purely coincidental.

For our buddy Mark Stricklett, who's trying very hard to get us to join the twentieth century—even though it's almost over! All the best . . .

# Prologue

John Rourke's thoughts went back to another time—his left foot stomped the clutch pedal hard to the Saab 900 Turbo's firewall, his right hand jumping the stick from fourth into second. As he revved the accelerator with the toe in order to double clutch while the heel of his right foot rode the brake, his hands wrestled the wheel into so tight a right turn that the car entered the alley on two wheels only.

Gunfire tore into the alley wall, bullets whining off the Saab's coachwork but not yet hitting a window. Rourke downshifted into first, the tachometer almost redlining before he could up-shift into second, the engine almost over-revving again before he could get into third. The alley was nearly too narrow for the Saab, but wider than Rourke would have preferred. The Mercedes from which the gunfire originated, sparks flashing from its fenders, was able to squeeze through as well. The Volvo which had blocked the road in front of him and would now turn down after the Mercedes should be a better fit still.

Rourke jacked the stick into fourth, the speedometer up to eighty-five or so he guessed; there wasn't any chance to take his eyes from his driving long enough to look. Submachine gun fire again, bullets rippling along a row of garbage cans, overturning them like a rank of dominoes.

At the end of the alley, late-evening traffic was light. Rourke was downshifting again into second, not daring to stop as he cut the wheel right and slipped between a blue delivery truck and a white Cadillac El Dorado. Rourke slipped the Saab's transmission into third, his eyes flickering toward the rear-view mirror, then the side-views. The Mercedes had turned out after him, and the green Volvo was beside it in the next lane out from the curb.

Traffic stopped for a red light.

He knew Munich not at all, really, and literally had no better idea of where he was at the moment than that he was "downtown" and his hotel wasn't in sight. On the other hand, the men who followed him almost assuredly knew the city reasonably well.

John Rourke's right hand slipped to his trouser waistband, finding the butt of the SIG-Sauer P-228 9mm. Celluloid superspies notwithstanding, it was only possible to bring one's own weapons along when one was illegally inserted into a foreign country or was working officially with the country's own secret service. This situation fit neither scenario.

Rourke was in Munich for the sole purpose of contacting a former KGB officer named Plotkin. Yuri Plotkin, on the other hand, was in Munich out of fear for his life. Plotkin was being hunted by the neo-Nazi underground because he carried in his head the names of powerful and highly placed European community leaders on whom the KGB had developed dossiers, the data therein implicating them as Nazi sympathizers, people who in the days before World War II would have been called "fifth columnists."

It was Rourke's mission to rendezvous with Plotkin—once he was able to refix his position and elude his pursuers (but not in that order)—so that Plotkin could download the information in his head then get out along an escape route the CIA had established for the Russian by way of returning the favor.

The very night of Rourke's arrival in Munich, he made his prearranged meeting with the local CIA station chief, Bernie Twillinger, at the bar in the touristy restaurant in his hotel. Twillinger gave Rourke the rendezvous time and place for meeting Yuri Plotkin, as well as keys to the Saab, but not a gun.

"Gun's in the car?"

"This should be a pretty clean job, Dr. Rourke, not what you're used to in Latin America,"

Twillinger laughed. "So, relax. You won't need a gun."

"I want a gun anyway."

"I can't get you one until tomorrow night."

"I'll make it through the night. Try for a .45 or a .357."

"I don't know very much about guns. Those are automatics, aren't they?"

Rourke exhaled, perhaps a little too loudly, too obviously. "The .45s can be either, and if you count the Desert Eagle, so can .357s. Want me to write a shopping list?" Rourke took the cocktail napkin from beside his double shot of Seagram's Seven and a pen from his pocket, then began to write as he spoke. "You won't find a Detonics that easily, so try for a Colt, either a Commander or a Government Model in .45 ACP. If you can't find either of those, get an L-Frame Smith & Wesson—a 681 or a 686 with a four-inch barrel—or a Colt Python, and those are .357 Magnums. Okay? Here." And, Rourke folded the napkin then handed it to Twillinger. "And I'll need the gun tomorrow morning, along with fifty rounds of ammo. If you get one of the .45 automatics, try to find me some extra magazines."

"Those are clips, right?"

"Not really, but you've got the general idea all right," Rourke said patiently.

"You won't be seeing our man until tomorrow night."

"Need time to clean the gun, check that it works properly." Rourke also intended to check out the rendezvous site before darkness masked anything he would be better off knowing about. That little detail, however, was nothing that concerned Bernie Twillinger. "So, tell me about Plotkin and these Nazis." There was a bossa nova playing over a speaker system, but barely audible. And that was a pity, because it was one of the works of Antonio Carlos Joabim—and John Rourke had always been a fan.

But he pushed the strains of "Desafinado" out of his consciousness and listened to Twillinger. "The Nazis aren't as big a deal as some people make them out to be."

"Is that official or only opinion, Bernie?"

"I work in Munich all the time, Dr. Rourke, and I feel I have a pretty good handle on things. The Nazis break down into three categories, really, the old guys who were Nazis during the War, the political theorists who banter over philosophy, and the skinhead types looking to bash some luckless Jew with a paving stone."

"You're wrong, Bernie. The philosophers are worth worrying over, because men die but ideas frequently don't die with them. Have three Nazis—the really dedicated ones who feel they're saving the white race or some shit like that—and you've got a plot. They're like fleas on a dog, because as long as they're left untreated they'll multiply until they become more of a threat than an annoyance. Remember the old Sax Rohmer character, Fu Manchu?"

"I suppose, why?"

"Well, the world will hear from the Nazis again, too."

11

"You and Plotkin should get along famously, Doctor."

"We'll see," Rourke told Twillinger, then sipped at his drink.

In the morning, there was a package at the hotel's front desk, inside it a SIG-Sauer P-228 (neither .45 nor .357, but perfectly adequate), one spare thirteen-round magazine and a box of 115 grain JHP Federal 9BPs, the only 9mm Parabellum load John Rourke ever bothered with.

Feeling brighter about the gun (the firearms-ignorant Bernie Twillinger could have brought him a .25 auto or something), Rourke disassembled the pistol, verifying its condition as much as he could without test-firing it. Totally unwittingly, Rourke was sure, Twillinger had provided one of the few semiautomatic pistols in which one could have virtually perfect confidence right out of the box.

The gun and the loaded spare magazine with him, Rourke went downstairs again and had breakfast, returning to his room to defecate, then make a telephone call to his wife. "So, how are the kids?"

"Michael's still fascinated with having a baby sister."

"Hope that lasts," Rourke told his wife.

"Sometimes brothers and sisters can be friends, like husbands and wives—sometimes."

"I'll be home soon."

"Why do you bother, John? I mean, for a man

of your skills to be zipping around the world chasing—who are you chasing today?"

"You know I can't—"

"Sorry, I forgot it's like being married to somebody who's in the Mafia or something. Keep the women ignorant. I forgot to ask! Is it time to get me pregnant again?"

"Sarah!"

"Look, you know I love you, but that's not our problem. Be careful. Annie's screaming like she's got her pants full."

"Fine. Love you too."

"Bye." She hung up.

John Rourke lit one of his small, thin, dark tobacco cigars and went to the window, staring out over the unfamiliar city. By nine in the evening, at least one section of it would be familiar enough.

As John Rourke took the Saab gently through the intersection, the light finally turned green, and he began looking for the few recognizable landmarks from his scouting foray during the afternoon. He didn't want to find them, lead the Nazis who pursued him—in a rather subdued manner now, to be sure—to where Yuri Plotkin was supposed to be. The cathedral steeple, the cafe sign, the fountain—none of these were in evidence, so Rourke's mind returned to the business at hand, the men in the black Mercedes and the lime green Volvo.

Rourke lit one of his cigars in the blue-yellow flame of his battered old Zippo windlighter, rolling down the window and feeling the slap of night air on his face. He smiled, thinking that he could always let one of the two pursuit cars pull up alongside, then, just like in the mustard commercials, lean his head out and ask to borrow some—he smiled, but doubted there was sufficient cross-culturalization for them to get the point. However, the idea might work as a means of killing some of them.

That there were no police following him was amazing; either that or indicative of the fact that Plotkin's intimations about official cooperation—at least at some levels—with the Nazis erred only in that they were conservative. It was possible that the men following him had some fix in with the local police, or at least with a few key officials.

Traffic was still moderate to light, as Rourke, keeping the Saab revving high in second, cruised along the street. There were illuminated windows, the shops behind them closed for the evening; and virtually every category of humanity Rourke could imagine walked the night, ranging from two rather obvious transvestites, to teens on the cutting edge of bizarre fashion, replete with Mohawk-style hair, colored purple or flame red, and blue jeans which were so full of holes they looked as if they'd been used for pattern-testing buckshot from a riot gun.

He was coming up to another light and the Mercedes was still behind him, but the Volvo was starting to pull up alongside. Rourke kept his window down, and the SIG was in his right fist the instant after he reset the gearshift into first.

14

The Volvo stopped beside him, windows down. Rourke turned his head and looked directly into the front seat. Two men, a little less than classic Aryan in appearance, looked straight ahead. In the back seat there sat a third man, something bundled in his arms—probably a submachine gun.

The man in the passenger seat, without even looking Rourke's way, said in a loud voice, "Doctor, you will turn right at the corner here and you will be followed. Should you do other than turn right, you will be shot." The man who'd spoken cocked his head toward the rear seat and now Rourke, as his eyes followed, verified that, indeed, the bundle was a submachine gun. Rourke almost laughed. The Jew-hating Aryan supermen were using an Israeli Uzi.

John Rourke mentally shrugged, then brought the SIG up to the level of his own chest and double-actioned the trigger, putting a bullet into the left temple of the man who'd spoken to him, blood and brain matter splattering the man behind the wheel. The left temple, aside from being convenient from Rourke's position, made an ideal target in that there was a bright red mark there, perhaps a forceps scar from his birthing process. But Rourke's attention immediately went elsewhere as he pivoted in his seat and fired two shots fast, the first into the thorax, the second into the mouth of the man in the back seat who was holding the Uzi. Rourke rotated slightly forward and fired a fourth shot as the Volvo's driver started to cross against the still-red traffic light.

The Volvo shot forward, the dead man slumped over the wheel, his right foot apparently stomping down in a death rictus over the accelerator.

Rourke's right thumb worked down his pistol's decocking lever and he slipped the firearm under his right thigh as his hand moved to the Saab's stick. But his feet were already working, his left hand cranking the wheel into a hard right.

The Volvo was into the middle of the intersection now, stopped in its tracks as it kissed bumpers with a bus. Rourke caught it in the Saab's passenger side side-view mirror as he finished the turn, already upshifting into second.

The Mercedes was right behind him.

But John Rourke had planned ahead.

His left hand caught the Saab's steering wheel into a tight right as he threw the stick into neutral and hauled up on the emergency brake. Rourke grabbed for the pistol and threw himself from behind the wheel, half falling into the street as the Mercedes slammed the Saab broadside.

The Saab skidded. Rourke ran. The Mercedes's radiator dumped its load into the street, a gusher of steam shooting upward as engine compartment met unibody construction support post.

Rourke wheeled, steadying his breathing as he aimed for the already shattered windshield, the Mercedes's driver's head partially through it.

Ten rounds remained in the SIG's original magazine. He used them, firing through the hole in the windshield and putting a bullet through the forehead of the driver. Rourke pivoted left, firing as the passenger-side door opened, killing the man there with two shots in the chest before the man's pistol—in the instant Rourke saw it the gun looked like a Walther P-38—could fire.

Seven rounds left. Rourke advanced on the Mercedes. As in the Volvo, there was a man in the rear seat, and like that man from the Volvo this man was armed with an Uzi submachine gun. Unlike the man from the Volvo, the man in the back seat of the Mercedes already had the gun up and ready.

As he started to fire from the driver's side rear door of the Mercedes, Rourke dodged left, behind the Saab. The glass in the Saab's "station-wagon back" (as the rear hatch was called ever since the old days of the Saab 99s and, perhaps before) shattered.

Rourke edged along the driver's-side left fender, keeping the engine block between him and the submachine gunner. The man was firing rapidly, long, ragged bursts, that would burn out the Uzi's magazine in seconds if the fellow maintained the same pace between the bursts. The thing with an Uzi, however, was that magazines were available in various capacities. Rourke once knew a man who had banked on just that, firing exactly twenty rounds from a thirty-two round magazine, then pausing while his foe approached, thinking the gun was shot dry, that only a twenty-round magazine was utilized. The remaining twelve rounds in the thirty-two-round stick ended the fight.

Rourke had no intention of making the same mistake.

There was a long burst which seemed to choke off prematurely.

Rourke had no choice but to assume that the incompetent firing technique so far displayed was real, and that the man had emptied his gun. Rourke jumped up onto the hood of the Saab, took one long step and was onto the twisted hood of the Mercedes. He bounded up onto the roof of the Mercedes as the submachine gunner was ramming the fresh magazine up the butt of his weapon.

Rourke didn't let him finish it.

The SIG in John Rourke's right hand fired, six rounds into face and neck.

Still standing on the roof of the black Mercedes, John Rourke thumbed the magazine release catch and did a tactical magazine change, replacing the spent magazine with the spare, thirteen rounds loaded now plus one in the chamber.

He jumped from the roof of the Mercedes—careful lest he twist an ankle—and ran. At last, police sirens were wailing in the night. He ducked into an alley at the middle of the block, thumbing down the de-cocker, shoving the pistol into his belt. Holding the empty magazine in his left hand, he loaded fresh loose rounds from the side pocket of his jacket with his right, still keeping a decent pace until he reached the end of the alley.

John Rourke stood there, catching his breath for an instant, continuing to insert fresh rounds beneath the magazine's feed lips. The sirens were louder now, despite the fact that he'd put some distance between himself and the two carloads of dead Nazis.

As he looked in both directions from the end of the alley, he spotted a fountain, and a cathedral spire.

"Plotkin," Rourke whispered, then started walking, pocketing the magazine and straightening his tie. It would be a walk of several blocks, but on the plus side, the walk would afford him time to be certain that he wasn't being followed again.

Two blocks past the cathedral, a magnificent old structure which looked almost too stereotypical to be genuine, he turned left down a wide street dotted with seen-better-days buildings of considerable age, all leaning against each other, it seemed, as if no one of them was able to stand alone. At the center of the block was the address he sought, but he didn't turn in.

Five minutes later, after walking round the block and checking both entrances to the building, John Rourke at last entered through the front doorway of the rooming house. If there was trouble in store, he'd rather have it when there was a wide street behind him rather than a narrow alleyway which could easily be cut off.

There were no doorbells, mailboxes or any other means of identification, but he already knew what he needed. Plotkin's room was on the third floor, overlooking the street, the second door from the stairwell.

John Rourke took the staircase slowly, but mounted the low treads two at a time, his eyes alternating from above and below him to the treads themselves, lest one were rigged with an alarm or a trip wire.

He found nothing out of the ordinary. When he reached the fourth-floor landing (as an American would reckon it), Rourke turned into the third-floor corridor. The hallway was long, running from side to side of the building, illuminated only by a bare bulb at the exact center. Plaster peeled within the gaps where paint—a kind of induction-center green—had once been. The runner of threadbare carpet was grey.

He went to the second door on the left, raising his left hand to rap on the door, his right hand behind him, holding the SIG.

After he rapped twice, the door opened a crack, a face peering through the crack. Rourke recognized the face from his briefing materials. "Plotkin, I'm Rourke, sent to work with you." Then, Rourke began the obligatory recognition routine. "Munich is lovely this time of year; what a pity I'm here on business."

"You would like the Alpine villages even more, I think."

"But I'd be doubly sad that I had no time away from my work."

"Life is a contradiction, isn't it?"

Rourke exhaled. "I hate those things."

"The ones in the KGB were worse, American. Wait a moment until I slip the chain." The door shut, then opened, and Rourke started inside, expecting what he saw next: Plotkin was halfway across the room, the pistol in his hand trained on Rourke's chest. "Tell me about yourself."

"Why should I, Yuri? If I'm not your American contact, then I'd probably know more about John Rourke than you do, so what good would it do?" Rourke's gun was still in his right fist, behind his back, and he would have guessed Plotkin knew it.

The pistol Plotkin held was a Ruger Standard Model .22, with the barrel replaced by one incorporating an integral silencer. Such weapons were made for the Special Forces and CIA during the Vietnam War. If this wasn't one of them, it was a clone. "Tell me something so I will not feel stupid for believing you are who you say you are."

"How about, I was followed by six men in two cars, one of the cars a lime green Volvo, the other one a black Mercedes." Plotkin's whole body tensed like a coiled spring. And then Rourke had a flash of inspiration. "None of the men looked particularly noteworthy except the man in the front passenger seat of the Volvo had a dull red birthmark—or something like it—at his left temple. I noticed it when I shot him."

"Gorin!"

" 'Gorin' doesn't sound too terribly Germanic, Plotkin."

"I do not know what he is, except that he is a devil!"

"Was," John Rourke corrected.

"Then—"

"All six men are dead or dying, but I'd bet on dead. Does that make you feel better?"

Plotkin lowered the muzzle of his gun. "I learned in my youth never to feel better because of a man's death. What is it the poet said?"

"Something about how each man's death diminishes me, you mean? John Donne. And, lest we forget and waste too much time, the passage goes on with, 'Send not to know for whom the bell tolls—' "

" '—It tolls for thee,' " Plotkin supplied.

"Yes. So, you have a list and I have an escape route. I have a feeling I'll be using it, too. I should be hot with the police and the Nazis by now."

"Do you have a notebook?"

Rourke, the pistol still in his right hand, looked at Plotkin's gun, then into Plotkin's eyes. "I pride myself on a good deal of ambidexterity, but it will take longer for me to copy down the names you're about to give me if I have to keep a gun in my hand."

Plotkin set down his pistol, then opened his hands, palms outward, toward John Rourke. "I learned to believe in God, too, over the years. May He help me if you are not who you say."

"And may He help us both to get out of Germany alive, hm?" Rourke belted his pistol, took out his notebook and his pen and relit the cigar that was in the corner of his mouth. "Don't mind, do you?"

Plotkin lit a cigarette, sat down on the edge of the bed and began to recite the list of names. . .

* * *

There was nothing to do but wait, sleeping in shifts for an hour at a time, thinking. To light a fire would have been madness. So, they waited in the cold, their stolen staff car more than a mile back and well below them, nearer to the battlefield than Rourke himself wanted to be. Deitrich Zimmer's Nazi forces had attacked the Nazi-like forces of a government which predicated its existence on warfare which did not exist. And, here was the first test. There might be the tendency for the defenders of the mountain city to congratulate themselves for having driven back the attack, but only if they were truly fools. Deitrich Zimmer's forces had probed the enemy, confirming whatever data Zimmer already might have possessed, making certain that Zimmer's superior technology and superior forces would prevail against the claustrophobic government here.

And, such would be the case.

Already, as Rourke watched through his binoculars, he could see Zimmer's land forces massing into a complex attack formation. And, soon the attack—perhaps a final attack—would begin.

After escaping the first battle, John Rourke and Paul Rubenstein had driven their captured vehicle as far as they dared, then abandoned it, moving on foot deeper into the mountains in search of a secure hiding place where they could wait.

And, while they waited, Rourke watched and remembered. The affair in Munich had been John Rourke's first encounter with Nazis, but certainly not the first encounter for the Rourke family. Rourke's father, in the United States Office of Strategic Services during World War II, had worked behind the lines in Europe and, for a period of three years, fought Nazis on an almost daily basis.

John Rourke's father spoke little of his experiences in those days, but those few of his friends who had survived, whom John Rourke had met while he was growing up, often did.

Time was of the essence now, but there was no way of telling when the forces of the Trans-Global Alliance would be able successfully to insert an aircraft and get them out of here. So, there was nothing to do but wait, rest—wait some more.

When the pickup came, they would be off to Deitrich Zimmer's headquarters at sixty-two degrees north longitude, one hundred and eighteen degrees west latitude. Sarah Rourke and Wolfgang Mann waited there. So did many nightmares.

# Chapter One

Was this consciousness, or a dream? Was this death? Her last memory was holding her new-born son clutched in her arms as a tall, evilly beautiful man aimed a gun at her head. And then there were swirling blurs, fragments of awareness, then dreams from which she never seemed to awaken. Now this. It was as if she were looking in a mirror and the mirror image was somehow able to move independently of her, while she herself could not move, could not even speak. She could open her eyelids and close them, the rest of her body numb and dead-seeming to her. Except for the dull throbbiing of her head.

She ached there.

"You are watching me, aren't you? I don't blame you. It's not every day you see yourself, is it? And, that's who I am. I'm you, but a little different. You make Penelope—wife of Ulysses—look like she was playing around, for goodness' sake. What kind of a woman are you? A glutton for punishment, I'd say. But, if you ever harbored any thoughts of getting even, hey, don't worry. I'll do it for you."

She wanted to ask the woman in the mirror who she was, even though she knew the woman was her. But she couldn't speak, couldn't do anything except blink.

"I'll bet you're confused, Sarah. Well, don't be! Because I'm Sarah, now. And I'm part of you, am you, really, except for a few differences. So, don't worry. I'm the latest model." And the woman who was her but wasn't, looked away, smiled, reached out her hand. A man's hand grasped her hand. "Wanna meet somebody?"

A man's face appeared in the mirror, the face instantly recognizable, yet not. It was John's face, or maybe Michael's face, but it wasn't either of them. "This is your son, in a way, but not really."

Sarah's head ached all the more and she wanted to close her eyes, drift back into the other nightmares, any one of them, because they were better than this.

But the Sarah in the mirror said, "Hey, now! You want to see your little boy, huh? This is Martin. I mean, it really isn't Martin, but he is. Just like I'm Sarah, do you see?"

Sarah Rourke finally could not stand it, closed her eyes, kept them closed. But there was only the pain, no fresh nightmare, and she kept seeing the mirror image, her own, and that of someone named Martin who looked just like her husband and her son but wasn't either of them . . .

His face was identical to that of Martin, which one time, early in her conscious life, a few days ago, she had seen with three different expressions all at once. One of them, Dr. Zimmer told her, was really Martin, but the others almost were. John was falling right into Dr. Zimmer's trap, following Dr. Zimmer's plan as slavishly as if he were one of the clones.

She asked him that. "Excuse me, Dr. Zimmer, but why don't you clone my husband and then you could use him, too?"

"I like it, Sarah, that you think of him as your husband. I truly do. And, as a matter of fact, I have considered your proposal. How would it be, for example, if John Thomas Rourke denounced the Trans-Global Alliance? Or, if he shot to death his Jew friend, Rubenstein? Hm? The possibilities are endless, not to mention that some of them are quite potentially beneficial and amusing. Let us just say for now that I have a number of options open to me, just as I did when I learned that 'your husband' was on the loose again. Leave it at that, my dear."

One of the Martins—no one would tell her which was which—added, "My father has some marvelous surprises in store, Mother dear." Was it Martin or an "Almost-Martin" who called her his mother?

"Almost-Sarah" brushed her hair, staring at herself in the mirror. The real Sarah could have been strikingly beautiful, and Almost-Sarah wanted to be. But Sarah—the original—was always too busy being Sarah to bother.

Almost-Sarah knew every detail of the life Sarah Rourke had lived. Although Almost-Sarah had no experiences by which she could actually compare (she was actually a virgin, although surgically refined so she would not appear so, and possessed of the real Sarah's memories), John Rourke, when he was around, was magnificent. It was hard for Almost-Sarah to imagine that anyone could be better sexually than he. He was so much a man, so perfect. And, of course, as Dr. Zimmer had explained, his perfection was his flaw, his weakness.

Almost-Sarah had memories of John Rourke naked beside her in bed, his organ brushing against her as he would roll over in the night. And these memories stirred her now as she examined her body in the mirror. But they were not her memories, really, because he had never made love to her, only to the real Sarah. And the real Sarah had never been with another man. So, perhaps any comparison was impossible.

Almost-Sarah's only real memory of "her husband" was a peek she sneaked when he came to sit at her bedside and wept that she lay comatose. She longed for him to touch her, not just hold her hand, and although she would do as Deitrich Zimmer had programmed her to do, trained her how to do, she would not be denied what she had

28

so suddenly come to crave. There were living creatures—some of these in the insect world—who killed after intercourse. And, she doubted that this would be a first among humankind.

After all, no one deserved death so richly, and with such magnificent irony.

She began to dress, still pondering whether or not Dr. Zimmer had cloned John Rourke. After all, his people had gotten into the secret hiding place for the cryogenic chambers all by prearranged plan, opened the real Sarah's chamber, just as they had Wolfgang Mann's, and taken cell samples, then resealed the chambers. What was to say that Rourke himself wasn't sampled, then cloned?

The process, she knew from the real Sarah's memories, was begun in the mid-twentieth century, with simple creatures, such as frogs. Almost-Sarah had never seen a frog through her own eyes, but recalled them vividly in memory when Michael, just a tot then, had raised tree frogs and she—the real Sarah—and John had gone all over creation it seemed in order to find live crickets for the frogs to eat. Almost-Sarah found herself smiling, remembering the time that the container of crickets tipped over and the little creatures were everywhere and all of them—except Annie who was too little then—had crawled around the floor on hands and knees, finding the crickets, picking them up and replacing them in the bait container.

John took Michael onto one knee and her onto the other, holding them both. Then she heard

Annie crying from the bedroom and went to change her and—Almost-Sarah shook her head, reminding herself consciously who she was, and who she wasn't.

As she zipped the coveralls closed, she refocused on the cloning process, still trying to understand Dr. Zimmer's overall plan. For example, as she well knew, the Wolfgang Mann clone Dr. Zimmer sent along on the expedition was expected to be discovered, his programming left imperfect.

The programming was, of course, the key to cloning's utility. Complex organisms were harder to clone than simple ones, but what had really prevented twentieth-century scientists and those in the intervening centuries from pressing onward were moral questions. The clone, albeit that it was made from the cells of the original organism, was a living, sentient being. As such, it could not be dismissed.

Dr. Zimmer had no such moral obligations. And Almost-Sarah felt a chill along her spine when she considered the real Sarah's set of memories and values—perhaps what the concept of "conscience" really meant. But her programming allowed her to resolve the moral conflict.

Almost-Sarah looked at herself once more in the mirror, then started from her room and down the corridor. She was about to check into a cell.

Why hadn't Dr. Zimmer just killed the Rourke family, instead of cloning them? If there was time and opportunity to take cell samples while they were in cryogenic sleep, then there was certainly an equal amount of time and opportunity for a lethal injection, even something as simple as a hypodermic filled with air that would cause an embolism when the air bubble reached the heart.

Dr. Zimmer had some sort of master plan, she knew, and he wasn't about to reveal it to anyone, except perhaps to the real Martin, who hadn't been out of the headquarters, as she understood it, for more than a year, his cloned doubles filling in for him.

What if Dr. Zimmer just died of a heart attack or something? Perfectly natural causes, she thought. He'd have to have told somebody. That only made sense.

But then the chill came again, making her body twitch with it. What if Dr. Zimmer would never die because he had had himself cloned, and would simply replace organs as required and, if necessary, simply have his mind programmed into a waiting clone kept in suspended animation, having a new, young body? He could go on forever, until time itself ended.

Martin, too, could live forever.

And, Almost-Sarah realized, so could she, if she did things just right and was very, very smart.

# Chapter Two

Wolfgang Mann was instantly alert, but didn't move. He had been lying on the quite comfortable cot in his padded cell, sleeping, but sleeping as he had always when in a combat zone, on one level of consciousness still alert to what was around him. The soft tones of the combination on his cell door being worked were what had brought him fully from sleep, but he pretended to sleep still.

The door opened outward and he could not help himself as he exclaimed, "My God, Sarah!" She half stumbled into the cell and Mann was to his feet instantly—catching her in his arms before she fell—holding her there for an instant—helping her to the other cot. "Sarah! You are alive!"

"Wolf? Wolf? Is it really—"

"Yes. I grew up an atheist, learned of God, and still I did not know. But I was praying, actually praying, that somehow you would be alive, that the cryogenic process had—but the bullet?"

Sarah's eyes looked past him. "Dr. Zimmer. The same bastard who shot me and took my baby—he saved my life, Wolf. I don't know why. But he's got to be up to something. But he operated on me and took out the bullet. I don't know when that was, but I've been in a kind of hospital up until just a few minutes ago. One of the doctors said I was well, my old self, said I could join my friend."

"Sarah!" Wolfgang Mann felt like a fool for not being able to say anything else but her name, but love could make men fools, he knew, or make them heroes.

Now that she was here, it was time for the latter if somehow he would be able to save her life.

His own life did not matter.

"How are you, Wolf?"

"Me?" Mann laughed, took his cigarette case and his lighter, the only personal possessions they had left him, then lit a cigarette. "I had a terrible headache when I first came out of the Sleep, and I was very weak, of course. But, you, you are alive, you seem your old self. I thought you would never recover, and that—"

"Did you really think that?" Sarah asked him, touching his face, her hand cool against his cheek. "Then why did you Sleep? And was it just you?"

"No, your husband was critically injured, but perhaps he has been restored as well. As to Michael and Annie and Paul—"

"Maybe we'll all be together again, if we ever get out of here. But why did you take the Sleep, Wolf?"

Mann inhaled deeply on his cigarette, looked away, stood up, paced beside his own cot. "Suffice it to say, Sarah, that I was a very lonely person, my wife dead, my battles fought—at least so I supposed. And—"

"Be honest with me, Wolf. Maybe this is all the time we'll ever have."

Wolfgang Mann turned around and looked at her. "All right. So, I will speak from my heart. I found myself fallen in love with you, which was hopeless, I knew, but I could not help myself. So, I took the Sleep in the hope that someday I would be near you, hear your voice, feel your touch—" And Wolfgang Mann laughed, the sound of it bitter to him. "And, here we are, are we not? The ultimate irony, hm?"

He looked away from her, not certain of his self-control, certain only that he was a fool.

# Chapter Three

Alan Crockett's horse, Wilbur, shook its massive head as Crockett reined him in. "Easy boy."

Emma Shaw's gloved hands tensed as she felt Crockett's body go tense under them. They were riding double and the only way successfully to do that was to hold on to the one who was in the saddle; in that way a horse was very much like the Harley-Davidson motorcycle John Rourke had told her about.

Crockett swung his right leg over the horse's neck and slipped down from the saddle. Emma pushed herself over the cantle and into the saddle, where the bedroll was tied in front of the horn. But as Emma Shaw started down, Crockett told her, "No, you stay mounted and wait here for me. If anything goes wrong, all the information I've collected these past three years and haven't been able to get back as intell to ONI in Honolulu is on laser discs in my saddlebags. It'll be your job to get it to the rendezvous. There's a map in the saddlebags, too. My last position—the camp from last night—is marked. If you can fly one of the new Blackbirds, then you can pilot a horse to a set of ground coordinates, okay?"

"Not okay at all, Professor Crockett! If that's who you really are!" She jumped down from the saddle, Wilbur skittering away a few feet. "We're in the middle of a war zone, enemy forces—we don't even know whose—all round us and you're going off somewhere? Bullshit!"

"Look, Commander. You are not in charge of me! Is that clearly understood? In fact, one of the principal tenets of my agreement with your Navy—"

"My Navy!"

"Whoever's Navy, then, but one of the operating principles agreed upon at that time was my complete autonomy to function however I saw fit while in the field. Is that clear to you, Commander? I didn't vanish from sight three years ago in order to get myself killed recklessly in what amounts to the final hours of my mission, so if it's some female instinct that's causing you such concern—"

"Look, Jack—"

"It's Alan, as you well know, Miss Shaw."

"Touché, already!"

"Fourteen days, Commander, is just enough

time to get ourselves killed if we hide with our heads in this proverbial sand."

"What are you talking about?"

Alan Crockett exhaled loudly, shaking his head as he told her, "Prior to the Night of the War, as it's commonly called, there was indigenous to Africa a great bird called the ostrich, its plumage at one time so much sought-after by foolish women as a means of adorning even stupider hats that the creature was nearly driven to extinction."

"I know about ostriches and I don't wear funny hats, Mack!"

"Alan, Miss Shaw. The name is Alan. My point, however, doesn't pivot on whether or not your particular concept of fashion happens to include silly hats. I am saying that we cannot afford to go through this territory blind to what there is around us, and that if we do we will surely perish. Each time I go out to reconnoiter, there is a chance, however slight, that I will not return, hence my warning."

The noise which had stopped them originally was increasing. It sounded as though somehow the size of the military force at the height of the high canyon wall to the south had grown almost exponentially. "Fine, then I'll wait, but be careful."

"That is most touching, Commander," Crockett smiled, his moustache making him look like a character out of a Victorian novel when he did so. She was not about to explain to him that she would have said the same thing to anybody, but assumed he knew that. "I'll return, but should I somehow be prevented from doing so, follow the map, reach the LZ in time and not before and don't forget about Wilbur. He's a fine animal."

"The last horse that got special treatment after the death of his rider, if memory serves," Emma Shaw told him, "was the one belonging to George Armstrong Custer. And, we all know what happened to him, don't we?"

"And touché to you, madame." Crockett took one of the two long guns from the protected saddle scabbards, one of these on either side of the rig. She had noticed the guns earlier, when they'd first seen daylight on the canyon floor, commenting to him that he had a rather odd choice in armament. He'd told her, "Not really. The guns are ideal for my circumstances." One of the guns was like John Rourke's rifle, a Lancer duplicate of the Heckler & Hoch HK-91 in 7.62mm NATO (so designated because it at one time was the official cartridge of the pre-War alliance). The other rifle was a .54-caliber Hawken, fitted with a percussion lock. He patiently explained, obviously thinking she knew next to nothing about guns, "You see, at times over these three years, I've run out of ammunition for the HK, once even for my revolver. And, it's no trick to run out of percussion caps, even though I can make them. But, it's far simpler to be able to switch from a percussion lock to a flintlock. I can fabricate my own powder in the field, if need be, you see, and flint can be obtained as well. So, I'm never without a firearm."

As he started up into the rocks along the canyon wall, she was going to ask him why he had taken the Hawken, his powderhorn and a possibles bag instead of the more modern cartridge weapon and some spare magazines, but Emma Shaw already knew the answer.

It was because she was a "girl" and he was a "gentleman" and, in the event he did not return, he was leaving her with the more practical of the weapons, under the circumstances at least.

Emma Shaw stroked Wilbur's muzzle, her eyes following Alan Crockett's movements as long as she could.

She'd learned also that Crockett was never without an ultrasmall vid-disc camera, and he would record whatever he saw at the summit for subsequent analysis. He was, of course, just doing his job by risking his neck, in much the same manner she'd nearly gotten herself killed during the bombing run on the gas factory at Eden City.

Crockett—and she was convinced he really was Professor Alan Crockett—was sometimes called "a modern-day John Rourke" and the comparison was apt. Although she didn't find him as desirable, she did find him nearly as irritating.

# Chapter Four

Paul Rubenstein awakened John Rourke carefully. He'd learned more than six centuries ago, in the immediate aftermath of the Night of the War, not to go up and just tap him on the shoulder when they were in dangerous circumstances. He merely whispered, "John." And John Rourke's eyes opened instantly.

But, he didn't sit up. The only detectable movement was the muzzle of a gun, this time in his pocket. It would be the little Smith & Wesson revolver John had lately taken to carrying in addition to his regular guns. "What is it?"

"Apparently Zimmer's SS Alpine Corps is looking for additional entrances to the mountain. Anyway, eight men are coming right toward us, about a half mile down."

John Rourke sat up, exhaled, then seemed to inhale quite deeply. As he exhaled, he spoke, "We'll have to be very silent about it, if we can't avoid a confrontation. Any word on a pickup, yet?"

"No, not yet." As soon as they'd taken this position on the mountainside and had the opportunity of surveying the terrain on the other side— it was suitable if the pilot knew his stuff—they'd called in for a V-Stol pickup. Helicopter transport would be too slow if detected, never have a chance to escape the fighter aircraft from Zimmer's force, which was still assembling outside the mountain community.

"I'll have a look," John told him, getting up into a crouch and starting to take out his binoculars.

Paul Rubenstein settled back against a rock and waited, wishing he still smoked.

This had all started out badly. First, of course, Sarah was shot in the head moments after delivering a child during an attack by the Nazis on Eden City more than a century ago, John himself was so critically injured as well that the only chance for either of them was cryogenic Sleep. They were placed in the Sleep in hopes that they would be kept from slipping closer to death, and that possibly the Sleep's restorative powers would at least help bring John back.

That happened, but there was still no hope for Sarah when all of them took the Sleep. Except for Sarah and Generaloberst Wolfgang Mann— no one talked about it, but it seemed obvious that

41

he loved Sarah and volunteered for the Sleep in order to be with her if or when she someday awakened—all of them had awakened just a short while ago. They found the world once again on the brink of war and destruction. And John, always respectful of Sarah, left Wolfgang Mann in the Sleep in the event that she would someday wish to return the German officer's love.

Then, of course, there was the business with Martin, the son stolen from John and Sarah just after his birth, thought dead, but in reality kidnapped by Deitrich Zimmer, raised as Zimmer's son, genetically altered so that his makeup not only included that of his birth parents but also of one of the blood relatives of Hitler.

And then the current crisis. Michael was in cryogenic Sleep, pretending to be Martin, who was now dead, dying accidentally when he and his father, John Rourke, fought. Martin was a brutish dictator and had, in the final moments before he fell from the open fuselage of a V-Stol, attempted to kill everybody aboard the aircraft with which he and the others had just been rescued from death.

In order to make Deitrich Zimmer think that his "son," Martin, was still alive, and thus trade for Sarah's life and the life of Wolfgang Mann, the deception was attempted. For all Paul knew, it was still holding up. But, once again, Deitrich Zimmer had turned things to his own advantage. Rather than a simple trade of Martin for a life-saving operation, there were extra conditions.

Zimmer, perhaps the most brilliant surgeon who had ever lived (he himself had survived for more than a century in cryogenic Sleep), was the only man who could remove the bullet he had placed in Sarah's brain, this her only conceivable hope of returning to life beyond the Sleep.

But Zimmer had other plans, and they involved John leading a mission to a mountain redoubt in upstate New York where once there had been a presidential war retreat and now, as they learned, there thrived a survival community purporting to be the United States government. In reality, it was a racist society based on the principles of Aryan supremacy and had promulgated a lie for centuries: that the outside world would not support life and that heavily armed forces consisting of Blacks and Jews constantly assaulted the community. To sustain the lie, the leadership of the community routinely executed select numbers of soldiers, "casualties" in a war which did not exist. This also served to keep population to manageable levels.

Somehow, Deitrich Zimmer had found out about this, and learned also that the remains of Adolf Hitler were brought to the mountain facility immediately after the Nazi leader's body was discovered in the ruins of the Führer Bunker in Berlin at the close of the War. The retrieval of these remains was Deitrich Zimmer's announced intent, in the hopes of somehow recovering useable DNA. But Zimmer's real reasoning became apparent when the clone of Wolfgang Mann, who accompanied John, Paul himself and the others on the mission, revealed the coordinates for a secret entrance leading into the mountain community.

Zimmer wanted conquest.

Paul shook his head, at once shocked yet filled with wonder at the mere fact that Deitrich Zimmer had been able successfully to clone another human being. The cloning process was simple enough, in theory. Each cell of the human body contained the genetic fingerprint of the whole. In theory, at least, the possiblity of duplicating a creature as complex as a human being was always possible, however unlikely. But Zimmer had really done it.

And, what haunted Paul Rubenstein now, was how and why? To clone Wolfgang Mann, Zimmer needed cell samples. The only way to have obtained them in time to "grow" an adult of similar age (barring that Zimmer had also discovered a means by which the aging process could be accelerated) was to have taken the samples years ago, decades ago. That meant that Zimmer would have obtained the sample material while Wolfgang Mann and all of them slept in their cryogenic chambers at a secret location in New Germany.

If Zimmer had access to Wolfgang Mann, he had access to all of them.

And the idea made Paul Rubenstein's skin crawl. Was there another of him out there, like the clone of Wolfgang Mann ready to die for his Führer, Deitrich Zimmer? And of Annie, too?

As John moved back from the ledge overlooking the mountainside, Paul Rubenstein wondered aloud: "Is there another John Rourke?"

# Chapter Five

John Rourke drew in the snow with his gloved fingertip. "Eight of them, coming up along this defile, with some type of sensing equipment in-use by two of them. The other six have their weapons in patrolling carries. The two with the sensing equipment are armed, of course."

"Four each is stiff odds if they're on the move and we have to be silent."

"Agreed, Paul," John Rourke told his friend. "If you can think of a viable alternative, I'd love to hear it."

"Unfortunately, there isn't one. We can't let them get above us, because, if they do, they could spot us inadvertently. Nor can we let any signifi-cant amount of time elapse between the begin-ning of our operation and terminating all of them. Otherwise, they'll call in for help and we're screwed."

"There are a couple of places which might be suitable for an ambush, one in particular," and he referenced his map in the snow with an $X$ to mark the spot . . .

The lead element was approaching, slogging slowly up the incline through thigh-deep snow, none of the party equipped with snowshoes, so the going was slow because their hands were occupied and they could not use their ski poles. But these were experienced alpine-trained troops and they moved well on their skis despite the limitations.

In a sabre-grip, clenched tight in John Rourke's right fist was the Crain LS-X knife, its twelve-inch blade freshly touched up.

Rourke had lent Paul the Smith & Wesson 6906 because of the suppressor fitted to it. Paul could hold his own against anyone, of that John Rourke was certain. But taking out four men with a knife under conditions of silence was a challenge for anyone and Paul was not as experienced with clandestine use of the edged weapon. Regrettably, John Rourke was.

The first man he had ever killed with a knife had been in Latin America centuries ago, and years Before the Night of the War. His father had, of course, taught him a great many things with edged weapons technique, and so had his training in Central Intelligence. And there was

46

his friend, Ron Mahovsky, the guru of Metalife Industries who action-tuned his double-action revolvers and whose Metalife SS Chromium M finish was something Rourke had always sworn by. Ron was possibly the finest knife man John Rourke had ever met, and Rourke learned a great deal from him.

Eventually, all of what he learned blended into a fighting style which was uniquely Rourke's own, martial-arts based, utilizing many of the elements of the kendo sword-discipline.

The first man was nearly to the notch of rock. Once this man passed into the notch, Paul would strike for the end of the patrol, where two men moved abreast. The suppressor-fitted 6906 9mm, if conditions were right, could account for these two and, with a great deal of luck, the other two. The important thing was speed enough that an answering shot would not be fired by the Alpine Corps personnel, because either the sound from a burst of caseless gunfire or an energy burst might carry far enough in these mountains that the personnel at the very fringes of the growing force of Nazi personnel preparing to storm the city would hear. Then, helicopters would go airborne, as well as V-Stols and, even if Rourke and Rubenstein could elude them, any attempts by a Trans-Global Alliance V-Stol to make an extraction would be frustrated to the point of the impossible.

The 6906 Paul had was fitted with a slide lock, but that was only for extreme conditions when even the mechanical noise of the slide operating would draw attention. The suppressor, made up for Rourke by the technicians at New Germany, was beyond anything available in the twentieth century. Noise reduction was all but complete, rivaling the "phut-phut" sounds of movie silencers.

Rourke's eyes were on the two rearmost men, his attention focused for the precise moment one of them started to go down.

And it happened. One of the men's bodies went rigid, then fell forward into the snow.

Rourke shifted his gaze to the men filtering through the notch below him and readied himself to jump. He couldn't be critical of their patrolling techniques, because there was no realistic way for them to have put a man on the high ground. But, in this day of flying video probes, one of these could have been employed and totally frustrated him. Thankfully, none was.

Rourke shifted his knife to a dagger-hold and launched himself from the rock overhang, down onto the back of the nearer of the two men, Rourke's feet and legs slamming into the second man. Rourke's right forearm pistoned downward, driving the Crain LS-X knife deep into the right side of the Alpine Corpsman's neck, then ripping it free as they impacted the now, Rourke rolling away. He was beside the second of the two men, the man down to his knees in the snow. Rourke's fingers spun the knife into a sabre hold and he drove it forward into the second man's thorax.

The second pair of men would have been the

logical choice to jump under other circumstances, but that would have placed Rourke between enemy personnel and Paul's friendly fire. Instead, Rourke had two men mere yards from him, both of them using sensing equipment, neither of them with a hand on a gun. Rourke wrenched his knife free, diving toward the nearer of the two men with the sensing equipment, driving the knife edge upward into the man's abdomen several inches below the sternum, letting the force of his charge drag the knife through flesh up to the bone.

Rourke rolled away.

The other man was dropping his sensor, going for his energy rifle. But John Rourke had planned ahead. The little A. G. Russell Sting IA Black Chrome which Rourke always carried inside the waistband of his pants was clipped to his gunbelt. Rourke freed the knife from its sheath, his left fist balling around it as he lunged forward from a half crouch.

The knife bit into the man just behind the jawbone at an upthrusting angle, gouging through into the mouth. Rourke was to his feet, smashing his right knee upward into the already dying man's crotch, Rourke's right fist hammering down against the exposed neck while his left hand freed the knife. Rourke spun round, toward the remainder of the eight-man patrol, his right hand filling with the butt of one of the two Detonics ScoreMasters that were in his belt. The guns were packed with snow, but not up the muzzle, and would fire reliably.

But, there was no need. Paul was just getting to his feet. The throat of one of the four men surrounding him was ripped open, Paul's knife in the chest of another. The two rearmost of the four were down dead, presumably from gunshot wounds. The suppressor-fitted 9mm was in Paul's left hand.

Paul nodded.

Rourke exhaled.

There would be a climb back to the ridge which formed one wall of the notch, but again John Rourke had planned ahead, snaking down a piece of monofilament line from the hollow handle of the Life Support System X knife, all-but-invisible in the snow. Rourke tugged at the line now and the full-sized climbing rope to which it was attached dropped down. The rope was secured around an outcropping of living rock above.

Rourke looked at his thinly gloved hands, his snow smock. They were covered with blood. His goggles were, of course, splattered with it. In the days prior to the Night of the War, a good friend of his who had specialized in training men for various commando units, had begun to teach various methods for sentry elimination which would minimize blood spray and its inherent risks. Even though modern medicine had made such worries all but academic, John Rourke was still careful to avoid direct contact. Old habits died hard.

Rourke washed the Sting IA Black Chrome clean with snow, then wrenched the larger Crain knife from the Alpine corpsman's body and did the same. "Keep tabs on things, Paul," Rourke said unnecessarily, the younger man nodding back. Then Rourke started up the rope. He would retrieve the weapons and gear secured above, then salvage the monofilament line for future use.

# Chapter Six

Alan Crockett was out of breath a little, so Emma Shaw waited until he volunteered information. All he managed was, "Let's get going, Commander. Have lots of company up above."

He swung into the saddle as easily as a man half his age, then extended his left hand for her to grasp. She did so, locking hands and wrists, and came up into the saddle behind him.

With his knees, he urged his mount ahead along the rocky, snow-splotched riverbank. The river gouged through the canyon as far as she could see ahead of them, and almost absently she wondered what had caused it. Perhaps some plate tectonics in the aftermath of the Night of the War, perhaps something else. Periodically, over the course of the early morning, Professor

Crockett had checked a radiation meter, but the levels were normal.

They rode on in silence for some time, the only noise beside the thundering of equipment from the canyon rim above and the clopping of Wilbur's hooves on the rocky trail the occasional snort as the animal exhaled a great cloud of steamy breath.

After several minutes, Crockett cocked his hat back on his head and lit a cigarette, then began to speak. "I would estimate that a full ten percent of the Nazi total force-strength is assembled above us. And there are some Eden forces, too, but only in token strength. The reasoning is pretty obvious, it would seem. The mountain city really exists."

"Mountain city?"

"Yes. During the early post-War period—I'm talking about World War II—there was a presidential war-retreat here in these mountains. It was abandoned for that purpose when it was deemed too vulnerable to a direct missile strike, as Soviet technology upgraded. For some time now, however, I've been picking up incidental intelligence data from land pirates and travelers concerning a survival community which inhabits the old war retreat."

"That's—"

"That's what?" Crockett asked her, looking over his shoulder. For the first time, she noticed that he had very pretty eyes, although she couldn't quite peg their color. "What?"

"I was going to say, that's hard to believe, but I

guess in a really hardened site they could remain unnoticed by aerial surveillance."

"Well, evidently, the Nazis have noticed them. Unless there's some colossal military exercise going on for training purposes, what's up there on the canyon rim looks like some sort of invasion force. If war with Eden and the Nazis is as close as you were telling me, I doubt they'd deploy such strength for maneuvers at this time. Therefore, logic suggests they have found the rumored community."

"Do you know anything about it, Professor?"

"Well, Commander, what I've heard isn't very reassuring—the principal reason I've never gone looking for the place. The land pirates—sometimes I'd travel with one of their bands for a while, but that's another story—they'd tell stories about finding human remains at times."

"Oh! Charming. Whose, did they know?" Emma Shaw asked Crockett.

"Just ordinary people, and no evidence to suggest they were residents of the community. If such a community has survived, it would have to have done so through advanced technology. A primitive society would have perished after more than six centuries, unless it resorted to cannibalism, and there's never been evidence to suggest that."

"So we may find ourselves caught between two opposing forces. But, on the plus side, they probably aren't cannibals."

"That, I am afraid, is a distinct possibility."

He began field-stripping his cigarette, despite the fact that it was filterless . . .

His field commanders were assembled inside the largest of the hermetically sealed tents. He stood before them at the small podium, his outstretched palms signaling them to be seated while he spoke. "Today is the stuff of history. We shall penetrate this mountain redoubt and liberate the Aryan peoples within from their self-proclaimed democracy, but most importantly to the future of National Socialism and of the world is that we shall recover the sacred remains of the Führer of all Führers, Adolf Hitler.

"It is possible, but only remotely so," Deitrich Zimmer went on over the muted sighs and exclamations, "that they shall have been imperfectly preserved. But! But, if there remains a single cell which can be extracted, the Führer will live again!"

With a spontaneity which brought a chill to Zimmer, running its course along the full length of his spine, the assembled field commanders rose as one, and shouted, "Heil Hitler!"

Indeed, Zimmer reflected, but he would not be the same Hitler; the new Führer would only have Hitler's spark of genius, for mastery of the moment and for inspiring supreme devotion. In other ways, the new Führer would be the true superman of which Adolf Hitler and the SS had only dreamed . . .

* * *

All through the night, and continuing past dawn, aircraft had overflown them, Natalia observing through electronic field-glasses. It was as if this were some great air-show for weapons of war, every conceivable type of aircraft in the Nazi inventory flying almost due east.

And still, the encampment surrounding their own plane remained unchanged. Some fifty Alpine Corps troops stood watch, their vehicles arranged in a circle about the aircraft where only she, Annie, the cryogenically sleeping Michael and the skitterish air crew remained, waited.

Annie came to kneel beside her in the open cargo bay. "The guys from the crew'll take the watch if you want, or I can."

"This isn't a watch, Annie, it's a hobby," Natalia smiled. "And I cannot say that I find it boring. There is something enormous going on. I can feel it inside me. Have you had any reactions?"

Annie was gifted—or cursed, depending on one's perspective—with an empathic sixth sense, to experience danger or suffering of those she loved. "I could sense some turmoil, but I don't really know. I haven't really felt anything odd or anything."

"Good. Have you checked Michael?"

"All the instruments are reading like they should. So far, so good," Annie volunteered.

But Natalia Anastasia Tiemerovna, Major, Committee for State Security, Retired, returned her gaze to the aircraft above. The traffic was

56

thinning, perhaps these were the last elements of the mysterious armada. And she wasn't so certain about the "so far, so good" thing . . .

Paul Rubenstein looked up from the radio, fixing the earpiece more securely as he spoke. "They're on the way, John!"

John Rourke asked, "From what direction? East, I hope."

"East. ETA is seventeen minutes to the coordinates we gave them."

John Rourke rolled back the cuff of his parka and the battered, brown, leather bomber-jacket beneath it, checking the black-faced Rolex Submariner on his left wrist. "We'd better get moving then." Rourke started gathering up his gear, the backpack, his HK-91, the climbing rope. Paul was doing the same. In seventeen minutes, they would need to get over the rise and down through the defile, the snow there God only knew how deep. But the skis they'd taken from the dead Alpine Corpsmen would help with that. Rourke had already adjusted the bindings, but didn't don his skis, now.

Herringboning up the mountain face would be at once exhausting and slow.

The skis, however, would get them down in quick time.

# Chapter Seven

Dr. Zimmer, before he left the facility, had explained to her, "There are many sides of the human personality, many facets, as it were. In restructuring Sarah Rourke in order to make you her near duplicate, it was unavoidable that some of these nuances of personality taken from the original would be altered in you. So, you must be careful, hm? Why, you might ask? Well, for a very simple reason.

"Personality is displayed through action and reaction," Dr. Zimmer went on. "Action can be calculated, but reaction cannot. This is why you must be careful, so that some reaction you display will not alert John Rourke that you are not Sarah, the real Sarah, do you see?"

"Yes, I think. I don't know, for sure."

Dr. Zimmer smiled, telling her, "When I sent out the clone of Wolfgang Mann, he was intentionally flawed. And I had two purposes in mind. First, I wished to have him plant the seed of suspicion in John Rourke's mind, but I also had a very real need for him to broadcast the entrance coordinates I required through the microtransceiver implanted in his mouth. After both of these tasks were accomplished, his usefulness was outlived. He was expendable.

"But you do not want to die, do you?"

"Of course not," she told him.

"Good. Then, if you do your job well you will live. Unlike the clone of Wolfgang Mann, you were not designed to be expendable. There is no reason that you should be. You are my finest creation, perfect in every way. Yet, you must still be cautious."

"I will be. But—"

"Yes?" Dr. Zimmer asked, smiling.

"Well, just what is the plan, I mean—"

He stood, began to pace back and forth behind his desk. "You are aware of the fact that I could have killed the Rourke family at the same time that cell samples were taken. You are also aware that I have most likely cloned all of you, or them, depending on your outlook. So, why did I not kill them?"

"Yes."

"Because I saw a need for the Rourke family, and also firmly believe that life, although expendable, should not be wasted. Do you understand the difference young woman?"

59

"Yes—well—"

He stopped pacing, looked at her as he leaned over the desk. His hands were clenched into fists and he rested his weight on their knuckles. His fingers, she remembered, were terribly long and graceful, like those one would expect of a pianist or concert violinist. "When I can use John Rourke and all the rest for my own purposes, I would be foolish merely to indulge some violent whim and be done with them, when the same result, after some patient waiting, will be achieved at any event. Rourke will serve my purposes. Then, after he has done so, I will no longer need the real thing. If you are careful and wise, you will be the most revered woman in the world. Let me ask you a question, hm?"

"Yes?"

He smiled again. "What is the end of power? Let us suppose that one has all the money one would ever require, that one can possess virtually anyone chosen from the opposite sex, that one exercises life and death over one's subjects. Then, why the quest for greater power?"

"I don't know. Is it a riddle?"

"To Sarah Rourke it would be a riddle, but to you it must not be," Dr. Zimmer said, starting to laugh. "Remember? You want to live on after your immediate usefulness is at an end. So, you should learn this lesson well. The ultimate end of power is ultimate power. Nothing matches it. I want to rule the world, but there will always be two sides. To have only one side, there would have to be a true Armageddon, and then I would be master of ashes.

"The true power," he told her, his voice lowered almost conspiratorially, "is to control both sides, to manipulate world events. That is the ultimate power toward which I labor, which I will possess."

As she lay on her back now in the bunk—her head ached a little—Almost-Sarah wondered what he had truly meant. Two sides, but one ultimate power?

Even though she could not comprehend his meaning, she was frightened.

Wolfgang Mann slept on the opposite side of the cell. After a century, he had not touched more than her hand, her arm, her shoulder. The real Sarah evidently engendered a kind of respect that was almost equally frightening to consider.

Almost-Sarah closed her eyes, recalling the real Sarah's memories of John Rourke. At last, sleep came.

# Chapter Eight

Thorn Rolvaag's voice was not as steady as he would have liked, but he was still little-used to speaking before the leaders of his own government and representatives from all the nations of the Trans-Global Alliance.

At least, this time, he was sitting at a conference table rather than standing at a podium, and not even at the head of the table. But the President of the United States, who had just come up from Mid-Wake, was now asking him a direct question. "Do I get it straight, Dr. Rolvaag, that you're saying we might be looking at the end of the world here?"

Rolvaag exhaled, tried steadying his hands. "Yes, Mr. President, we could be. There's no way to tell. At the moment, the fissure is opening toward the east, toward North America. So far, the fissure has remained stable to the west. At this stage, the possibility exists of a major cataclysm, or a final cataclysm."

The ambassador from New Germany interrupted. "How can we know, then, Professor? What I mean to say is that we cannot act on so little information, can we?"

"I see several choices, sir," Rolvaag blurted out. He hadn't wanted to list the options as he saw them just yet, because they sounded wild, insane. But he was into it now, and these were the only options he had. They were based on computer scenarios he still had being rerun in the event of an error; but, he did not think there were any errors. "The worst-case scenario, I'm afraid, is for the end of the planet's existence. If the fissure continues and dead-ends, that's one thing. But the fissure could split against the North American plate and follow the old course of the Western Hemisphere's ring of fire. That would mean that we'd see volcanic activity of a magnitude unprecedented in human history. The interim effects would be incalulable, but the end result seems inescapable. The Pacific Basin would, in effect, separate from the remaining body of the planet. The exact mechanism for human destruction is only speculative, but nonetheless certain."

"If that happens, Dr. Rolvaag, when?" the president asked.

"Those calculations are still in the works. Not immediately, but not in a hundred years, either.

We'd be talking months at the least and perhaps a decade at best."

"What are the other options, I mean for averting disaster, Professor," the ambassador from Lydveldid Island queried.

"Well, we can attempt to divert lava buildup, hence pressure, all along the trench, then carefully utilize nuclear explosions—those would be the only things powerful enough, and I have no idea of the explosive force we'd ultimately need, perhaps all of the nuclear weapons in existence on the planet. We'd have to seal the trench to prevent further expansion."

"What of the side effects of such a thing?" the ambassador pressed.

"Those can be calculated, I believe, but use of such explosives would present a certain amount of unavoidable risk."

"If nothing worked to stop it, Doctor?" the president asked, his voice sounding almost too controlled.

"Well, then, uh—we'd have only two choices."

"They are?"

"Well, Mr. President, we could wait around for eventual extinction, mass death, really—"

"Or not wait around," the president said, finishing Rolvaag's thought for him.

"Yes, sir, not wait around, but leave. Some few of us, persons younger than ourselves, persons best suited not only to survive, but to thrive."

"Elsewhere," the president said.

"Yes, elsewhere than here."

"You're the scientist, Dr. Rolvaag. What are

64

the chances of finding an 'elsewhere' as we've been putting it?"

Rolvaag looked the President of the United States squarely in the eye. "Opinion or fact?"

"Try both."

"Fact is that ever since the Night of the War, we—as a race, the human race—have done nothing to find out anything about what's out there. Presumably, the Eden Project records which were recorded in the fleet's computers, might tell us something. But the government of Eden won't release any scientific data because it might have military implications," and he said what was on the tip of his tongue. "That's a pile of crap as we all know. But, beyond that, we don't have any data."

"That's the facts, right? What's your opinion, Dr. Rolvaag?"

"Opinion, Mr. President? I believe that out among the countless billions of stars there is a hospitable place. The trick is finding it, which could take an almost incalculably long period of time."

"Does the technology exist, should such a course of action ultimately prove necessary, to—" the president seemed to be struggling for the right phrasing.

"Send out an ark," the Icelandic ambassador supplied.

"Yes," the president said.

"It could be gotten together," Rolvaag told them, "if we all pulled together, pooled our scientific talents, our resources."

"And the war we're currently preparing for? That could deplete a wide range of needed resources, isn't that correct, including the nuclear warheads that might obviate the planet's destruction?"

"Yes, Mr. President."

"And the fissure, Professor Rolvaag," the Icelandic ambassador began, "was likely precipitated by the destruction on the Night of the War?"

"Yes. I'd say that's very possible," Rolvaag told him.

"So, mankind has brought about his own undoing through war, and his last hope for salvation will fail because of war. What fools we are," the Icelander suggested.

"But we must consider another human trait, Mr. Ambassador," the president said. "That's the will to survive. No matter how bleak it appears, we have only to recall past adversities—from the recent past and all throughout time—to see that even if the means of survival eludes us now, there is still hope."

Thorn Rolvaag was beginning to wonder. But he said, "Six hundred and twenty-first years ago, one country alone launched one hundred and thirty-two human beings into space and they survived. So, perhaps—" Rolvaag let the sentence hang.

"Let us remember what they became," the Icelandic Ambassador said sombrely. And Rolvaag had no words to counter his words. The Eden

Project became Eden, and Eden had nothing to do with Paradise . . .

Martin Rourke Zimmer let himself into the cryogenic laboratory. There was a palm-print reader beside the vault door and it would only respond to his own palm or that of his father, Deitrich Zimmer. The forces of the new Reich and those of Eden were in position for the attack against the mountain community in the wastelands along the northern Atlantic coast, their objectives the securing of a strong outpost near the easternmost edge of Eden and, of even greater importance, the retrieval of the Führer's remains.

Martin Zimmer's father, Deitrich Zimmer, had personal charge of these forces, and (with Martin's considerable assistance, because it seemed he had a natural talent for strategic and tactical planning) was beginning the final plan for ultimate victory.

This was really why Martin Zimmer entered the cryogenic vault where the bodies of the clones were kept. The process was not easy, of course, as the bestial things which had preceded these ultimate creations of genius attested.

But there were, at last, the required replicants or clones.

It was like the wax museum at Eden City, really, except the figures were never wholly visible, but only partially so as the wisps of bluish gas would part, then reassemble. There was another difference, too. Within the cryogenic chambers were living human beings.

"Father! And how are we, hm?" He stood before the chamber which housed the clone of John Thomas Rourke. "You'll soon be out of there and leading a marvelously interesting life—as soon as we have the real brain to download into that empty thing of yours. Now, here's a question, Daddy. What if we got you to hump the clone of my mother—who may already be getting herself humped by Wolfgang Mann, of course. But, would the two of you make me again? Or one of them?" And Martin gestured next down the line of chambers toward the clones of Annie Rourke and Michael Rourke.

He walked past them and stopped before the chamber in which Natalia Anastasia Tiemerovna rested. Like the others, she was naked. Unlike the others, however, she was exquisite, as physically perfect as one of the goddesses of Nordic legend. Soon, she would be his.

Yet, Martin sighed, it would be fascinating to experience the real thing, if only just once, with her kicking and screaming because she knew what was happening. He'd have to see if he could arrange that. He looked at the sleeping clone of his birth father, saying, "You wouldn't mind if I screwed good old Natalia, would you, Daddy?"

# Chapter Nine

The black-and-white camouflaged jet aircraft was already visible in the distance, terrain following over the icefield, and perhaps already visible on Nazi sensing equipment as well.

John Rourke and Paul Rubenstein were at the height of a steep, windswept slope, at the midway point down the mountain, still a considerable distance from the icefield where the V-Stol would land. It could only remain on the ice for moments at the most before having to take off again. Well beyond the icefield there was a sheer drop, and through his binoculars Rourke could see a canyon wall beyond. Within it, shimmering like a ribbon of silver from a Christmas card, there was a river, snaking eastward.

John Rourke lowered his binoculars and

checked the bindings of his skis, looked at his friend and asked, "Ready?"

"Makes me wish I'd spent more time in Vermont than Florida when I was a kid, but yeah." Paul had skied, he'd told Rourke once in conversation, but had never considered himself good at it. Yet, Paul was a better athlete these days than he had been in his youth, was in top physical condition and, if he was careful, would do all right. "Just remember I'm not Jean-Claude Killy or James Bond, okay?" Paul laughed.

"Well, the resemblance is uncanny, actually," Rourke told him, "but I'll try to keep it in mind." Rourke checked his gear, then pulled down his goggles and readied to dig in his poles. But, behind him, he heard a high-pitched whistle. Rourke craned his neck, turning to look back up the slope. About two hundred yards back, already in motion, there was a contingent from a factor he had failed to even consider: land pirates.

Paul saw them too, saying hurriedly, "Those assholes won't only draw attention to themselves, but to us. Idiots!"

"We've got rifles, warm clothing, things they want, need." There were four vehicles, improvised things, tracked, welded-up snow-tractor Frankensteins cobbled together with parts from junked transportation defying Rourke's imagination. One of them was once, it appeared, a mini-tank of the type with which Rourke was familiar from New Germany, during the last days of the great war with the Russians.

The four were arcing along a ridgeline paralleling the slope along which Rourke and Rubenstein had to travel. "Let's go!"

"I'm with you!" Paul shouted.

Together, they dug in their poles and jumped off onto the slope . . .

Wilbur climbed like a mountain goat; there were goats in New Germany which Emma Shaw had seen once during a Trans-Global Alliance field exercise.

But it would have been unfair to ride the horse as he struggled, so instead they scrambled along with him, Alan Crockett leading the animal, Emma Shaw behind. "Wilbur, you're a gentleman. I've been behind you for almost an hour now and you haven't done anything to make me regret it, yet," she announced.

Crockett evidently heard her, calling back, "Well, we still have a few minutes left of this trail until we reach the canyon rim. There's still time for Wilbur to disgrace himself."

She started to make a crack, but instead something she heard made her look upward so rapidly that she nearly lost her balance. Coming low over the far wall of the canyon she saw a German V-Stol, cammied up for operations over snow-covered terrain, but clearly, from its fuselage markings as it passed overhead, an allied craft, neither Nazi nor Eden.

"Hey! Look!"

"I saw it." And Crockett urged Wilbur along the trail more rapidly now.

Emma Shaw's palms began to perspire within her gloves and her mouth was suddenly dry . . .

Deitrich Zimmer looked up from his notes, the radio operator standing before him at stiff attention. "Forgive me, Herr Doctor, but you wished to be informed should—"

"Yes, yes, I know." Zimmer took the note from the young soldier's hand and read it. An allied aircraft had been detected coming in below usual scanning levels from the east. That would be for Rourke and his Jew friend, of course, just as Zimmer had anticipated. He looked up from the transcription and told the young soldier, "You will notify all commanders in the sector that my orders concerning this aircraft are to be carried out to the letter." The young man was scribbling hurriedly in his pad. "Reiterate to them that under no circumstances is this Allied aircraft to be interdicted." And Zimmer waved the young man away. The thing about heroes—and Dr. John Rourke certainly was one—was that they were so wonderfully predictable.

# Chapter Ten

By the time they reached the summit of the canyon wall, Emma Shaw heard gunfire, conventional small arms and heavier cartridge arms. The aircraft she had seen overflying the canyon was coming in for a vertical landing on the ice field, but it was neither the origin nor the target of the gunfire. The origin was a group of vehicles—four of them, as motley a collection as she had ever seen—riding recklessly along a ridgeline paralleling a smooth, snow-swept slope. There were two men on skis coming down along the slope, one of them moving quite easily it seemed, the other moving steadily but with considerably less apparent grace.

"Land pirates," Alan Crockett said very simply as he crouched beside her. Then he took her by the shoulder and turned her around. "That V-Stol's big enough, isn't it? You're a pilot."

"For Wilbur?" Emma looked at Alan Crockett, then at his horse. "The cargo bay, you mean, big enough to handle—"

"You know what I mean. Let's go." And Crockett didn't say another word. He wrestled Wilbur up from the snow, great clouds of it rising as the animal's hooves settled and it shook itself. Alan Crockett almost literally vaulted into the saddle, throwing down his hand for her to grab him at the wrist. She did and he swung her up behind him. "We ride toward the aircraft. You have to promise me that you'll get Wilbur out of here."

"He's not your *horse*, he's your *friend* and you love him."

But Alan Crockett didn't answer her. Instead, he dug in his heels and rasped, "Gyaagh!" Wilbur, despite his docile appearance, lunged ahead, across the ice field, toward the aircraft . . .

There was a mogul, and Rourke forced the heel ends of his skis apart, bearing down on the toe ends, but only slightly. As he started to turn, Rourke twisted his upper body, his left shoulder pointing away from the mogul. As his knees bent, he drew the heel ends of the skis into his new direction, almost imperceptibly throwing his weight to the outside ski, jabbing his poles deep into the snow and thrusting forward.

He was accelerating, hoping that Paul saw the mogul in time.

74

But there was no time to look back toward his friend. The nearest of the four land pirate vehicles was closing from the left, gunfire emanating from the open hatch in the crude turret at its top, bullets lacing through the snow mere feet from where Rourke skied.

The land pirates might be some of those who worked hand-in-glove with the Eden Defense Forces, or independents. But Rourke was mildly surprised that the gunfire had not already attracted Nazi forces.

There were rocks ahead and to the left. Rourke christied again, veering toward them, then dug in his poles, twisted his body left and skidded to a lateral halt in a spray of wet snow.

Paul was coming fast, but controlled, and Rourke shouted to his friend over the gunfire and the roar of the vehicle engines, "Make the plane! I'll be right behind you!" Rourke kicked out of his bindings, then dove to cover behind the rocks as Paul skied past.

Rourke loosened the sling for the HK-91, bringing the rifle to his shoulder, cheeking it as he bit away his right outer glove. He thumbed the selector off 0 to 1, settling the .308's sights on the gunman in the lead vehicle's turret. As a burst of automatic weapon-fire rang across the rock near him, John Rourke squeezed off his first shot.

The HK-91 was a true rifleman's rifle, in the World War II sense of the term. It was accurate, rugged and fired a manstopping cartridge. It wasn't a spray and pray gun in a caliber that many experts—himself not included, because he'd always found the .223 adequate in antiper-sonnel work—considered questionable at best.

Leading the tracked vehicle ever so slightly, Rourke's finger finished the trigger squeeze with the rifle's sights settled on the throat of his target, thus allowing for terrain variances which might raise the head or lower it, still giving the opportunity for an instantly killing shot. The man's head snapped back and his weapon—it looked like some sort of belt-fed machine gun fitted with an improvised stock and vertical front hand-grip—sprayed upward.

Rourke looked over the rifle's sights, searching for a chink in the vehicle's armor. And, he found one, a slotted panel; at the front and through which the driver viewed the terrain. The slot seemed to be about three or four inches high and at least twice that wide. Rourke inhaled, let out part of the breath, held the rest in his throat and began the trigger squeeze. Such a small target on a moving vehicle would be a dicey shot at best, but if he connected, the following vehicles would have to stop or pull off the ridge-line in order to avoid striking this one.

Rourke led the target less, mentally adjusting for elevation as he squeezed the trigger again, then again, no ricochets visible this time, and for a moment no sign that he had struck his target. Then the vehicle began to swerve, cut a sharp right and started straight toward Rourke's position. But the rocks which formed the boundary for the ridge-line got in its way. The vehicle slammed into the low rock wall and stopped dead.

The vehicle behind it, the bastardized German minitank, swerved, but not in time, striking the first vehicle broadside.

Rourke didn't wait for the rest, mowing the safety off fire, slinging the HK crossbody in a patrolling carry, then throwing down his skis as he pulled on his gloves. He stomped his feet into the bindings, grabbed up his poles and dug in, launching himself back into the trail Paul had already cut through the snow along the slope.

Ahead, Paul was midway between the base of the slope and the aircraft which was parked on the ice field. A half dozen commandos were in a defensive formation around the aircraft, and in the distance, coming toward the aircraft from the deep canyon Rourke had observed earlier, there were two people riding double on horseback.

Rourke reached the base of the slope, then dug his poles into the ice in earnest.

This was cross-country skiing now, the skis themselves better suited for it, but the going slower.

Rourke looked back.

Two of the land pirate vehicles were making their way down from the ridge-line, onto the slope. If their weight didn't prove too great, they'd make good time—perhaps too good. Rourke worked his poles as hard as he could, tucking his body down to minimize wind resistance.

Paul was nearly at the aircraft now. The commandos—six of them—divided, three of them coming across the ice toward Paul, dropping prone to its surface, bipods folding out from the fore ends of their weapons. The other three fanned out and waited for the horse-mounted personnel.

As Rourke started to look away, the horse foundered on the ice and fell, the two riders jumping clear. The horse's body skittered along the icy surface, its off foreleg bending, twisting.

Rourke quickened his pace, summoning all the speed he could now. He looked behind him. The two land pirates' vehicles were coming fast, leaving the slope and starting across the ice.

Gunfire came from the commandos facing Rourke, their positions such that they could shoot toward the vehicles without Rourke himself being in their lines of fire. Rourke kept moving . . .

She shook her head, pulled off her helmet, her hair falling over her eyes.

"Wilbur!" It was Crockett shouting. Emma Shaw looked from Crockett and toward the animal. It was down, its left front leg twisted. And it was obvious that the animal's leg was broken, badly. Professor Alan Crockett was up, running, his cowboy hat pulled low over his eyes, his dark clothes snow-splotched, his face a mask of violence and anguish, his western-style six-gun in his right fist, its long barrel angled slightly upward. And he shouted to her, "Remember the

78

saddlebags, Commander! Remember the saddle-bags!"

"I'll remember, but—" Emma Shaw drew her .45 from beneath the parachute-fabric poncho, racking the slide. These men from the aircraft were friendly forces, and common sense told her to run toward them. But she didn't, scrambling to her knees and running instead after Alan Crockett. But as she looked toward the aircraft, she could have sworn that the figure nearest to it, a man on skis, of average-looking height, was somehow familiar.

Dismissing the notion, she followed Crockett, shouting after him, "Alan, don't! We can get the horse aboard. We can—"

But he was on his knees beside the animal, cradling its head, and before she could reach him, Crockett abruptly stood, putting the re-volver's barrel on line with the animal's head. There was a single shot, louder-seeming than the gunfire that was coming from the far side of the aircraft. Wilbur's body twitched once and was still.

As she reached Crockett, he was already cut-ting his saddlebags free from the rest of his gear, a small pocket knife in his left hand. "Get the bags and get out of here! I enjoyed your com-pany, Emma Shaw!"

She moved her hand to touch him, barely felt at his sleeve and Alan Crockett was gone, run-ning, toward the two land-pirate vehicles, only his six-gun in his hand. Emma Shaw picked up the saddlebags.

And she realized suddenly that every man—or woman—had his own definition of what it was which was important enough to die for, what principle could not be violated. "Alan!" But she only called after him once. He was a man alone, whether by fate or design, and the one companion whom he valued—only a dumb animal, some would say, one of God's or nature's humblest creatures, really, for all the myth surrounding them—was dead by enemy action, albeit accidental. All the loneliness, all the solitude, and the one thing outside himself on which he could rely, in which he could trust, was gone.

Some would say that Alan Crockett lost his mind; others would understand, as she did. Emma Shaw picked up the saddlebags, then ran toward the aircraft . . .

John Rourke could feel the pulsing of the lead vehicle's engine in the air around him. Bullets and energy bursts impacted the ice near him. He kept going.

There was a woman running toward the aircraft now, and a man in dark clothes and a western hat running toward the land pirate vehicles. With only a long-barreled handgun—the only visible weapon—he shrugged past one of the commandos who tried to hold him back, ran on, toward the land-pirate vehicles.

Paul was at the aircraft, firing toward the land pirates. The female figure was nearly to the fuselage door.

Gunfire tore into the ice in front of Rourke, and as he tried to turn away, an energy burst struck the side less than a yard from him, and the surface beneath Rourke's skis rose, collapsed and Rourke was momentarily airborne, slamming down onto the ice, his bindings breaking loose, his body twisting, rolling, skidding.

John Rourke shook his head, clawed at his rifle on the ice beside him. The nearer of the two land-pirate vehicles was tracked like the one he had disabled, its frame was that of an old truck, enclosed in the bed, firing ports there crudely armored. The vehicle was closing, bearing down on him.

But as Rourke shook his head to clear it, tried shouldering his weapon, he saw the black-clad man jumping onto the running board of the vehicle's cab, stabbing his long-barreled revolver through a vision slit. Almost instantly, the land-pirate vehicle began to swerve. The vehicle just behind it tried turning clear. John Rourke had the HK-91 to his shoulder, firing at the joint between two sections of armor plate on its cab, firing out the entire magazine, then buttoning it out into the snow, drawing another magazine from his musette bag, ramming it up the well. He cycled the first round into the chamber, resumed firing.

The first vehicle overturned, the man who had attacked it with little more than his bare hands jumping clear.

The first vehicle's cab separated from the bed, rolling over again and again in the snow. Rourke

81

brought his attention back to the second vehicle. Gunfire from the commandos near the aircraft was opening up on it now. Rourke kept firing. The second vehicle swerved, skidded, nearly overturned. Bullets rang off the heavier of the armor plates, peppered the others.

There was a blast from a squad energy cannon, then another and another, the energy bolts spreading out of the armored engine compartment.

The vehicle stopped.

Rourke pulled another single magazine from his musette bag, was to his feet, running.

At the far edge of his peripheral vision, he could see the black-clad man with the cowboy hat. Men were piling out of the first land-pirate vehicle. And the man in black just stood there, taking them down one at a time until his gun was empty. Rourke ran toward the fray, shouting, "Get out of there, man!"

The land pirates swarmed over the man in black, the man's pistol barrel flashing in the sun, swiping across skulls until finally he was swamped by his enemies. Rourke at last had a clear field of fire around the overturned truck, and bringing the HK-91 to his shoulder opened up. At the range, there was no need for real marksmanship, just shooting.

The commandos from the aircraft were suddenly there, Rourke ordering, "Let's help that man! Come on!" Rourke safed the HK-91, letting the rifle fall to his side on its sling. From beneath the snow smock he drew ScoreMasters, one in each hand, running forward.

The range was point-blank, and he opened fire, killing three of the land pirates before he reached the man in black.

The commandos swept past the first vehicle, toward the second one, that was stalled out yards away in the snow. Rourke dropped to his knees beside the man.

There were knife wounds—more than Rourke could immediately count—all along the man's torso, and blood dripped from the corner of the man's mouth. In his right hand, the man still grasped his long-barreled handgun. Rourke recognized it, a Colt Single Action Army, almost certainly a Lancer copy.

As Rourke belted his own pistols and reached out to examine him, the fallen man in black opened his eyes and what was almost a smile crossed the fellow's lips. "Dr. Rourke, isn't it?"

"Yes, but we've never—"

And the man in black began to laugh, the blood flow from his mouth increasing. As Rourke started to say, "Be still so—" the man in black said through clenched white teeth, "When she told me you were alive, I really didn't believe her, thought perhaps it was the shock from bailing out over enemy territory, or maybe she was just crazy. I think sir, that she loves you."

"Who—what—"

The man in black closed his eyes, then opened them quickly again. "It has, sir, been an honor."

"And you, sir, are either the bravest or most foolish man I've ever met."

"There's a fine line—" And the face of the man in black suddenly went rigid and his head cocked back into the snow.

Rourke felt for a pulse and there was none.

As he thumbed closed the man's eyes, Rourke finished the man's words, ". . . a fine line between the two."

From behind him, John Rourke heard a woman's voice, a voice he knew very well and at once wanted to hear again but was afraid to hear. "John. That was Alan Crockett. You probably never heard of him. He was an archaeologist, a survivalist like you, he was—"

Rourke turned around as he stood. Her hair needed combing, there was dirt on her left cheek, and tears were flowing from her eyes.

Emma said, "Hold me. Please?"

"Yes." John Rourke walked the few paces toward her very slowly, folding her into his arms, her head resting against his chest. They needed to be off the ground quickly, out of here and away. But there was something John Rourke needed to do. "Will you be all right?"

"Uh-huh."

"Hold my rifle, then."

Emma Shaw took it from him and Rourke turned back toward the dead man; Emma had called him Alan Crockett. Rourke walked back toward the man, dropped into a crouch. He opened the dead man's hand, hefted the handgun, shoved it into his belt. Then he took Crockett's right hand and arm, hauling the arm across his own shoulders, slinging the dead man up into a fireman's carry as he rose. In the distance, Paul and the commandos from the plane were settling with the remaining land pirates.

"We've got to hurry!" John Rourke shouted, starting toward the aircraft, the dead man in black over his shoulder, Emma Shaw falling in beside him. It felt good to have her there.

# Chapter Eleven

She had told him about this man named Alan
Crockett, how Crockett, a college professor, ex-
plorer, archaeologist, weapons expert and survivalist, had helped in faking his own death so
that he could work for these past three years
deep inside enemy territory as a field intelligence
agent. And she also told him about the man and
the horse.

John Rourke closed his eyes as he thought
about it again.

Emma was asleep in the seat beside him.

A human life had to have a focus, something
internal or external, which kept it moving, gave
it purpose. Often, the external force was inter-
nalized, became symbolic of all the things in life
that were good or bad or important. John

Rourke worked once with a man named Sterrett, on an assignment in Latin America against a guerilla band paid for by the drug cartel.

Sterrett's equipment was state-of-the-art, except for a spare knife that Sterrett carried lashed to his web gear. It was stag-handled, but the crude brass guard, however serviceable, was an abomination.

At a rest stop once, Rourke's curiosity got the better of him and he asked Sterrett, "What's the story of that knife?"

"This? My dad's."

"He carry it during the War or something?"

"No. He gave it to me. You know how when you're a kid, Rourke, you get stuff, don't even give it a second thought. Well, I got this knife from him. Wasn't the world's best, but I really thought it was something. Then this one day, a couple of weeks after my dad died, I realized it was the only thing really—I mean something tangible—that I still had that he'd given me. I've been carrying it ever since. And you know what?"

"No."

"It's really not such a bad knife after all. Holds an edge okay and—anyway, it's got a purpose."

The knife. Alan Crockett's horse.

John Rourke was certain that Sterrett would have willingly risked death to retrieve the knife, or to somehow avenge its loss or destruction.

John Rourke opened his eyes, staring down at the different but identical-seeming snow field below them. The V-Stol would be landing in Lydveldid Island in less than ten minutes. Then, off again, back to North America, but as part of an attack squadron.

A few Nazi and Eden Defense Force aircraft had closed to within a mile of their aircraft, but only after they were airborne, then fallen away after a brief, halfhearted seeming pursuit.

And John Rourke could not help wondering why, yet at the same time think that he might know. He looked at Emma Shaw's face while she slept, how peaceful she seemed, exhausted as she had been, and how beautiful, although she was the kind of woman who would never consider herself anything more than pretty enough.

They would be on the ground at Hekla Airbase, named after the once partially destroyed, since rebuilt Hekla community within the mountain volcano of the same name, in only minutes. As he gently checked Emma's seat belt, he considered the current situation. He was pitted against the most intelligent adversary he had ever encountered, and it was not silliness on his part to view the conflict as personal. Zimmer's every move seemed to have made it so.

Rourke looked at the face of his wristwatch. In the days Before the Night of the War, a Rolex was very much a status symbol. He wore one simply because it was an extraordinarily good timepiece. But many persons, wishing the supposed status that the watch conferred by its name, bought fakes. Some were outright counterfeits, others made to closely resemble the real thing.

What had they been dealing with—he and Paul—in their encounter with the fake Wolfgang Mann? A counterfeit, or something closely resembling the real thing. A true counterfeit—and perhaps Zimmer had that ability—would have maintained its identity and signaled the just-discovered entranceway's coordinates surreptitiously, rather than shouting them to the night sky. But something designed to only closely resemble the real thing, yet be just enough different that the deception would be discovered immediately or even eventually—why had Zimmer done this, except for the one obvious reason, to alert him—John Rourke—to the fact that he—Zimmer—had perfected the process of cloning a human being?

If this was Zimmer's intent, then for what motive, and toward what end? Merely to have his work admired? Rourke dismissed that; Zimmer's ego was great but Zimmer's intellect greater. Indeed, Zimmer would be a dedicated believer in the dictum that the end always justified the means. The means were the creation of human beings from the cells of unwilling donors, then using such beings however Zimmer saw fit. The Wolfgang Mann clone had an explosive charge inside his body, was intentionally doomed.

Zimmer might well have used a clone as the source for his new eye.

If Zimmer had cloned Wolf, then Zimmer could have cloned all of them and, indeed, as Rourke had already surmised, the woman he'd thought was Sarah was not Sarah—perhaps. There could be duplicates of them all, himself included. But again, to what end?

Why, if Zimmer had the ability to penetrate the cryogenic repository in New Germany in order to obtain cells for cloning, why hadn't Zimmer just killed them?

The answer seemed inescapable: Zimmer had some means by which he could record the electromagnetic impulses within the human brain, and he needed the brain to be active in order to do this. So, Zimmer wanted his clones to be programmed with the "minds" of the unwilling donors. That in mind, then still to what end?

In Eden, Rourke had discovered statues of himself, seen his face on the coinage. There was even a motion picture glorifying him. All this under the aegis of a man who was his enemy? To what end?

Dictators built personality cults around themselves, not their enemies. Yet, Zimmer had built such a cult around his enemy. Why?

For some reason which John Rourke could not as yet discern, Deitrich Zimmer needed him alive and free and fighting, hence the halfhearted pursuit by enemy aircraft while their own aircraft escaped.

Rourke's inability to discern Zimmer's intent bothered him less than the very real possibility that Sarah and the real Wolfgang Mann were part of the plan, and might well be sacrificed by Zimmer in order to bring the plan to fruition.

"Damn," Rourke rasped as he lit a cigarette.

# Chapter Twelve

The coffee was hot, but coffee could be drunk hot or cold and, often, it tasted little different. Drinking coffee these days was like a byte of racial memory, because only extremely costly coffees contained caffeine, and caffeine was the major purpose behind coffee's popularity in the first place. Yet, people still drank coffee and claimed that it helped keep them awake; Tim Shaw did.

This morning, Tim Shaw drank coffee just because he liked the taste. Although he'd had little sleep, he couldn't have been more alert. Word had just reached him by telephone that his daughter, Emma, missing in action after her Navy fighter plane went down, was alive and well and safe with John Rourke.

Shaw was alone in his office at Honolulu P.D. headquarters. The door opened, his son Ed standing just on the other side of the doorway. "Mind if I join you, Dad?"

"Come ahead, Eddie," Shaw told his son. Ed still wore black battle-dress utilities and combat boots, not yet having the chance to change after the battle with the saboteurs right in the heart of downtown. The BDUs were still stained with the contents of the fire extinguishers from when they had flooded the inside of the armored truck.

Tim Shaw had showered and changed, unable to stand himself, even cleaned his guns. But that was the advantage of giving the orders instead of taking them. Someday, Eddie (who gave a lot of the orders now, because Eddie was the SWAT Team's tactical commander) would give the orders. "Pretty good news about Emma, huh? The girl's tough."

"Yeah, but tough doesn't mean invincible, Eddie. Tough people get croaked every day."

"You know what I mean, anyway—so, you think the Nazis are gonna try for you? I mean, you set yourself up with that TV crew after the fight, just in case the bad guys didn't know who you were. Only thing you didn't do was have 'em flash your home address on the screen."

"Hey, I tried," Shaw said, grinning at his son. "I figured we could start us a little business on the side, Eddie, you know, sell nostalgia stuff and shit like that. But we've gotta get us a phone number with operators standing by and the whole routine. Maybe we can get our own TV

92

show, call it "Honolulu SWAT" or somethin', huh?"

"You laugh, Dad, but if these guys come for you in force, to get their revenge for all the damage you've done, you could wind up with the old tail in a sling."

Ed Shaw reached into the top right-hand drawer of his desk and took out his .45, laying it on the desk. "Not so long as I've got my friend here. To be honest with ya, Eddie, I hope the fuckers try it. And we can be ready for them. See, I can sleep, take it easy, catch up on the tube, shit like that, while they come to get me. They're gonna be workin' hard. And you're gonna be workin' hard, too. I figure, right about now, our little Nazi buddies are shittin' bricks and spittin' nails 'cause we nailed so many of 'em right after they first got here, then got those lowlife schmucks they were gonna use to do the missile heist. They can't be too happy, anyway. So, I agree, they're gonna come after me, teach me a lesson, that kinda stuff. What they don't know, I hope, is that I want them to do it, and you and the guys from the SWAT Team are gonna be ready and waiting."

"This could take a long time, Dad," Ed said, grabbing the chair opposite Tim Shaw's, turning it around and straddling it.

"Yeah, but it won't. Wanna know why, Eddie?"

"No, but you'll tell me anyway."

Tim Shaw lit a cigarette, leaned back in his chair and rocked his feet up on the corner of the desk. "If we dish up an opportunity our little

Nazi saboteur buddies can't resist, and it's comin' up pretty soon, what are they gonna do? I'll tell ya, Eddie." And Tim Shaw swung his feet down from the desk and leaned across toward his son. "Before they hit this super-attractive target, they're gonna hit me. And since we wasted the no-talent bums the Nazis sent on the missile job, they're gonna figure they've gotta come after me themselves. Six of them left maybe, right? So, maybe they'll bring some of their damned fifth-columnist saboteur hoodlum whackos with 'em. More the merrier. We just get to put the bag on more of 'em. And that's your department. Just like when you had that supermarket job when you were a kid, Eddie. You're a bagger. I'm the sale coupon that brings 'em into the store."

"This could get you killed, Dad. Emma'd be so pissed with you, it'd be the first time the living ever haunted the dead."

Tim Shaw laughed. "That's cute, Eddie. And, God knows, you might be right. You think of a better shot at nailin' these guys, I'll be happy to try it." And Shaw took the cigarette out of the corner of his mouth and looked his son hard in the eyes. "But you better hurry, cause I'm goin' home tonight and I might cut out early."

Eddie didn't say anything.

# Chapter Thirteen

Natalia stood up so suddenly that Annie was startled. "What is it?"

"Answer a question, Annie. Do you think men are smarter than women, just because they are men, I mean?"

Annie Rourke Rubenstein just stared at her for a moment. "That's a hell of a question to ask! I mean, we're in a plane in the middle of an ice field and we're surrounded by enemy forces and—"

"That is exactly why I asked you the question in the first place, Annie. So, give me an answer." Natalia lit a cigarette.

Natalia had finally relented and let the air crew keep the watch, Natalia returning with her to the sealed portion of the fuselage where they could at least get out of their arctic gear for a little while. "I don't think so, no. I mean, each person's an individual and sex doesn't have anything to do with intelligence. I mean, studies have confirmed that men are usually better with math, especially the kind that involves spatial skills, and women are usually better with languages. But if that were always true, there wouldn't be any female mathematicians or any male writers, I guess. What are you driving at, Natalia?"

Natalia leaned back in her seat. "I think there's something very seriously gone wrong. Is that correct English?"

"Why do you keep asking me about your English? You've been speaking English perfectly ever since—"

"But then it was a second language and I always had to think about it. Who am I going to speak Russian to these days, except maybe some sailors or some land pirates, unless I go back to the Urals. So, it's more important to me. Notice? I'm using more contractions."

"Contractions weren't common in American speech until after the westward expansion period in the mid-nineteenth century."

"That's useful to know," Natalia said, smiling. "So, you'd agree with me? Men aren't necessarily smarter, and women can at the worst be just as smart."

Annie stood up, dug her hands into the pockets of the heavy woolen skirt she wore and started pacing the aisle. "Well, sure. But, what's your point?"

"If things aren't going right, then maybe the plan we have been following needs to be altered."

Annie turned around and just stared at her. "And?"

"I think we need to start the process of getting Michael out of cryogenic sleep."

"But—"

"Let me finish, all right?"

"Fine, so finish," Annie said, sitting down again. "But, if we take Michael out of cryogenic sleep we'll be screwing things up for rescuing Mom, maybe."

"Even when I still—well, that's not the right way to put it. But, before Michael and I got together, when I was still lying to myself that your father and I could—"

Natalia let the thought hang unfinished. "I know what you're saying, but I never would have—you always had all our best interests at heart, my mother's included. You're saying men don't have a monopoly on honor; everything about you has always proven that men don't have the monopoly there, and you know that."

"And I still have Sarah's best interest at heart, but we won't save your mother by getting Michael and ourselves killed. I think the situation has changed." And she laughed, adding, "Call it 'woman's intuition.' Or whatever you want."

Annie shook her head, "But what'll happen when Daddy gets back with—"

"Adolf Hitler's remains? Can you see John Rourke unleashing that on the world? Assuming,

I mean, that Zimmer could do anything with them."

"If the situation had changed," Annie started, leaning forward, perching on the edge of her seat, "wouldn't Daddy have signaled us?"

"A radio transmission or anything else could be intercepted. You were raised to be independent by your father, and my uncle raised me the same way. Maybe John's assuming we'll do something. Your father's like that. All I know is that whether John Rourke assumes we'll do something or not, I think we should. If we had to make a stand this way, Michael would be helpless. If we had to flee and the aircraft were disabled, we'd have no means of bringing him, so we wouldn't flee and we would all be killed. We both know that. Michael's your brother and my lover."

"We should wake him up," Natalia said after a long pause. "I just know that we should, all right?"

"We'll wake him up, but he's going to be pissed."

Natalia smiled. "Get your gear. Of course he'll be angry; he's just like his father, isn't he?" And Natalia smashed out her cigarette, stood and grabbed up her gunbelt.

They dressed in the rear of the sealed portion of the cabin, swathing themselves in their arctic gear . . .

Natalia actuated the control for the cyanide gas. If she made a mistake, Michael would be dead in seconds and nothing could be done to change that. Annie had volunteered to do it, but Natalia used the same logic she had with John, six hundred and twenty-five years ago, that if something went wrong, it was better this way. Before Annie could argue, Natalia touched the controls.

There would be a few seconds before they would know for certain that the cyanide gas release was successfully disengaged, but the awakening controls were already at work. Natalia looked at Michael's face through the swirling gas, then could stand it no longer and looked away. Annie was staring at her from within the scarves and hood which covered everything except her eyes. Natalia had to talk, or scream. "One time Vladmir and I were on a job, in Iran. You know, sometimes the Soviet Union was popular with the Iranian theocracy, sometimes it was not. This was one of the latter times. We had to reach one of our agents who had been getting information on the Israeli effort to support the Americans prior to President Carter's failed attempt with that helicopter attack."

"I remember Daddy telling us about it."

"Well," Natalia went on, "the only way for Vladmir to get in unmolested—you see, he didn't do well with languages—was to take me along, because it would be all but unthinkable for someone to molest a party with a woman in it. Anyway, I had to wear this chadarlike thing. I mean, the true chadars are head to toe—"

"That's a veil."

"Yes," Natalia told her. "But this thing just covered me except for the eyes, sort of like we are now, covered except for the eyes. It was hot, and I hated it, but there was one big advantage."

"What?" Annie asked her, seeming genuinely interested.

"I could carry a submachine gun under my clothes and nobody was the wiser." She looked back at the cryogenic chamber, at Michael's face. There was movement there, the eyelids fluttering just slightly. He was the most beautiful man she'd ever seen—one of the two most beautiful. The readouts on the control panel were looking just as they should. "He's coming around."

"He's going to really be mad. He just did this so we could get Momma out."

Natalia said to Annie, "We will not free your mother by means such as this. And I know that somehow. If Zimmer will not perform the operation to get that bullet out, I have ways of making him, ways that were taught to me."

The best method with the cryogenic chambers was to let the sleeper awaken himself, and Natalia moved away from the chamber, leaning back against one of the fuselage ribs while she waited.

It could take only a few minutes or as long as close to an hour for Michael Rourke to come out of the Sleep. Natalia Anastasia Tiemerovna, after all these years, was an expert on judging such things.

And, Michael would be irate.

She was fast becoming an expert on Michael Rourke, too.

# Chapter Fourteen

It was the largest of several briefing rooms located at the allied airbase at Hekla. And it was filled with pilots and ground personnel. Sitting in the front row, in fresh gear, her face washed and her hair combed but (Rourke suspected) time to do little else, was Emma Shaw. She would lead one of the fighter groups which would back up the ground attack.

John Rourke stood at the podium, an enormous video display screen behind him. The data obtained from the late Alan Crockett's discs was en route both electronically and physically (by transatmospheric insertion flight) to Hawaii, some of it already acted upon.

On the podium was a control panel. With it, Rourke could instantly summon any of the digitized video images within the computer. He wasn't fully familiar with the system's operation, but after a short briefing knew it well enough to use it for his purposes. The principle behind the system was one with which he did have some familiarity, from the days Before the Night of the War. Digitizing video for the purposes of off-line editing was just coming into its own, then, with equipment such as the EMC-2 editing computer. Rourke participated in the making of several training videos and, always a bit of a technology buff, took considerable interest in the editing process.

The idea was the same. He would be editing the bank of images within the computer so that he could utilize the proper images to illustrate the battle plan.

With the fingers of his right hand, his left hand resting on the podium, Rourke started punching in the time-code numbers for the digitized frames he had preselected. "All right, ladies and gentlemen, we've used up precious time already, time we may not have. But, that was necessary in order to assemble the required forces. This will be your only briefing, why it is being done en masse, as it were.

"We have a dual mission," Rourke went on. "The first portion of that mission involves doing as much damage as possible to the Nazi and Eden forces assembled in upstate New York in preparation for an assault against the Aryan Supremicist regime which controls the one-time presidential war retreat. From the video images provided by the late Professor Alan Crockett," Rourke said, changing video images as he spoke to a close-up of the assembling enemy forces, "we have a reasonably detailed idea of force strength. If we can do severe damage to this force, we'll be neutralizing a substantial portion of the Nazi forces in North America.

"We need to accomplish that," Rourke told them. "Even now, cargo lifters are en route to a drop zone where what armor we could muster on such short notice will be employed, these units originating in Lydveldid Island, France and New Germany. The bulk of the damage we hope to do, however, will be accomplished from the air. Squadrons from those areas already mentioned as well as carrier-based aircraft stationed in the North Atlantic will all participate. We'll have the Nazi forces severely outgunned in the air, but they'll have the superior numbers on the ground.

"Meanwhile, as this attack is going on, a second phase of the operation will be getting underway. This second phase concerns a ground attack against Nazi headquarters in Northwestern Canada. The bulk of the enemy forces which will be engaged in upstate New York, originated at this Nazi base and, because of that, with these forces otherwise engaged, we have a rare opportunity to take over the base, if possible, or destroy it if necessary.

"The ground attack on the Nazi headquarters complex," Rourke continued, aerial surveillance photos of the base and its environs now on screen, "will consist of two elements. The first will be comprised of a group of volunteer commandos, Navy SEALs and German Long Range Mountain Patrol personnel. This unit will infiltrate the Nazi headquarters complex for a specific personnel-related mission.

"The second element of the ground attack will be launched on a signal from within the Nazi Headquarters complex or at a specified time, whichever comes first. At that time, air support— exactly two squadrons, because that's all we can spare—will come in and knock out anything outside the complex itself, or at least we hope. Commander Shaw will lead one of the two squadrons and will be overall commander for the two fighter squadrons.

"Each of you has a standard mission pack, detailing map coordinates, unit strengths, logistics, mission statements and all other necessary data. I must emphasize, however," Rourke said very slowly, "that the commando operation against the Nazi headquarters is only partially related to the primary objective. All of the personnel involved in this phase of the operation are volunteers. The survival of the commando force is not a primary objective. Questions?"

He would have gone in alone after his family, just he and Paul both would have, but Paul saw to it that word got out and in less than a quarter of an hour, John Rourke had a list of volunteers five times the size he could practically employ. He was genuinely touched.

# Chapter Fifteen

Emma Shaw jumped out of the half-tracked transport truck and waved the driver on. She could catch another one on her way to the other end of the airfield. Her helmet under her arm, her just-washed and still slightly damp hair making her freeze in the subarctic blasts, she ran toward the cargo lifter which was still boarding. For a moment, she didn't see John Rourke, but there was a knot of men in black BDUs near the rear cargo doors and she ran toward them. As the knot of men broke, she saw John, who had been at their center. "John!"

John Rourke looked around, waved, said something to one of the men still beside him, then walked toward her. Dressed as he was, he looked even taller than he normally did, all in black, black jump boots, black BDU pants, a black sweater beneath a black parka, the parka open despite the cold. He was bare-headed, and the wind touseled his hair almost wickedly.

Emma Shaw stopped, stood there, just watching him. She was head over heels in love for the first time in her life, and she was certain for the only time. And he was a married man, readying himself for a rescue mission, to save his wife.

He stopped just a few feet away from her. "I just—" Emma Shaw began.

"I couldn't see you after the briefing, everybody coming up and asking stuff, uh."

"Look, I, uh, I just wanted to tell you—"

"What?" John asked her.

"I, uh—I want you to know that we're all pulling for you to get your wife and family out of there and that it all—" And Emma Shaw started to cry and cursed herself for it, started turning her face away so he wouldn't see, but she was certain he'd seen her already. And, in the next instant, she felt his arms around her. "I'm sorry!" Emma blurted out, letting him hold her, resting her head against his chest. "This is so fucking dumb of me!"

"No." That was all he said. She felt his fingertips raising her chin and she tried blinking back her tears as their eyes met. "I love you." Then he let go of her and walked away.

Emma Shaw stood there, the wind so cold now that her body was shaking uncontrollably. He boarded the aircraft, never looking back. But he'd said that he loved her. Her knees were weak.

She muttered the word, "Asshole!" She was talking about herself . . .

John Rourke saw her through the window, then looked away, locking his chair into position and looking to his weapons. Once the aircraft began to taxi, he would secure them. The chair was vastly more comfortable than the old bench-style seating from the air drops in the days Before the Night of the War. The chairs allowed position adjustment and had fold-down desk plates, much like the old Thompson chairs of his high-school days. The little desks accommodated last-minute note taking, tasks like that. John Rourke began field-stripping one of the ScoreMasters, pulling the magazine and emptying the chamber first. One of the pleasures of the Detonics system was that there was no removable barrel bushing with which to contend, and the basic Colt/Browning design field-stripped much more simply. One merely aligned the slide of the empty pistol with the disassembly notch and worked out the slide stop. He closed his eyes.

Emma Shaw.

A man shouldn't say what he had said and then just walk away. It wasn't right. "Paul?"

Paul was forward in the fuselage, going over details with the jump master, and looked back when John Rourke called his name. "John?"

"Keep an eye on this, huh? Be back in a second." And Rourke picked up the two subassemblies of the ScoreMaster, folded back the desk just enough to slide out from behind it, put down the pistol's parts and started aft.

The cargo doors there were still open and Rourke ducked past a pallet with snowmobiles packed aboard it, walked onto the ramp and down to the runway. Emma had probably gone already. It was exceedingly cold, a fact of which he was doubly aware because he had left his coat in the aircraft. But, as Rourke walked around the tail section coming up along the left side of the craft, he saw her, standing where he'd left her.

"Emma?"

She looked up, didn't move.

John Rourke stood his ground about three yards from her, the engines starting to rev, deicing beginning. "I just couldn't go away without—"

"What did it mean when you said you loved me? What am I supposed to do, now, John? I'd like to know."

"I don't know."

"Did you mean it?"

"Yes, I meant it." It was necessary almost to shout because of the increasing mechanical noise.

"So, what am I supposed to do?"

"I told you that I don't know."

"Should I wait for you, to see what happens, and then if nothing happens, just pretend you never said it?"

"I shouldn't have said it," Rourke told her.

Her shoulders dropped and her gloved hands balled into tiny fists, her helmet falling to the runway surface, rolling, stopping a few feet from her. "But, damn it, if you shouldn't have said it and you knew you shouldn't have said it then you said it because you really feel it, right?"

"Yes, I really feel it."

"I love you!" Emma Shaw bent over to pick up her helmet, brushed the snow away from it, then looked at him. "I love you! Know why I said it? Because I feel it too, damn it!" Sticking the helmet under her arm as a football player would have carried a ball, she broke into a run, away from the aircraft.

Rourke stood there for several seconds, watching her, then just closed his eyes.

There was nothing else to say, nothing he could tell her, although there were things he wanted to tell her. That he respected her, that he cared for her, that he loved her—but there was nothing that he could do about it because of the way that he was made.

And, somehow he thought Emma Shaw knew all that already.

John Rourke looked after her for a second longer, then turned and walked back into the aircraft.

# Chapter Sixteen

Michael Rourke, too weak still to dress, sat wrapped in a blanket, the thin, very loose-fitting jumpsuit that was standard cryogenic Sleep attire, beneath it. His metabolism wasn't quite what it should be, yet, and he was cold. The important thing now, of course, was to consume plenty of fluids, get his kidneys and urinary tract flushed out, then get some nourishment into his body. He was so weak that he was almost too weak to listen, but he made himself do that, as Natalia, who sat opposite him, spoke. "And that's why we—and it was really my decision—thought it was the best thing to get you out of the Sleep. Do you agree?"

Michael exhaled, closed his eyes, opened them again. The weakness was something that could

110

not be avoided, especially because he had forced himself out of the chamber a little too soon. He was paying for that now.

But, he said, "I think I follow your reasoning. I mean, if we have to, I can always go back. So, yeah, I guess you guys did the right thing. I don't know anything for sure, now. Get me some more water, huh?"

And Michael Rourke leaned his head back. His father and Paul were off tracking down Hitler's remains because Zimmer had made that a condition of the deal for getting his mother the operation she so desperately needed in order to be truly alive again. And a virtual Nazi aerial armada had left the area, flying east, in the same direction his father and Paul had gone.

He considered what this had to be doing to Paul, and what a magnificent person his brother-in-law, Paul Rubenstein, really was.

Natalia returned with a glass of water, helping Michael to hold it, tilting the cup for him. Annie had left them to be alone for a little while, which was sweet of her, but under the circumstances, he didn't think he would have had the energy to kiss Natalia on the cheek. "You're gonna have to get me up and moving pretty soon; just let me rest a little while longer. If you're right, I'm going to need to be ready to move. The thing is, we can't even try to get the plane airborne, because if we initiate anything it might trigger a response from Deitrich Zimmer and he might kill Mom."

"I know. You just rest a bit, and we'll get you up and around. I should make love to you like this, when you're too weak to move. And, you wouldn't have to."

Michael felt himself smiling. "If you're trying to raise my blood pressure, it's working."

"Good. But we need it in the arms and the legs most of all," she told him, smiling brightly, then leaning forward and kissing him on the cheek. "I did not want you to be helpless if Zimmer's forces tried something, and I just have this feeling that—"

"You've been hanging around with Annie too long, with her feelings about things. Trouble is, she's always right," Michael added . . .


Both ScoreMasters were field-stripped, cleaned and reloaded, as were John Rourke's other guns. The Crain Life-Support System X knife's primary edge was touched up, although it really hadn't required it, as were both edges of the A. G. Russell Sting IA Black Chrome.

And John Rourke was left with nothing to do for twenty minutes or so but think, about Sarah, abut the mission to save her and Wolfgang, and about her and Wolfgang, and about the rest of his family, his son and daughter and Natalia. Rourke shook his head. He had loved Natalia, in many ways still did, but it was not like the feelings he had—totally irrational—for Emma Shaw. She was extraordinary, and—like many men, Rourke imagined—he was at once mystified yet fiercely attracted by the openness of her love for him.

But it wasn't right, and he had spent his entire

life trying to do what was right. He had almost betrayed that life, in a moment of weakness when he'd thought that Sarah was dead. If he had, he would never have forgiven himself. Fidelity was something John Rourke had always viewed as being implicit to marriage, even if the marriage were not "working out" as people sometimes so euphemistically put it. His and Sarah's marriage had never been known for "working out," nor had they ever made any secret of that.

That he even had told Emma that he loved her was disgraceful, Rourke thought, and wrong for her. He was being the sort of man he had always considered beneath contempt, leading on a woman, taking advantage of her.

He forced thoughts of Emma Shaw from his mind, focusing on Sarah, how lovely she was, how good it would be to have her with him again.

But, it had rarely been good between them.

And, it was the same for his parents. John Rourke lit a cigarette, a cigar too offensive in the confined quarters of the aircraft. The men of the commando unit—American SEALs, German Long Range Mountain Patrol personnel—were all deep within themselves, some listening to music with earphones, a few of them playing cards, others sitting with their eyes closed. Rourke closed his eyes again.

His father and mother had never fought, nor was anything even suggested that they would not stay together, but it was very hard to have imagined them friends in the true sense of the word, which they probably had been once, before war,

113

hot and cold, kept his father away. They were married for quite a few years before the War with Hitler and Tojo, Rourke's father working for what would later become known as the National Security Agency. Rourke had accessed his father's personnel file once—something he wasn't supposed to do, of course—through a friend in NSA.

John Rourke's father and mother rarely did things together, and it seemed obvious that they no longer had very much in common. When his father was home, there was an extra plate on the table, but rarely was there conversation between a man and woman who were often separated for protracted periods of time.

In those days, as he learned much later from that very same personnel file, his father worked through the transition from World War II OSS and Cold War Central Intelligence Agency. For a brief period, there was no real transitional agency, and his father worked as a security consultant for one of the international oil companies.

And, always, unfailingly, when his father was home they—he and his father—spent a great deal of time together, shooting, prowling the woods, building things, talking.

It was as if whatever had existed between his parents had ceased to exist anymore.

There were pictures of his parents locked arm in arm, smiles on their faces, the perfect happy couple.

There were pictures like that of John Rourke and his wife, too.

The jump master's voice made him open his eyes. "Excuse me, sir, but we've picked up a tail wind. We'll be over the drop zone in about twelve minutes."

"How are weather conditions?"

"Perfect night for a drop, sir; heavy, high cloud cover, a little snow, nice and soft," the man laughed. "I'll be getting the men formed up."

"Thank you, Sergeant," Rourke told him, nodding.

John Rourke sat up in his seat, running a last-minute mental checklist. It was good to have something to do.

# Chapter Seventeen

In these high-tech days, airborne troops utilized a new jump method incorporating state-of-the-art control systems. The talented man or woman who was thoroughly conversant with the necessary techniques was able to navigate to the center of a bull's eye target with uncanny accuracy under a wide range of weather conditions. These were high-altitude, high-opening jumps, or HAHOs. The opposite of the current method was the old HALO jump, high altitude and low opening. Since it was no longer employed in warfare because it could be inordinately dangerous, John Rourke elected to employ it now.

The wind rush tore at his clothing, whistled through the tiny gaps between flesh and helmet. It was bitterly cold and his flesh numbed with it, albeit that not a centimeter of skin was bare. John Rourke had been jump-qualified since his early teens, skydiving for fun then; but, the exhilaration of the jump never left him.

By utilizing the same high-tech instrument packs as were employed in the standard method, however, the potential for precision landings was just as great.

His arms extended, legs forming a V-notch, Rourke floated through the night sky, his eyes alternating between the men surrounding him, Paul among them, the darkness below, and the instruments on his chest pack. Not only were there dual digital altimeters and wind-speed gauges, but there was a constant readout from the global positioning satellites. The global positioning system had been implemented Before the Night of the War, but those older satellites had long since fallen from their orbits and burned in reentry. There were few of the new global positioning satellites in place, the system growing again; but, one of the geosynchronous units was positioned over the eastern coast of Greenland and in a perfect location for their operation to take advantage of.

The readout from the global positioning satellite provided a constant update in degrees, minutes and seconds of both longitude and latitude, so by slightly altering the vector of one's body (assuming a reasonable amount of skill in doing so), it was possible to keep to a relatively precise flight path. One of the greatest advantages of the system was that it was totally passive, no signal necessary from the person using it, as had been the case with the original.

Rourke was little worried about himself or the bulk of the commando force, beyond ordinary concern at least. But, he was worried about Paul Rubenstein, Paul unused to jumping, but game enough to try. Rourke's eyes scanned the night sky around him now for some sign of Paul and found it. His friend was easily picked out, the least graceful because of his inexperience, the most rigid in body language of the commando team. Nonetheless, Paul was with them and well within the descent path. The two most experienced jumpers in the unit had volunteered to fly with him, flanking him on the way down lest Paul should get in trouble. Rourke doubly admired his friend's courage. And, Paul would be indispensable once he was on the ground—of all the men Rourke knew now or had ever known, the one Rourke most counted on.

His eyes back on his chest pack once more, Rourke mentally ran a weapons check. Everything was secured. The double Alessi shoulder rig with his twin stainless Detonics CombatMaster .45s was stowed in his gear. His two ScoreMasters, the larger .45s which he normally carried holsterless in his belt, were this time carried in matching full-flap military holsters, fabricated of waterproof black ballistic nylon and lined with waterproof black doeskin suede, these suspended from a military pistol belt, one gun on each hip. The only other firearms on Rourke's body were the HK-91, slung tight against him in a drop case, and the little hip-gripped .38 Special Centennial, this latter secured within the right outside pocket of his coat, instantly to hand if needed.

The knives which John Rourke carried as a matter of course—the A.G. Russell Sting IA Black Chrome, the Crain Life-Support System X and the little Executive Edge Grande pen-shaped pocket folder—were supplemented by a knife given him by the leader of the contingent from New Germany, Captain Klein, his name by some biological accident well-descriptive of his stature. What the fellow lacked in height, however, was offset by build; Klein was one of the most muscular men Rourke had ever encountered. Captain Klein warned, "Herr Doctor, you have jumped often enough to know, I am sure, when there is a certain type of knife which can prove itself when others cannot."

Rourke smiled in return, saying, "I was planning on finding someone from whom I might borrow a switchblade, yes. I've never liked the things, although I admit their utility under circumstances such as these."

"I am a student of edged weaponry, Herr Doctor, and I have come to the realization that in the past such knives were often cheaply fabricated and unreliable. Allow me to present you with this one, however. I would consider it a personal favor and a great honor were you to accept it, not as a loan but as a gift. I acquired several of these a number of years ago and always have at least two spares with me."

Rourke thanked Ernst Klein, accepting the

knife. The handle slabs were of synth-stag, so identical to the real thing that it was difficult to realize they were man-made. And the action of the knife, the blade geometry and finishing, all bespoke a quality which Rourke had rarely seen in switchblade knives.

The switchblade was in the pocket opposite the one carrying the little revolver, ready for instant one-hand opening and use with the parachute rigging should circumstances demand this.

The jump goggles Rourke wore were capable of being switched back and forth instantly (at the flick of a toggle) between standard and vision intensification. The controls were wired along the outside of Rourke's left sleeve to a master alongside Rourke's left palm, this so that one would not be forced to alter a flight vector in order to change the mode of the goggles. Rourke flipped to vision intensification. Below him, the countryside became only somewhat more visible, but sufficiently so that it was possible to make out some few of the more significant terrain features.

The perspective between aerial photo and the real thing was always difficult to grasp in the first instants. Usually, it required some visual cue to serve as the identifier which suddenly made the mosaic of dissociated images take on order and meaning. Such was the case now. There was an iced-over lake, its westernmost shore forming what looked like the partial profile of a man with a large, bulbous, hooked nose. Rourke's attention focused on this until the other details, like pieces of a jigsaw puzzle, started reforming in his mind, falling into place.

To the northwest of the oddly shaped noselike shoreline lay a progressively widening notch which had once been a river course, perhaps in the past as recent as Before the Night of the War or in a past more distant still. The commando team would move along the south wall of the notch until it widened some five miles further out, deepening as well, forming a gorge of considerable depth and breadth. At the point where the broadening and deepening began, however, the commando team would follow the terrain upward, toward what would be the height of the gorge.

Some six miles beyond this point lay the north face of Mt. Wolseley, named after the courageously controversial Victorian-era British soldier, Field Marshall Sir Garnett Joseph Wolseley. The mountain would most assuredly have been renamed by the Nazis, whose headquarters redoubt lay both within and atop it.

Rourke's eyes still alternated between his physical surroundings and his monitoring of his chest pack. The readouts, in red diodes, were brilliantly bright, but not harmfully so, when viewed through vision intensification. And soon it would be time for chute activation.

Rourke switched from vision intensification to standard, then back again, trying to fix the terrain features as firmly as he could, through normal vision. After several tries, he had these with his own night vision.

Altimeter readings were nearing the magic

number. Coordinates as played from the global positioning satellite signal were as perfect as they could be, judging from the computer scenario for the jump.

Rourke slowly reached up, pulling the rip cord for his primary chute.

There was a sudden loss of aerodynamic stability, the rustle of fabric in the wind, then a jerk as his body was caught up, torn upward, his shoulders and back feeling the snap. Immediately, his eyes glancing once to the chest pack, Rourke's hands moved to the shroud lines, playing them as he alternately watched the dark shapes below him and the coordinate readouts. As he looked around him, the other chutes were open as well. He sought out Paul, located him, breathed a figurative sigh of relief that his friend's chute had opened properly. Therein lay the true danger for the novice: jumping out of an airplane wasn't difficult under satisfactory conditions, nor landing that dangerous (provided one knew how to fall); but panic, should something malfunction, could kill.

There was no equipment chute, because it would have to be opened via a static line or radio activation. And, a manless chute could not navigate.

Therefore, all the equipment they would utilize was carried on their bodies.

The ground seemed to be rising quite rapidly now, Rourke fighting his shroud lines as wind gusts tore at his chute. The objective was to land near the noselike feature on the lakeshore, not to be blown miles off course. There was no time to look for Paul or anyone else, and the altimeter and coordinate readouts were superfluous now. By manipulating the shroud lines, however, he slightly altered the vector of his descent, the chute sweeping him over the shoreline, almost too far.

And suddenly the ground was racing toward him and Rourke flexed his legs for impact, the wind gusting into his chute in the very last second he was airborne, starting to drag him. For an instant, Rourke thought that Captain Ernst Klein's gift of the switchblade knife would somehow prove prophetic, but Rourke was able to roll, capturing the shroud lines as the wind and the snow it drove whipped almost cyclonically around him. For a few seconds, Rourke fought the shroud lines, but at last he had the chute itself, crushing it with his body weight.

Quickly, he began bundling the parachute into his arms, his eyes darting from side to side as he scanned the night, both for the others of his unit and for any sign of enemy personnel. Of the latter, there was none.

Rourke turned his gaze skyward. Four of the chutes were just coming down, all to the north, but not far. Rourke looked to the mission clock set into his chest pack. Eleven miles of hard travel lay ahead, and every second lost might be critical. He attacked the crushed parachute as if it were an enemy he had to subdue . . .

It was like a roller-coaster ride at an amusement park when he was a teenager. Paul Rubenstein had never liked amusement-park rides, except the tamer ones, simply because he'd always reasoned that if someone were that desperate to feel like vomiting, it was cheaper and easier just to stick a finger down the throat. But, when a girl or some of the other guys would nag at him to try the ride and, on rare occasions, he would, he almost invariably enjoyed himself.

The airdrop was just like that. There were rational arguments galore against even considering it, but he knew he had to be with John for this mission, so he did it, made the jump. And, despite a few microseconds here and there of unadulterated terror, in restrospect now, Paul Rubenstein realized he'd enjoyed it. At the back of his mind, there was already the growing desire to do it again, to willfully addict himself to the adrenaline rush of jumping out of an airplane into darkness as deep as shadow, then glide through the air like a soaring bird, have time dilate where seconds seemed like an eternity, where commitment was total.

He could write about the experience in his journal, if they made it through this one and got back.

The odds, of course, were stacking up against them, him and John Rourke. Over the course of six hundred and twenty-five years, they had been in battle after battle, met danger after danger, survived when by all logic they should have perished. Yet, they were still here, on their way to the next brush with death.

Like a gambler on a winning run at blackjack

124

or roulette, the odds were with the house, and if the house won, they perished.

In the midst of the Navy SEALs and German Long Range Mountain Patrol personnel, it was hard to imagine failure and its price; and, if he had ever dwelt on that price, he would not have survived in the immediate aftermath of the Night of the War, nor since.

The idea was to keep going, hoping to cheat the odds, but dismissing the possibilities for doing so. Most people who knew John Rourke would have said that John's motto was, "Plan ahead." Indeed, John lived by that dictum. However, even more apt would be, "Give it your best and never give up." He had learned that from John Rourke and he would do that, until or unless the odds did catch up with one or both of them.

Paul Rubenstein shrugged his shoulders under his pack and checked the digital readout on his compass—a passive receptor for global positioning satellite transmissions, virtually identical to the instrumentation on the chest pack he'd worn during the jump. If it read correctly, they were on their way toward the very heart of Deitrich Zimmer's Nazi threat.

Annie, Natalia and Michael were the primary objective, the main objective the headquarters itself, wherein they would find the real Wolfgang Mann and Sarah, John's wife. And John might find horror.

# Chapter Eighteen

Buckling on the last of his weapons, Michael Rourke looked at Natalia and at his sister, Annie, asking, "Since this was your idea, ladies, what now?"

"We should wait," Natalia told him, "and observe. Come aft with me and we will see."

He'd already been aft once, taking only a pistol, freezing cold (because of his then still-depressed metabolism) and feeling both exhausted and slightly silly at the same time, a blanket wrapped around him over his coat. He saw nothing for his trouble beyond what the two women had told him to expect. But Michael Rourke agreed with their assessment of the situation. Something had already gone or was in the process of going off the graph of the plan, which altered the conditions under which they could expect to operate.

They lay on their stomachs atop stacked cargo mats, looking out with night-vision binoculars through the open rear cargo doors, his sister to his left, Natalia to his right. "One of us should go out there and reconnoiter."

Michael recognized the pilot's voice from the darkness behind them. "That's a good way to get killed, Mr. Rourke."

"Agreed, Lieutenant, but it's just as easy—perhaps even easier—to get killed because we don't know what's going on. And don't use my name in the open like that. If they have long-range sound equipment trained on us—parabolic microphones or similar—you could have blown the whole operation."

"I'm sorry, sir. I just wasn't—"

"Hopefully there's no harm done," Annie supplied.

"Perhaps you are right about fresh data being required," Natalia said. "I'm the most experienced, so—"

"No way," Michael told her. "I won't let you."

"You won't let me?"

"Look, guys, we could be getting listened to right now," Annie implored.

Michael jerked on both their arms, then started back, keeping low to avoid getting into the line of sight of any sensing equipment, then slipping through the doorway leading to the main compartment, standing as he did so, stepping aside and waiting while the others followed. "That's

127

the last of us," the navigator whispered hoarsely. They closed the door leading aft and Michael sat down. "Shouldn't we—?" the navigator started.

"One of you go forward, two of you go aft, and be ready for anything," Natalia ordered.

Michael inwardly laughed, realizing how close to near dismemberment the crew had come; if anyone had questioned Natalia's orders after what he had said to her and she had answered back, it would have been a huge mistake.

The three crewmen took up their stations, the compartment was empty again save for Annie, Natalia and himself. Michael looked at Annie, saying, "Sis? How's about keeping the pilot company in the cockpit?"

Annie looked at him for a moment, shaking her head as she shrugged out of her parka. "Fine," was all she said, leaving the compartment.

Natalia was out of her coat, pacing the aisle. Michael still wore his, a bit cold. "So, what's on your mind?"

"Why are you ordering me to do something? I'll do what I feel is best, just as I always have, Michael!"

"I figure it this way, all right? We run the defroster system on the engines, which will get the interest of anybody watching the aircraft. If they don't have a full sensor array on us, they will then. I slip out just before that. You and Annie and the crew make yourselves a little noticeable. You restarted the cryogenic chamber, so they'll be getting a readout on that. That means everybody's accounted for, so they won't suspect someone skulking around. That's basically it."

"It could work, unless they already have what we're doing, which is possible. Annie and I discussed things before we revived you. I wasn't thinking."

"So, you're angry at me because you're angry at yourself."

"That is not—"

"And there's another reason I won't let you go out there," Michael said, knowing he was pushing things hard.

Natalia wheeled toward him, lit a cigarette, her surrealistically blue eyes hard pinpoints of light, aimed into his soul. "There's a lot of stuff you can do better than I can; and, I'm very well aware of that. But a man thinks differently than a woman, sometimes. Even if the woman is better at something, and it's dangerous, even a little—"

"Oh, don't be silly!"

"What do you want me to say?"

"Not that!"

"Fine, then! I'll lay my cards on the table. I want you to have my children, and I'm old-fashioned enough to figure we should get started on that after we're married. So, be my wife, marry me, okay?"

"Michael?"

"Fine," Michael told her, shaking his head in mock disgust. He stood up, walked over to where she stood, legs spread, feet squared as if she were going to fight someone. He took her right hand in his, dropped to one knee and asked, "Will you marry me, Natalia?"

"I—"

"Well, will you?"

Natalia's hand went rigid. "I—yes."

"Good." Michael took the cigarette from her hand, stubbed it out, then pulled her down to her knees, in front of him, his arms enfolding her, the fingers of his right hand entwining in her almost-black hair, cocking her head back. Her lips parted. Michael kissed her, then stopped. "You really mean it? You'll marry me, Natalia?"

"Yes, I'll marry you, Michael. Yes. Yes. Yes. I will marry you. I will be Mrs. Michael Rourke and I will have your babies, as many of them as you want. Is that what you want to hear?"

Michael drew Natalia close to him, kissed her hard on the mouth, feeling her hands touching at his neck, his face. It was what he had wanted to hear.

# Chapter Nineteen

Michael Rourke heard the crunch of snow under his boots and stopped in his tracks. If he could hear it, so could the enemy. He dropped to a prone position, edging forward on knees and elbows through the swirling windswept snow, the visibility so poor that, unaided as his eyes were, he could see little more than a few yards ahead.

As if in a radio play (there was an entire collection of fully soundscaped radio drama from the Atlanta Radio Theater in the library at the Retreat), like the slamming of a door or the tapping of a boot heel on a staircase, perfectly on cue, the noise of the aircraft engine deicers began and, once again, Michael Rourke could rise to his full height and move more quickly through the night.

All ears and all audio-sensing would be on the aircraft, all eyes and video-sensing as well.

Natalia was going to marry him. It wasn't as if her agreement was a big surprise, but it just felt better somehow knowing that she'd said yes and that it was as official as it could be under the circumstances.

Annie would know by now, probably be crying her eyes out with happiness, and certainly planning what she'd wear to the wedding. But, Annie was like that, one of the toughest and most intelligent and competent persons he knew, but on the other hand classically, almost stereotypically female in her fascination with clothing and the like.

He would tell his father that he and Natalia were at last going to get married. That would not be easy, even though his father expected it. It still would not be easy, because his father had loved Natalia, in many ways still did. At first, when Michael had realized what he felt for her, the situation which preexisted between her and his father bothered him greatly. Afterward, after their first time together, he realized that he'd really never had any choice at all; what his father had once planned for, counted on taking place between them—Michael and Natalia—was right all along.

Michael reached the nearest rock outcropping and dropped behind it. There would be perimeter defense systems set up. Under normal conditions, Michael Rourke could have worn special infiltration goggles designed to detect electronic countermeasures, by both visual and auditory means. But the keening of the wind and the blowing snow would obviate the usefulness of any such device now. So, it was back to good old stealth and a little luck.

Michael Rourke started moving again . . .

The ground abruptly dropped off before them and John Rourke signaled a halt. He flipped his goggles to vision intensification, perusing the sprawling terrain in greater detail. There were no land pirates in these parts, the climate too inhospitable except for persons possessing state-of-the-art equipment. Rourke himself wished that they had the snowmobiles, but these would be air-dropped only after the attack on the Nazi headquarters was well under way and no element of surprise would be sacrificed. They would be the means of escape from the Nazi facility with the rescued prisoners, two of the snowmobiles specially outfitted to two small trailers that were portable life-support chambers, in the event that Sarah and/or Wolfgang Mann required these.

For now, however, it was foot travel, and six miles more of hard terrain lay ahead. John Rourke turned to the man behind him, rasping through the toque which covered his face. "We're heading for the high ground. Pass it on and get moving."

"Right, sir!"

John Rourke shrugged his shoulders beneath his pack and kept moving through the numbing cold . . .


Hawaii had been noted for its tropical warmth, the closest place to paradise on Earth, Before the Night of the War. Tim Shaw was glad he hadn't lived in those days. Warm weather was something he'd always disliked, but he was never exactly fond of bitter cold, either. To him, the current Hawaiian climate was paradise-like. There was frequent rain, often there was dense cloud cover and, when the sun shone (as it still did quite a bit over the islands), there was usually a cool breeze off the Pacific and a light jacket or sweater was the order of the day.

But he was in shirtsleeves now, his knit tie down to half-mast, his sleeves rolled up, an open bag of pretzels beside him. He'd kept his shoes on, despite his predilection for removing them, because if the Nazi saboteurs came after him tonight for their revenge, he didn't want to be caught barefoot.

Half stuffed between the sofa cushions was his .45, the hammer down over an empty chamber. The little Centennial was tucked in his trouser waistband. He lit a cigarette and hit the play button on the remote control unit for the vidscreen.

Despite his profession, Tim Shaw was not overly fond of cop movies. And, despite the period in which he lived, he wasn't particularly fond of modern movies. The morality was too complex for his tastes. For entertainment to be genuinely entertaining, at least in most cases, he felt it should be basic. And, there was nothing more basic than the Western.

The Western was a uniquely American art form, and rarely practiced in this day and age. He doubted seriously that a really good, authentic Western could still be made, certainly not as good as the old ones.

The video he watched was old indeed. The cast included a young John Wayne, a beautiful Claire Trevor, a brilliantly debauched Thomas Mitchell, in the heroic saga of a stagecoach traveling west.

When he was a young man, Tim Shaw had actually gone down to Lancers and bought a reproduction of the Winchester Model 1892, had the barrel cut back to sixteen inches, had a hoop lever fitted to it and, almost religiously, practiced roll-cocking the rifle, just as John Wayne had done with such quiet authority. Eventually, Tim Shaw got it right.

At about the same time that he mastered the art, he matured to the point where he could no longer fantasize that such a skill would ever be useful to a twenty-fifth century cop in Hawaii. And he hung the rifle on the wall. Tim Shaw's eyes drifted from the screen to the rifle—it only came down from the wall for an occasional range session or a cleaning.

And, he laughed at himself as he grabbed a handful of pretzels. It wasn't the gun, or the epoch in history, but the spirit. Maybe none of his cowboy heroes carried a Lancer reproduction of a stainless steel Colt Government Model .45 automatic, but that didn't matter. The idea of standing for justice was what was important, not the tools which aided the man or woman who stood.

Over the centuries of mankind's existence, battles were fought with bones and clubs and swords of all descriptions and guns ranging from the Single-Action Army or the Winchester lever-action to the M-16 and AK-47. The reason for the battles never changed. There were good people and there were bad people and sometimes violence growing out of the conflict between them was an unavoidable necessity.

The trick of it was for the good guys to shoot straighter than the bad guys.

Tim Shaw shot straight. Now, all he had to do was wait for the chance.

# Chapter Twenty

The nearest of the hermetically sealed tents appeared to be the command post. Michael Rourke's right hand held the copy of the Crain knife old Jon the Swordmaker had made for him more than a century ago at Lydveldid Island. In his left hand was one of the two Beretta 92F 9mm pistols from his double shoulder-holster rig.

There was an advantage to thinking on a level that was more low-tech than what was considered state-of-the-art. When someone wished to know what was going on inside a military tent these days, all sorts of electronic gadgetry could be utilized. Why bother to physically approach the tent, perhaps go inside, risking life and limb? Therefore, such direct physical action was little guarded against.

Michael hesitated. If he sliced through into the tent, he could avail himself of whatever classified materials might be inside; provided they were *en clair*, he would have useful data. On the down side, however, he would—in relatively short order—alert the enemy that something was afoot.

As he'd moved along the perimeter of the encampment which surrounded the aircraft in which Natalia, Annie and the crew were waiting, he'd detected several anomalies. First, although there were quite a number of vehicles and tents, there seemed to be very few personnel. Either guarding the aircraft was suddenly a low-priority task or this was just a show. With all the equipment Natalia and Annie had reported seeing, flying east, Michael Rourke now wondered if the mission to the east were some sort of emergency, or preplanned. If preplanned, why have two operations going simultaneously when, it appeared, there was a shortage of personnel? Or, was that planned, too?

His father and Paul had flown east, in their attempt to fulfill Deitrich Zimmer's bizarre demand in exchange for performing the required operation on Michael's mother. Was this some elaborate trap to capture his father and Paul, but then why not all of them, himself, Annie and Natalia included? And, he—Michael—was supposed to be Martin, in cryogenic Sleep, part of a trade for Sarah Rourke's life. Was it that Deitrich Zimmer just didn't care about Martin, that this was all a sham? Or, was this casual attitude toward Martin all part of a plan as well? Did Deitrich Zimmer know that Martin was dead? Then, why the charade?

Michael Rourke reached a decision: He was damned if he entered the tent to steal information, yet might be damned if he didn't. Glancing from side to side, double-checking his earlier assessment that he'd bypassed the tent's rather lackluster intruder defense system, he stabbed the knife into the fabric and, just as in the old videotapes he'd watched at the retreat, cut his way into the Arab/Indian tent.

There was a pneumatic hiss as the point where the knife penetrated the fabric, a rush of warm air wafting toward Michael's few centimeters of exposed skin—he wore no goggles. Quickly, Michael lengthened the cut and stepped through, squinting his eyes against the brighter light. There was no one about in this compartment and, as rapidly as he could, Michael sealed the rift in the tent's outer wall with the modern equivalent of duct tape. Like his father, Michael Rourke planned ahead.

He waited near the tent wall for several seconds, until his eyes were fully accustomed to the brighter light. He listened for the slightest sounds. There was the clicking of a computer keyboard from the next room. There was the low hum of music, perhaps from an audiodisk player. There was no other sound, except the barely noticeable whisper of the environmental conditioning, which heated the tent and circulated preheated air.

Michael pushed back the hood of his parka. Beneath it, he wore a black toque, the hoodlike garment masking his face completely except for the eye holes. He left the black hood in place. If he were discovered, there was no sense in advertising his identity.

Opening his coat against the warmth, a pistol in one hand again, the knife in the other, he crossed the small room—it was used for storage of message blanks, coffee, innocuous things like that. There was also a box of grenades. Michael already had some of his own.

He reached the doorway leading to the main section. His ear to the doorway, he could only hear the keyboard clicking louder, the music more recognizable. There was a nostalgia craze in Eden these days, he'd heard, and evidently this was something the Nazis were not immune to, either. The song playing was an electronic arrangement of one of Elvis Presley's big hits. At the retreat, there was an original record (a big black vinyl disk) with the song. Annie was always a big Elvis fan, as was Michael's mother.

There was no other sound.

Michael stuffed the Beretta into the waistband of his trousers, his sweater pulled up enough that he could grab the pistol's butt if need be. He turned the knob as slowly as he could, listening for the slightest squeak, attentive to any alteration in the rhythm of the keyboard clicking beyond.

If the computer console were oriented to face this doorway, Michael would be forced to use the gun. If not, he might be able to do what he needed to do silently. The door open now about six inches, Michael peered through.

The computer operator's back was to the doorway. There was no one else in the main compartment.

Three desks, a radio set, various monitors, a second computer console and a stack of assault rifles were all that remained in the compartment. This was a typical field command post, communications equipment, data processing, all instantly portable. Michael was beginning to wish he'd brought Natalia along. She was good with computers, just like Paul. He was not more than adequate, but learning.

He continued opening the door, widening it at last until he could slip through.

The snow had already melted from his boots. The floor of the structure was a carpetlike material. If he could approach silently enough, there was at once the chance that he could do what he came to do unmolested and that he would not be forced to kill the man sitting at the computer keyboard.

Michael Rourke, the knife in his right fist in a sabre hold, started moving, walking slowly toward the Nazi.

During the five years in which his father had left cryogenic Sleep and joined Michael and his sister, many things were learned. One of the skills his father taught them both had to do with the versatility of the knife as both a tool and a weapon. "You know how much I'm into guns, guys, right? But, if I had to choose one weapon only, I'd choose a knife. The reason for that is because a good knife, that isn't abused, can be used over and over again. But, eventually, especially with semiautomatics which shuck empty brass everywhere, you'll eventually run out of ammunition. Even if you have the facility to reload your own, eventually the cases will become unusable. A flintlock rifle, probably the most practical survival weapon you can have—you can make your powder, your shot, mine your flint—will cease to function under conditions of extreme dampness, can't be used in water at all, needs to be reloaded between shots.

"A good knife, on the other hand," their father went on to say, "doesn't run out of ammo, can be used regardless of weather conditions, won't fail you unless you use it improperly. You know I like big knives for some purposes. One of the reasons is that with a really large knife, you don't always have to use it as a knife in antipersonnel work. You can use it as a club."

There were two ways of doing just that (although a third way was to keep the knife sheathed, but this was dangerous in that if the knife were needed as a knife, time would be wasted ridding the steel of the leather or fabric). The first of the two ways would work well with a single-edge knife absent sawteeth. One utilized the spine of the blade. The second method worked with any large knife.

It was the second method which Michael Rourke was about to employ. He was fewer than four feet from the man at the computer console, still keeping his concentration on things other than the man himself. Whether it was some sixth sense only activated in times of mortal peril, or just coincidence combined with superstition, there was an old rule in sentry removal, applicable here: don't think about the target.

Michael rotated the knife slightly in his hand, primary edge out. As, very quickly now, he closed the gap between himself and the Nazi who was typing away at the computer, Michael Rourke's right arm raised, then arced downward, crashing the left flat of the blade downward. Steel contacted skull and, with his left arm, Michael caught the man as the Nazi slumped, unconscious, from his chair.

Michael lowered the fellow to the floor. From the pocket of his parka, Michael withdrew the modern equivalent of Flexcuffs, binding the Nazi computer operator's wrists behind him, then the ankles. With a piece of the duct tape he'd used to close the cut in the tent wall, he closed the man's mouth, first checking with his gloved fingers for any obstructions to the air passage, dentures (uncommon these days) or the like.

Michael left him beside the chair, then went to the tent's main entrance.

There would be guards outside, but there was nothing to indicate they had been roused. This was almost too easy, and perhaps it was that way because it had been planned to be. Had Michael killed the man working at the computer console, it would not have bothered a man such as Deitrich Zimmer at all.

Regardless of whether or not this was some elaborate setup, Michael set about his work.

The music disk was playing the Kurt Weill/Bert Brecht song from *Three-Penny Opera* about a fellow named Mack who was well known for his blade work. Michael sat at the computer console, exploring the program in which the now unconscious man had been working. The program revealed forces strength data, and from what Michael was able to determine, the Nazi headquarters some five miles distant was severely undermanned.

That made even less sense. Michael printed out the data which seemed most interesting, after the file was loaded into the printer's memory buffer, beginning to search the hard disk for additional data. At last, he was able to access another file. This contained information which, by all rights, didn't even belong in a system the primary purpose of which was expediting a military operation. Why was it there? The data concerned Dr. Zimmer's experiments with cloning human beings.

Zimmer had, the file related, successfully discovered the means by which to record the electromagnetic impulses of the human brain. He could probe through the brain—probably not very pleasant for the subject—and extract data. This was of considerable value to his military intelligence operations. No longer were torture, drug therapy or any other technique for the extraction of information against a subject's will required. Zimmer's probe replaced all of that. Michael realized, as he disgested the information, that the main fault intrinsic to Zimmer's new technique was the sheer volume of information which would be obtained. There was no one specific area of the brain which held "memory." There were, instead, cells throughout the brain, billions of them, and within these were subtle electrochemical connectors which strung together.

When one saw a tall, four-legged animal with an odd sort of chair on its back, myriad receptors processed and interpreted the data which instantly allowed the identification of the creature as a saddled horse.

The volume of data which would be extracted by, in essence, recording the brain was enormous, too much for even the most sophisticated of computers to process. Hence, the cloning. Zimmer had available a "bank" of living human beings kept in a state of suspended animation (probably cryogenic Sleep) whose sole function was the reception of such data.

Trans-Global Alliance Secret Agent X was captured, the electromagnetic impulses within his brain recorded, the information downloaded into one of cryogenic sleepers awakened for the specific purpose of receiving the information. The cryogenic sleeper, according to the data, had previously implanted within his or her brain an electronic device which could be utilized to stimulate pleasure or pain.

Should the human being receiving the downloaded information be endowed as well with the original subject's will and concurrent desire not to release the data, it was a simple matter to manipulate these pleasure and pain centers in order to convince the human receptor that answering all questions and divulging all information was the correct thing to do.

Michael instantly wondered why Zimmer went to all of the trouble. Why not simply place such a device in the brain of the interrogation subject? As Michael Rourke read on, that question was answered. Recovery from such an operation was estimated at a rate of seventy-five percent. What if the subject died? Then, the intelligence data would be lost forever. And, it was possible that while performing the operation the subject would be "damaged." That could mean specific areas of memory loss, tiny details which might prove vital—gone.

Michael regretted his meager German, because much of the data was in vocabulary which was well beyond him. Natalia, on the other hand, had perfect German.

The first file was printed and Michael set about printing this one. The notes beside the computer console dealt with forces deployment, specifying guard rosters and the like for the encampment surrounding the aircraft.

It was obvious to Michael Rourke that the information—in the file—was intended for him or one of the others from the family to see, to use. But, why? Was there some secret ally within the Nazi headquarters? Or, was it Deitrich Zimmer, manipulating them to his will?

Michael Rourke scanned through the rest of the files, finding few things of any real interest.

As soon as the file concerning Zimmer's cloning experiments and the other data pertinent to them was printed, he would be on his way.

# Chapter Twenty-One

The night was moonless because of the cloud cover, but through the vision-intensification binoculars, John Rourke was able to survey the encampment surrounding the aircraft clearly.

The rear cargo doors were open, and figures huddled there in the darkness behind a barricade, one of them using glasses similar to his own. They were the two women, he decided, Natalia and Annie. Near them, the cryogenic chamber in which Michael was ensconced was visible as well.

It was time for a very important decision, that being whether he would divide his force and simultaneously infiltrate the headquarters complex and attack the encampment here, or quietly penetrate and overtake the encampment, then

147

move on with his full force to the headquarters, that force supplemented by Natalia and Annie and, if possible, an awakened Michael.

Through the glasses, John Rourke studied guard deployment, apparent strength. The encampment was grossly undermanned for its size, and this struck him as extremely odd. Once he had awakened from his last session of cryogenic Sleep and ascertained that the world was, once again, at war, he had studied everything he could get his hands on concerning this new enemy, only to find that it was an old enemy which should have been extinct by all rights. The philosophy of racial superiority as an excuse for state-sponsored terrorism was not only vile, but insane.

In all that John Rourke had digested concerning the Eden Defense Forces and their Nazi allies, he had never found reason to accuse the enemy of poor generalship. Yet, here it was. The position could easily be overrun by a platoon of ordinary soldiers with a good plan behind them, or roughly a third that many men who were possessed of specialized training and the right amount of determination.

He had those men, and the determination was self-evident in their dedication; one did not become a United States Navy SEAL or a German Long Range Mountain Patrol commando without it, much less survive past one's first mission. And, the men with Rourke were seasoned veterans.

Added to this, Rourke knew the position taken by Commander Washington's Hawaii-based

SEAL Unit. Once he felt sufficiently confident that he could contact this unit without betraying the presence of his own team in the area, he would have an additional thirty-six battle-hardened men under his command.

There was something wrong. Perhaps it was a trap. He said as much to Paul Rubenstein who lay beside him just behind the lip of the ridge of ice and snow. "Looks like it to me, John. What'll we do? Bite?"

"Maybe. Dispatch two men—make it three— to make contact with Commander Washington's force. Have Washington and his men move up to along that ridge and then fan out on either side." Rourke gestured to the opposite edge of the ice field. "There and there. Tell them to be in position by—" And John Rourke rolled back the cuff of his snow smock and the storm sleeve of the arctic parka beneath it. The luminous black face of his Rolex Submariner read nearly 2:30 A.M. "Have Commander Washington get his people in place and ready to move by four on the dot. They'll attack openly using fire and maneuver elements and a lot of small-arms fire. At a few minutes before four, you'll take half of the team and infiltrate from the far side, over there," Rourke said, pointing to the north.

Paul, peering through his own night-vision binoculars, volunteered, "That outcropping of ice would be a good point."

"Agreed. I'll start the rest of the team from here. We meet in the middle of the camp. Get as far as we can before Commander Washington's people get everyone's attention focused on them, then we finish what we've started. Have the messengers impress upon Commander Washington that we've got to strike so rapidly that the Nazi Headquarters won't be alerted. It's far enough away that even in this clear, cold air, the gunfire won't be picked up. Make sure the messengers get it memorized. Nothing written down."

"Gotcha," Paul nodded, then started edging back from the ridge.

John Rourke returned to studying the encampment. If he could pull this off quickly, there was indeed the chance that Nazi headquarters would not be alerted and there would be some element of surprise remaining when he began the infiltration. That might prove crucial to saving Sarah's life. But, he could not abandon his son and daughter and Natalia in order to ensure that.

The cold was getting to him and he shifted position slightly, monitoring the schedule as the guards patrolled, searching for signs of electronic countermeasures, gauging distances. This would be quick and dirty or it wouldn't work at all and a lot of good people might die, his family included.

# Chapter Twenty-Two

The ready room was quiet as a funeral, except for two pilots in the far corner laughing over something in a magazine and the sound associated with the vidscreen dominating the far wall. The mission was as understood as it ever would be. As soon as the appropriate signal came in from John Rourke, her two wings would scramble and be airborne over the target in under thirteen minutes, using a modified atmospheric insertion technique.

Emma Shaw lit a cigarette, her eyes glued to the vidscreen. It was either by accident, or because of someone's perverted sense of humor. The movie was the story of John Rourke's heroic struggle to save his family during the final days prior to the Great Conflagration.

The actor who played John—she'd always thought he was handsome, albeit a bit "pretty" before—was nothing compared to the real thing.

It was the end of the movie, when the special-effects blue-screen skies caught fire and John Rourke stood heroically barechested, a pistol in each hand, fighting off the last of the helicopters under the command of Rozhdestvenskiy, the KGB commander who was John's nemesis after the supposed death of Vladmir Karamatsov. The actor who played Rozhdestvenskiy did such a good job of portraying an evil bastard that, afterward, he was unable to take any other sort of role. He eventually took his own life, instead.

It was kind of sad watching him die, here. The actor who played John flexed his pectorals, almost sneered at the last efforts of his enemy, the stars and stripes blowing in the breeze behind him as he defiantly stood his ground.

It was really like that, she knew. John, when she'd pressed him once, had admitted that "events were similar, but there wasn't anything heroic about it, really."

The helicopter was coming in for the kill, Rozhdestvenskiy hanging out the side, firing an old-fashioned AKS-74 assault rifle. Missiles were firing off the weapons pods. Bullets richocheted off the rocks around John, explosions impacting near him, the fabric of heaven renting around him as ball lightning rolled through the sky and the air crackled with electricity. Great special effects, but the real thing must have been terrifying. A quick cutaway shot of Soviet troops dying on the ground, their bodies aflame, electrical currents arcing from them.

John's twin stainless Detonics pistols were in his hands. The actor shouted, "Come an' get me, you son of a bitch!" But Emma Shaw could not picture John ever talking like that under the circumstances. He was just as capable of being foul-mouthed as the next person, herself included, but only when there was a purpose. Rozhdestvenskiy couldn't even have heard him.

Close-up of Rozhdestvenskiy firing his rifle, empty brass flying toward the camera.

A jump cut to John, bullets pinging off the rocks near him.

Calmly, coolly, John waited. The flag flew. The lightning rent the sky. And then, John fired. His bullets tore unerringly into Rozhdestvenskiy's chest. When she'd mentioned this part of the movie to John—he was obviously embarrassed that she'd seen it—he said, "A lucky shot under the circumstances. I have no idea where or what the bullets struck, although it's true that I was aiming for Rozhdestvenskiy." On screen, the pilot was struck by a fusilade of bullets as Rozhdestvenskiy's assault rifle went wild.

The helicopter started to spin, augering down toward the ground, the fireball, as it exploded, nearly enveloping John.

As John made a mad dash for the access tunnel into the Retreat, he looked back over his shoulder, perfect jaw line hard set, eyes gleaming with pride. The stars and stripes still flew.

She'd asked John why he'd risked everything

to raise the flag above the Retreat in an act of defiance against men who would be dead in minutes anyway. "It had very little to do with the men out there, or the flag as a national symbol. A man named Reed, a captain in Army Intelligence, died trying to raise a flag over the Soviet facility which was called 'the Womb,' where the KGB Elite Corps planned to survive for five centuries and lie in wait for the Eden Project. Captain Reed didn't quite make it, dying in the attempt. So, I figured—Reed was a good man, and a lot of good men and women died because of what happened. I did it for him, for them, maybe for me. It was foolishly reckless, Emma."

"Would you do it again?" Emma Shaw had asked.

Then John smiled, lighting a cigar with that old beat-up lighter of his. "Yeah, I probably would. It was an irresponsible thing for me to—"

"It was beautiful," she'd told him, wanting to kiss him and hold him and be taken by him so badly that her breasts hurt just thinking about it even now.

It was the next to last scene in the film, John Rourke standing in near total darkness, as if guarding the cryogenic chambers in which his wife, his son and daughter, his friend Paul (whose Jewish heritage was neglected in the Eden film because of the government's policy of anti-Semitism) and Natalia slept.

John Rourke laid down his pistols. Tight shot on those, then a quick cut to his face.

The last scene began with the American flag,

154

which had started as a reflection in John's eyes (which was impossible, because the flag was on top of the mountain and he was inside the mountain), blowing in the wind, the sky burning around it but never touching it, the camera drawing back and gradually encompassing more and more of the terrain as the destruction closed over the planet, the mountain itself consumed in flames.

Fade to black, then the end titles began, then the music rising. She'd taken an evening-school adult-education course once in understanding the movies. It was fun, but not very practical.

Sarah Rourke was played by a woman named Elizabeth Horton Dane; in real life, Sarah Rourke was played by a woman who was more dead than alive and whom John was willing himself to die for, even though she probably hated his guts, or certainly would when she found out about the fate of their third child, Martin. John was the last of the real heroes, he and Paul Rubenstein, really.

Emma Shaw lit another cigarette from the burned butt of the first one. If she hadn't had a mission just ahead of her, a really stiff drink would have been a wonderful thing just now.

# Chapter Twenty-Three

The nonalcoholic beer tasted all right, but this time Shaw felt stupid drinking it. He'd had three of them the previous night and been tempted to switch to coffee. Instead, he convinced himself that one real beer wouldn't hurt.

As he got up to go toward the kitchen and retrieve one, he picked up the .45 and stuffed it into his trouser band.

It was good knowing that Eddie and the guys were out there, keeping an eye on the house. But there was little comfort in the plan that he had essentially dictated to Eddie in his office that afternoon just before leaving for home. "This is the only way it'll work, Son. I know it gives ya the willies, and it doesn't go down too hot with me, either, but there's no choice, all right?"

"Fine, we respond when the first shot goes off and what if somehow they were able to slip right past us and they're using suppressed weapons and you don't get off a shot at all? Ever think about that, Dad? Emma'll have your ass for breakfast when she finds out, if you're still alive for her to get to."

"Who's gonna tell her, Eddie? She's like her mother, worries too much. Women are all like that. You should know. The second I even think one of those Nazi fuckers's got his ass in the house, I pop off a shot and you guys close in. Couldn't be simpler, right? Relax already."

There was always the possibility that Eddie was right, Tim Shaw realized. The Nazis might slip past, might use suppressed weapons and he might get dead very quickly, too quickly to trigger a round and call in the cavalry.

It was the chance he was taking because he didn't have a choice.

Yet, things were starting to look rather discouraging. It was almost time to hit the sack and still no bad guys. He'd strip and get into the sheets just like he was supposed to, but he wasn't cool enough to close his eyes and sleep. If they came, he wanted to be wide awake.

Tim Shaw opened the refrigerator and peered inside. There was some chocolate pudding, but that might screw up his stomach, when he was nervous (and he counted himself as being honest with himself to admit that he was), he had a little lactose intolerance. All he needed was to be farting when he should be shooting.

As he took his beer, Shaw had an awful realization: he would be at his most vulnerable when he was in the shower tomorrow morning.

Detail-stripping a J-Frame Smith & Wesson wasn't a picnic, but the Government Model Colt was a snap after all these years. Tim Shaw shrugged his shoulders. He'd take it into the shower with him. And he laughed. Years ago, he'd known this guy who'd cleaned his .45 by running it through his wife's dishwasher, field-stripped to major components, then lubed up afterward. It was a cute trick, but Shaw had never seen a lot of practicality in it. In an old gun magazine on microfiche, he'd even seen an ad Colt had used showing a .45 auto in the dishwasher. "Hell, who cleans 'em?" Shaw laughed to himself aloud. The virtue of a big-bore handgun, among other things, was that it really didn't have to be cleaned that often to keep running.

On impulse, before closing the refrigerator door, Shaw tapped down his pockets. The spare magazines for the Colt, a Lancer reproduction, were there and so were two speedloaders for the little Smith, also really a Lancer. He used the old seven-round magazines for the Colt, liking those better, giving him eight in the gun plus fourteen more. And he had a grand total of fifteen rounds for the .38. Eight and fourteen made twenty-two, plus fifteen gave him thirty-seven rounds. If that wasn't enought to get him by until Eddie and the Honolulu SWAT Team got on the scene—"I'm fucked anyway," Shaw said aloud.

He kicked the refrigerator door closed and

twisted off the cap on the beer bottle. The beer, his favorite, was something he had John Rourke to thank for. At the Retreat, Doctor Rourke had kept a case of Michelob. Better than a hundred years ago, Rourke gave a bottle of it to a lab technician at New Germany to reproduce for him. The lab technician not only produced a supply for Rourke's Retreat, but gave a case to New Germany's primary alcoholic beverages distributor. As the story went, the man—his name was Balthazar Schmidt—fell in love with the taste and decided to manufacture it, even duplicating the labeling. Today, Balthazar Schmidt Breweries produced an entire line of pre-War liquors and beers, all faithful formula duplicates of the originals.

There was a story going around that the executives at Balthazar Schmidt were trying to work out an endorsement deal for Dr. Rourke. Shaw didn't think Rourke would take it. On the other hand, he would have.

As Tim Shaw opened the bottle and took a sip, he looked into the front of the microwave oven, in which he could see his own reflection, and said, "This is Dr. John Rourke, hero of the War Between the Superpowers, telling you that—" Behind his own reflection, Tim Shaw saw the bedroom door down the apartment's hallway. The door was half closed. Tim Shaw's bedroom door was never touched, unless it was one of those increasingly rare occasions when his daughter, Emma, came over to spend the night. Otherwise, it remained open, just as it had been when he'd gone in the room earlier and put his wallet, his keys and his money clip on the dresser.

Shaw made himself laugh, took a long pull on the beer and slowly, very slowly, turned away from the microwave so that whoever was inside the bedroom or down the hallway wouldn't notice him staring at the reflection. "Yeah," he said aloud, as if the earlier beers had really had alcohol in them, "If I were John Rourke, I'd be sittin' pretty on all those endorsements. Lancers? Hey, 'I think the Lancer reproductions are just as good as the real thing. I use them; why don't you?' Keep me in guns—and money—" And Tim Shaw threw the beer bottle into the sink and wheeled toward the hallway.

The smart thing to do would have been to fire a shot, but if he had accidentally bumped the bedroom door and caused it to swing partially shut, he'd blow the whole thing. This way, brandishing a weapon in the direction of the assumed bad guys, if they were there they'd do something.

They were there.

There wasn't even a sound as loud as a balloon bursting, just a phut-phut sound and microwave oven's front panel shattered and Tim Shaw fired the .45 down the hallway and threw himself left, toward the front room.

The vidtape he'd just put in had passed the length of its pause and the regular programming cut in, an announcer selling life-insurance benefits to veterans. Tim Shaw dove over the couch as bullets tore into the doorframe between the kitchen and the front room.

160

Shaw's head struck the end of the coffee table and he muttered, "Damn it to—" Gunfire impacted the couch and Tim Shaw went flat, stabbing the .45 up over the arm of the couch and pivoting the muzzle right and left as he fired four more shots.

Three rounds were left. Time to change magazines. Tim Shaw grabbed for the fresh one in his left pocket, made a tactical change and hunkered down between the couch and the coffee table. "Hey guys, you fucked up. I wanted you to come visit me, motherfuckers! You kill innocent civilians and you murder children and their teachers. Come and get me fast before the good guys get here and bust your ass! Come on!"

There was more gunfire now, all of it suppressed.

Tim Shaw was mentally ticking off the seconds. In about another minute, his son and the Honolulu P.D. SWAT Team would be kicking in the doorway at the front and the back and nail the Nazis between them. "Yeah, you shits! Come and get me!" Tim Shaw glanced up over the couch and, sure enough, six men with submachine guns were coming to get him.

# Chapter Twenty-Four

Time dilates when life hangs in the balance. Tim Shaw didn't learn that truism during his first gunfight, but instead had it forever hammered into his understanding of the world when he was just a child.

His father, Emma and Eddie's grandfather, had always been big on water sports, a natural thing for someone living in Hawaii, even with the colder post-War climate. They'd been out on an all-day fishing trip and Tim Shaw had been pestering his father, Ed, from the very start to give up on the fishing and take out the water skis. It was the last time he ever water-skied until after he was married and his wife, Emma and Eddie's mother, got him to try it again.

After the Great Conflagration, the only place

where life survived in any true diversity was in the oceans. And sharks were ultimate survivors. His father had gotten the boat going along pretty well when the craft hit a swell and rolled over it. Tim Shaw never rolled over it. He lost the rope, the skis, the whole thing—and his cool. His legs and arms thrashing around in the water, he shouted to his dad.

Then he felt something slam against him, knocking him below the surface, knocking the wind out of him, too. As he opened his eyes, he saw the snout, the dorsal fin, cutting through the water away from him in a long arc.

Sometimes, when he'd take Emma and Eddie swimming when they were kids, he could still see that dorsal fin, like a keel on a boat turned upsidedown, cutting through the water, turning toward him. It was all in slow motion, the whole thing.

His father was suddenly there.

Tim Shaw remembered that his fists were balled up and he was going to fight the shark even though he knew the thing would kill him, eat him alive. But his father was leaning over the boat, a .45 automatic in his hands, shouting, "Swim to me, Timmy! Swim!" And Tim Shaw swam. It was only years later that he realized what his father was doing, using him as bait for the shark. The shark came up through the water and straight at him. His father's .45 boomed, boomed, then boomed again. Then there was silence. So suddenly that he almost threw up, the water was filled with blood. A life preserver was flung into the water and the next thing Tim Shaw knew, he was safe in the boat, his father's arm clamped around his shoulders.

What Tim Shaw realized years later was that if his father hadn't made him swim, the shark could have struck from any angle that it chose and he would likely have been killed. But, swimming as he did, he drew the shark after him so that his father could kill it.

It was the same situation now. If he stayed put, since a sofa wasn't an ideal defensive position, he'd be killed.

Another thing he'd learned about time dilation during periods of extreme danger was that people didn't experience it in the same way. The six men with submachine guns who'd come after him weren't experiencing it at all, he realized. They didn't think they were in danger, for if they had thought so they wouldn't be here.

Tim Shaw was already moving, one gun in each hand, a slug from the .45 nailing one of the six men in the chest just as the coffee table exploded under the impact of a long burst of automatic weapons fire. The little .38 Special in Shaw's left hand stabbed outward, toward the man who'd fired the burst, and Shaw's trigger finger was already snapping back, a bullet hole appearing in the submachine-gunner's forehead.

Bullets tore into the wall. Shaw had run for the apartment's exterior wall. His neighbors in the adjoining apartment were quietly evacuated, but the kid had tropical fish in a tank and there was no sense ruining the kid's day. And, one direction was just about as good as the next.

Bullets tore out a chunk at the corner of two intersecting walls as Tim Shaw ducked into the guest bathroom. He stabbed the .45 around the corner just beneath the damaged corner anyway and fired two rounds.

He backstepped, into the bathtub, wishing it were one of the old-style tubs he'd seen in period films—cast iron instead of fiberglass.

Back to the wall figuratively but not literally—he was on his knees inside the tub, crouched as low as he could—Shaw swapped magazines for his pistol to the last full spare. He made a quick reload on the second gun, spilling the five empties into the tub, ramming the speedloader against the Smith's ejector star. Snatching the .45 from under his armpit where he'd stuck it, in the same instant he rolled the cylinder of the little revolver closed against his thigh.

The bad guys hit the doorway, the first one playing hero or just naturally foolish. Shaw let him have one from each gun, killing him with one in the chest and one in the neck.

The last three men wouldn't be as careless. Shaw threw himself down as flat as he could into the tub, knowing what was coming: the three surviving men would spray their submachine guns through the open doorway.

There was a short burst, choked off as the sound of unsuppressed gunfire rang out from beyond the bathroom doorway.

"Eddie!"

Tim Shaw was up, stepping over the bathtub, advancing toward the doorway as he hugged his body flat to the wall opposite the sink.

The gunfire kept coming, as if there were a small war going on in his living room. One of the three ran past the doorway, blood spraying from a wound to his right thigh, his mouth open in a scream.

Tim Shaw fired in the same instant as a burst of unsuppressed fire came from the hallway.

The man had already been dying; now he was dead.

"Dad?"

"In the john, Eddie. Six down?"

"There were seven."

And Tim Shaw suddenly realized he had to urinate. The nonalcoholic beer was like that with him. He dropped the little .38 into his pocket, upped the safety on the .45.

Shaw set the cocked and locked .45 auto on the flush tank, unzipped his fly and did what he had to do. He could hear his son's voice from the hallway. 'The seventh guy was waiting outside the door, just in case you made it that far. You all right?"

"Yeah, hey, peachy keen. Hey, remember what you and Emma said when I told you there was a tub in the guest bathroom?"

"No. What'd we say?"

"Said it was a bad idea. Good thing I don't listen to you guys." He shook, zipped, flushed and picked up his pistol. "Any of 'em alive?"

"Nope."

"What they look like?" he asked, stepping past his son and into the hallway.

Before his son could answer him, one of the SWAT Team members bent over the nearest of the dead men and pulled the hood from his face. "If that guy's a Nazi, I'm gonna be the next Miss Hawaii. Just hitters. Damn it!"

"Check 'em all," Eddie ordered.

One by one, the six dead men were unmasked. Three of them were guys Tim Shaw had seen in lineups, and none of them had anything close to the classic Aryan look.

"He's still out there, Eddie, whoever the fuck their leader is. Still out there. And this is either gonna bring him after me or send him to ground."

"You nearly got—"

"Agh—I nearly got a beer, that's all I nearly got. Get the news people over here. I want all the coverage we can get. This time, no screwin' around. I'm gonna call their leader a coward, tell right on the air that he's a chickenshit afraid to come after me. See what he's made of."

"Dad, what if he comes after you with a bomb or something?"

Tim Shaw stepped over one of the dead men as he walked into the kitchen. He opened the refrigerator door and took out a beer. "No bomb, Eddie. He'll either make a run for it 'cause he knows he's too hot or he'll come after me himself, up close, real personal. And he'll be smarter than these schmucks. It's just gonna be him and me, Eddie."

167

"Hey, no way!"

"Hey—remember who runs this fuckin' TAC unit, huh? I'm gonna tell him it's just gonna be him and me. Either way, we're rid of him"

"What if he—"

"Heck, if he gets me then you get on the damn television and call him out. Long as this Nazi shit's runnin' around the islands, we got more civilian deaths to look forward to. You tell me what choice we got, huh?" Tim Shaw twisted the cap off his beer bottle and took a long pull.

Tim Shaw took another bottle from the refrigerator and handed it to his son. "Here, have a beer." And he called out over his son's shoulder, "Any of you guys want a beer, help yourselves." His son was speaking out of love, and Tim Shaw knew that. But he was speaking out of duty. The only legitimate function of a police officer was to protect the citizens who paid his salary. None of the rest of it mattered at all.

Eddie took a swallow of beer, then said, "Where you gonna do this stupid shit?"

Tim Shaw laughed. "The OK Corral's closed for repairs. I figure the mountains near Emma's place. No civilians to get hurt. And I know those mountains. He doesn't."

# Chapter Twenty-Five

Michael had been back for almost five minutes. After embracing him, making certain that he was all right—her own behavior amazed her at times—Natalia set about reading the two print-outs Michael had smuggled back.

Annie and the crew members were guarding the aircraft against what Natalia considered an almost inevitable attack.

The number of troops on hand at the Nazi headquarters complex was ridiculously meager compared to what any decent commander would have maintained. The material regarding the cloning of human beings and the recording and downloading of the mind was like something out of a nightmare. "What do you make of this? I mean, its existence in that computer? Was the computer just a terminal into a central system?"

"Not that I could tell. Looked to me like they were set up to modem data back and forth as required, but who the hell loads a field computer with top secret data anyway?"

She lit a cigarette. "They seem to want us to know the contents of these files, would you agree?"

"My thoughts exactly," Michael answered, nodding. She heard him exhale, her eyes on the documents. "Deitrich Zimmer must have counted on one of us hitting the command tent. But, why? How did he know we'd do it?"

"What if he knew that Martin was dead. Zimmer specified the number of people who could accompany your father when he returned Martin for the deal. If Zimmer knew that Martin was dead, then he would be able to assume that because of the number he specified, the entire family would come along, even you, posing as Martin. You did that before, remember?"

"For what purpose?"

"Put the two files together, darling, and what do you have?"

"An invitation to go visit Nazi headquarters and greater urgency than ever before to get Mom and Wolfgang Mann away from him."

"Exactly," Natalia agreed. "And, if curiosity gets the better of us, we'll all come. He will have the entire family in one place at one time."

'Still doesn't make any sense. Why didn't he

just bomb the hell out of the cryogenic repository in New Germany and kill us while we slept?"

"I will have to coach you in your technical German," she said, smiling. "It seems clear that the only way Dr. Zimmer's little mind experiments can be performed is when the subject's brain is active. When we were in the Sleep, our brain-wave activity was at a reduced level. What if he wants what is in our heads? What about that? What do you think, Michael?"

"To what end, Natalia?"

She looked up from her reading. Michael was stretched out in one of the chairs, his long legs extending well past the table before him. "What if he sees a Rourke family that is alive and well, as of much more potential value to him than a Rourke family that is dead? What if he is almost daring us to come, by telling us his plan ahead of time, making his plan so irresistible that we cannot avoid walking right into it? I think Dr. Zimmer laid out this data as an invitation."

"And we'll accept, won't we?" Michael asked.

No answer was necessary. Natalia Anastasia Tiemerovna knew that they would . . .

The digital diode reader on the mission clock—there was one built into the receiver for the positioning device—showed ten minutes before the appointed hour for the attack by Commander Washington's force, and ten minutes before the hour was the time John Rourke had set for the two-pronged penetration against the camp.

John Rourke tapped the man beside him on the shoulder and started forward on knees and elbows over the ice, toward the camp. The problem was that the perimeter security system looked too obvious, the manpower was obviously dangerously low for the enemy and the only thing that was missing was an engraved invitation . . .

The attack on the city within the mountain, at which Deitrich Zimmer now stared, would be costly.

The fools within it were not the ones who would exact the toll.

He would.

Zimmer looked away from the window and stood up, pacing along the fuselage toward the coffee urn at the rear of the craft. He preferred not to have servants attending him, as extraneous people often interrupted, however unintentionally, one's thought processes. He poured a cup of coffee into a china cup set on a saucer, the cup and the saucer ordinary in color and design. Neither was he a man of excess. When there was the need to impress with power and influence, he was fully capable of summoning all the trappings. But he needed them not at all, and for himself preferred a more modest approach to life.

Zimmer sipped at his coffee. The urn's contents were always kept at a drinkable temperature, because he drank his coffee rapidly. There was no need to waste time experimenting with the contents of one's coffee cup just so that drinkability could be ascertained.

His attack on the self-styled Aryans within the mountain would begin in moments, and then of course the Trans-Global Alliance forces would arrive on the scene, to harrass his forces, perhaps even to engage. But they did not know with what they would be dealing. While the bulk of his force would be inside the mountain, safe, the bulk of the Trans-Global Alliance forces would be exposed. They would regret that.

Meanwhile, John Rourke and his loyal associate would be about to attack the supposed headquarters complex. Zimmer had personally seen to it that Rouke could find it. Dr. Rourke's entire family would be inside that complex.

And, if the primary plan failed, the woman—whom John Rourke would not be wholly convinced was the clone of his wife—Sarah Rourke was even convinced that she was a clone—would either kill him, which would be regrettable in a way, or she would be killed by him. In either event, Rourke was finished. Knowing Rourke as he did—they had been enemies for better than a century—Zimmer was as certain of John Rourke's behavior as he was that the sun, if it rose, would rise in the east. After all, this could be the last second of eternity, although Zimmer seriously doubted it.

If Rourke survived, the minds of Rourke and his family would be his, to do with as he wished.

"Lovely," Zimmer said aloud, then sipped again at his coffee.

The play was about to begin, the invitations all neatly answered, But, what the Rourkes and the Trans-Global Alliance did not suspect was that this was the beginning of the final act.

# Chapter Twenty-Six

No one living had ever witnessed what Anton Gabler was about to precipitate. The prospect, when he considered it at any great length, caused him to become partially erect. Power, after all, was the ultimate aphrodisiac.

Purposely, even though he did not have to answer any biological need, he had gone to the restroom, his intent merely to be able to see his own face in this moment before he made history, remember the set of his features, be forever aware of the power he was about to exert.

Anton Gabler took the small brush from the right outside-pocket of his lab coat, worked back his short hair with it, getting the front—exactly cut only this morning—at the precise angle to set off his profile, rather than distract the viewer's eye from it.

There should have been photographers and videographers ready and waiting, to record this. Instead, there was only the automatic video camera which constantly monitored all activity within the bunker.

The button—he had made certain of the color was red. Red was the color of blood, and of the sun when it was dying in the night sky. Red signaled anger. In some cultures, Before the Night of the War, it had signaled happiness.

No anger consumed Anton Gabler, only passion. And the passion was not for death, but for immortality. He, of all the scientists under Deitrich Zimmer, was the Herr Doctor's choice to lead the project, and the obvious choice to execute it in this final moment.

The Herr Doctor saw the potential in him; of that, Anton Gabler was certain.

Finished with his hair, he pocketed the brush, trying to decide whether or not he should avail himself of the opportunity to urinate. He decided against it. After all, the moment was approaching when he would hold his finger poised over the button. The historic moment was one he wished to savor.

Anton Gabler walked through the doorway, careful to check the door behind him, making certain that it was properly locked. This was his own private facility, and there was always the possibility that some jealous person might attempt to use it.

As director of the project, one had certain pre-reogatives, and with these came responsibility. In order for others, younger scientists, to strive to be their best, to attain his level of excellence, the example had to be set, the rigidity of how he looked down from the heights maintained, so that they would, in turn, aspire to these heights on their own.

Satisfied that the bathroom was locked, Anton Gabler walked carefully, evenly, along the corridor toward the double doors at its far end. Armed SS men stood on either side of the doorway, and even then it was necessary to be admitted by voiceprint and visual computer identification. This was good, because such power as he was about to wield could not be allowed to fall into the wrong hands.

Whenever he was not personally present, Gabler locked all access to the controls, to the master program. After all, not just anyone was allowed to detonate the first nuclear device to be used in six hundred and twenty-five years.

# Chapter Twenty-Seven

The buttstock of the M-16 tucked up tight to her cheek, Annie Rourke Rubenstein hissed from beneath the scarf covering her mouth, "Be ready. they're coming."

The three with her manned various weapons. The captain had a caseless assault rifle, but the copilot and the radioman/navigator crewed an energy cannon.

Michael and Natalia, outside the aircraft, had energy weapons and conventional assault rifles.

If Michael's and Natalia's supposition, based on the intelligence data Michael had gathered within the Nazi camp, were correct, this attack wouldn't be much. But anytime enemy personnel were advancing toward her in vastly superior numbers she took it seriously.

Beside her sandbagged position—which would be of little use in the event of a direct hit from an energy weapon—lay the Detonics ScoreMaster. If she needed a handgun under these circumstances, it would only be because the enemy had closed on her position. Under such circumstances, her father had taught her to rely on nothing less than a .45 ACP or a .357 Magnum. The latter caliber was unavailable to her.

Annie had another worry, more serious than her own safety. If Deitrich Zimmer's Nazi forces were attacking the aircraft, that signaled that all bets were off, and her father, John Rourke, and her husband, Paul Rubenstein, might be in even graver danger. There was no way to know. She took what little comfort she could from the fact that she had felt nothing, no sympathetic pain, or sense of imminent death, as she had always felt since awakening from the Sleep for the first time one hundred and twenty-five years ago. The doctor who had treated Natalia during her breakdown had discussed the phenomenon with her—Annie—and said that it was somehow intertwined with the fact that she had pubesced quite early after leaving the Sleep. In documented cases of psychic phenomena, as affecting women, there was usually a link to the onset of the menstrual cycle.

Annie didn't know whether that was scientific silliness or valid, but that she could experience empathic response with those for whom she cared a great deal, was a fact of her life. For once, she was happy for it. No news was good news ...

*   *   *

She disliked the new weapons as impersonal things. In the final analysis, battle should be face to face between enemies. The energy rifles both she and Michael would use in a matter of moments were built for an age of sloppy marksmanship. A good, solid hit wasn't required, only that the living target be within the blast radius. That would, at least, produce debilitation. A solid hit would cause death.

With a cartridge arm, the determined man or woman, pumped on his own adrenaline, could survive a bullet to the heart long enough to take the life of his killer. Not now.

Natalia imagined that some of her discontent with the current technology stemmed from her background as a dancer, then in the martial arts. Guns were always useful, and weapons of honor when in the hands of men and women of honor, but there was nothing as reliable as the blade. The knife she had carried with her for well over six centuries was secured in the right outside pocket of her parka, the Bali-Song. If the enemy, who vastly outnumbered them, closed, it would come to that.

Without planning it, only realizing it after she'd done it, Natalia reached out and touched Michael's gloved hand.

"What is it?" Michael asked.

"I love you," Natalia responded.

180

# Chapter Twenty-Eight

As President of the United States, Arthur Hook knew that he was considered not only his nation's leader, but leader of the free world. The free world these days encompassed the nations of the Trans-Global Alliance. The enemy of the moment in humanity's never-ending struggle was an old enemy, one never properly defeated the first time.

Although he rarely had the time anymore, he'd made the time for himself today, visiting the place in Mid-Wake which was his first love: the United States Navy Center for Marine Research. It was the world's finest aquarium, because the aquarium surrounded the observers.

His security personnel were vehemently opposed to his leaving the main complex at Mid-

Wake, to venture out more than two miles to the Marine Research Center, but he finally just ordered the security people to do as he told them. And, he was transported here in a minisub, four other minisubs surrounding it and three attack submarines standing by to assist.

The problem with being president, he had once told an interviewer, was that the constraints it placed on the little, ordinary things, were outrageous.

Although always a reader of history, he had fallen in love with the view through the center's aquarium windows when he was just a student and had been lucky enough to get a clerical job here. On his break time, he would come to the windows and just watch life unfold before him. The glass—it wasn't really like ordinary glass at all—was designed to intensify available light, making the view without as clear as day, but casting no light on the sea creatures, thus altering their behaviors not at all.

He studied a striped sea catfish, special sensory barbels or "whiskers" extending from its lower jaw to aid in locating food, as they schooled near to the window. He envied them the simplicity of their lives. Eat, reproduce, perhaps die prematurely, but never the need to carry the weight of the species on their shoulders. He carried that weight.

At the end of World War II, the United States and its allies made two horrendous mistakes. First, the advice of the generals should have been taken, the German Army—the Wehrmacht—re-

182

armed and set against the Soviet Union. Second, the useful Nazis who were true Nazis—not the ones who were legitimate scientists impressed against their will or by circumstance into missile research and other programs, but the ones who were true believers in Nazism—should have been eliminated, by whatever means necessary.

As recorded in the memoirs of Commander Robert Gundersen, USN, Captain of the USS *John Paul Jones*, John Rourke had recounted once during that historic voyage the story of a Latin American military officer. The officer was a friend of one of Rourke's own friends. During a meeting once—social—the retired officer told Rourke's friend, "The problem with the United States, *amigo*, is that you never win a war. You win all the battles, but then leave the field. Your nation did not win World War II. If you had won, you would have seen to it that those who caused such destruction were rendered unable to do so again; you would have taken the territories which were controlled by the vanquished and established governments there which would forever be allied to your own political interests. Look at Germany and Japan. They are world leaders in both industry and finance. They are gradually destroying their adversaries from the period of World War II, and your nation helps them to do this. The people of Germany and Japan would be just as well off, perhaps better off, if your nation controlled them, and your nation and the world in general would not be in peril."

Arthur Hook had read the memoirs so often

that he'd memorized this passage, almost certainly a paraphrase. The message, however, was clear. American military personnel had fought and died only so that the political leaders could sell out the hard-won peace.

Today, as he quietly observed the infinite variety of life, this course of past action was about to bear its final fruit. Doctor Thorn Rolvaag's estimates concerning the trench which was growing inexorably toward the east were, as best Hook's scientific advisors could determine, right on the money. That meant that unless the enormous crack stopped of its own accord—unlikely—something would have to be done to stop it. The chance of such an endeavor succeeding was remote at best. Rolvaag's whimsical alternative, a race to launch arks for humanity into deep space, was impractical considering the time frame.

Chances were excellent that humanity was about to perish and sink into oblivion. And, as Arthur Hook watched the catfish on the other side of the glass, he was reminded of another quotation, from a work vastly older. "As ye sow, therefore also shall ye reap."

# Chapter Twenty-Nine

Gruppenführer Croenberg's eyes were grey-blue, but the most extraordinary feature about him was his head itself. Shaven, the skin was very tight and, according to the intelligence dossier, it was possible to see a vein occasionally pulse beneath it.

Croenberg's English, normally accented, could be perfect when the need arose. Disguise was something he had been known to employ on at least two occasions. In his fifties, he was tall, vigorous and, judging by the results of his activities on behalf of the SS, exceedingly intelligent and remarkably clever. That he was ruthless seemed obvious, but there was always a pattern to his activities. Croenberg, it seemed, was as cold-blooded a killer as had ever been born, but only killed out of necessity as he interpreted it. Nothing suggested a pathological blood lust.

Manfred Kohl's voice interrupted James Darkwood's thoughts. "Remember, that sleeve pistol he carries, hmm?"

"7.65mm, muscle-group activated or something like that. I remember," Darkwood told his friend. "You just remember, we're talking making a deal, not a hit—unless it comes to that."

Kohl took off his glasses, wiped the lenses with his handkerchief, the circles under his eyes glistening slightly with perspiration. "I was not happy that we were volunteered for this mission, James."

"I know."

"I am reminded of the words of Winston Churchill, when he was speaking of Joseph Stalin, to the effect that he would make an alliance with the devil in order to defeat Hitler."

"And you think asking Croenberg for help and offering him a deal in exchange is making a pact with the devil."

Manfred Kohl put on his glasses, shrugged his shoulders. "I think it is possibly so. You are an American. I am a German. For me, perhaps, the concept of a Nazi is more real. And, this man is a Nazi."

"If we defeat Eden and Zimmer's Nazis, if we can save a lot of lives by doing this—or even one life—it's worth it, maybe. Hell, I don't know." Sometimes, there was an advantage to having orders to follow rather than decisions to make.

Kohl shook his head and sighed, then started

186

moving again, Darkwood falling in beside the taller man.

They had been enjoying their first few hours of R and R after a dangerous mission in Eden City and a difficult escape when they were hunted down by New Germany Military Police and told to report to the office of Generaloberst Nauert as quickly as possible. In the next breath, they were told that transportation would be provided and to climb into the car.

Generaloberst Franz Nauert was New Germany's chief intelligence officer, one of the real powers in the Trans-Global Alliance's intelligence hierarchy and at once respected and reviled. He was respected for his personal toughness, that he had risen through the ranks, had as much field-agent experience behind him as anyone and more than most; Franz Nauert was reviled for the assignments he sometimes made.

This turned out to be one of them.

In khaki shorts and a T-shirt, his pistol in a Lancer copy of the pre-War DeSantis GunnySack fanny pack holster, Darkwood was told to sit down and listen. Kohl, a little more presentable-looking, sat down as well.

Generaloberst Nauert's English was perfect; and, doubtless because he knew their files inside and out, he knew that Manfred Kohl's English was perfect but James Darkwood's German, however adequate, was not perfect. The Generaloberst spoke in English as he paced back and forth behind his enormous, ornate desk.

"A rare opportunity presents itself to us, gentlemen. You two men are the best men available for the job at hand, so it is yours. I will make this meeting exceedingly brief, as I assume that you will both have a few things to do before your flight leaves—" And Generaloberst Nauert checked the watch on his left wrist. It was obviously a Steinmetz, and quite expensive-looking, Darkwood remembered thinking. "There is a significant rift in the organization that has been so painstakingly assembled by Deitrich Zimmer and his late son, Martin. This is a chink in the armor of the Eden-Nazi front. We must take advantage of it.

"You are both familiar with Gruppenführer Croenberg?"

"Yes, Herr Generaloberst," Manfred Kohl answered for them both.

"Good. He is their best man, the toughest of our adversaries. And, he has proposed an alliance, of an extremely temporary nature, of course. Yet, this may be just what we need in order to defuse the current crisis."

"Excuse me, sir," James Darkwood interrupted. "Aren't we just putting off the inevitable?"

'Until we are better prepared? Possibly."

"Won't they be better prepared too, by then, I mean?" Darkwood persisted.

"I do not make such decisions, nor do you, Darkwood. We all follow orders, do we not?" Generaloberst Nauert didn't wait for an answer. "You will travel to Eden City; appropriate travel

188

documents and the like are in readiness so that you should not have any real difficulties in getting around the city. There, you will meet with Croenberg and he will provide you with data which should enable us to anticipate Zimmer's current scheme before the elements of it can be realized. Do it. That is all."

It was all, Nauert dismissing them with a flourish of the hand, sitting down again at his desk and turning to his computer console. They stood, walked out, were driven to their BOQs where their gear was already packed. After quick showers and a change of clothes, they were airborne, landing at a predesignated landing zone about fifty miles from Eden City. The field was just that, a field. Yet it was adequate for the V-Stol which brought them in.

How they had managed it through the Eden Air Defense shield Darkwood was not certain, except that this might also have been part of the fix. A car was waiting for them and, after inspecting it for explosives and monitoring devices (they found neither), they drove to Eden City, using their papers to enter legally.

Much of the city was in ruins and security was tighter than Darkwood had ever seen it. Some fires still burned, but as best Darkwood could tell, the chemical weapons facility—Plant 234—was totally destroyed. The fires looked to be from downed aircraft and surface-to-air missiles, all due to Eden weapons systems, not those of the Trans-Global Alliance.

Sirens filled the dawn air as they stopped at the

appointed doorway. It was a private apartment building, quite well-to-do looking.

Two Eden police stood guard at the doorway with energy rifles. Darkwood and Kohl presented their security passes—they bore Croenberg's own signature—and were admitted to the foyer.

Darkwood rang the appropriate bell and stared up into the video monitor. It would either remain black, or, if the person on the other end were so inclined, show a picture. There was a picture, the face was Croenberg's face. "Do not identify yourselves. I recognize you both. You are admitted. Take the elevator to the fortieth floor."

"Which apartment?" Darkwood asked.

"The fortieth floor is the apartment, gentlemen."

The screen went blank, the door buzzed and, as Kohl opened it, Darkwood said, "I knew that; that he had the whole fortieth floor."

"Bullshit, as you say."

"Fuck you, as you say," Darkwood answered politely.

The elevator doors opened the instant Manfred Kohl pushed the call button and James Darkwood entered first, his pistol drawn.

'What good will a handgun do if this is a trap, James?"

"Beats me. Force of habit." But, James Darkwood didn't put the pistol away. Distrusting Nazis was habit, too.

# Chapter Thirty

John Rourke looped the garrote over the sentry's head, then wheeled and snapped the sentry up onto his back, partially severing the head from the body, but more importantly stifling any potential for sound. Rourke slowly eased the dead man to the snow, leaving the wire where it was, unsheathing his knife as he moved along the side of the outermost tent.

There were seven tents in all, one for hospital use, one for command and communications, one for field repairs, the remaining four for personnel. Rourke's observations of the encampment had confirmed this almost too easily. He kept moving, two of the German Long Range Mountain Patrol commandos and two of the SEALs with him.

At the front of the tent, Rourke signaled a halt. An ordinary soldier, not even Alpine Corps, was passing, about ten yards away, too much in the open for Rourke to get to him without an alarm being raised.

Rourke drew the suppressor-fitted 9mm from his belt. This was all but immoral, penetrating this camp so easily, the men who had been left here staked out like goats left to bait a wild predator into a trap. Was that their true function?

The aircraft, well beyond the encampment, looked safe enough, but about three dozen men had begun advancing on it at almost the same instant Rourke and his personnel had begun their infiltration. This left the encampment even more poorly manned.

In about three or four minutes, as Rourke judged it, the troops advancing on the aircraft would be in position for an assault, their obvious intention. But they were all afoot. Why were the armored half-tracks still parked in the encampment's motor pool?

None of this made any sense, except that there was danger here, more than he could fathom.

The soldier stopped walking, took cigarettes from the pocket of his parka and pulled down the lower portion of the toque covering his face. "Shit," Rourke hissed under his breath, readying the suppressor-fitted 6906 as he did so.

The soldier fired his cigarette with a lighter, as he did so, his face turning toward the side of the

the tent where Rourke and the four commandos waited.

There was no choice. Rourke stomped his right foot and stabbed the pistol toward the target, pulling the trigger, then again and then a third time, the first bullet hitting the voice box, the other two the head.

The soldier collapsed silently enough into the snow.

Rourke looked toward the troops advancing on the aircraft. They were nearly in position. "We go tent to tent. Move it!" Rourke rasped. The two SEALs fell out, their knives going to work on the tent wall, Rourke and the two Germans running around toward the front of the tent. There was no guard. Rourke stepped through the flap opening, the two Germans at his heels.

No one was inside the tent, except the two SEALs who had just cut their way in. "Next one!" Rourke wheeled toward the opening, running now for the next tent. If someone appeared, he'd shoot. There was no time for anything else.

He saw no sign of enemy personnel between this tent and the next. "Same method," he hissed, the two SEALs going to the side of the tent, Rourke himself and the two Germans going to the front.

No guard. No one inside.

"Deaton, Hines, hit the hospital tent and watch it." There was no need to tell American military personnel, "Remember we don't make war on wounded." But Rourke did add, "Watch out for the other teams." Paul's men and the others from Rourke's group would be moving about the encampment as well.

As Rourke started toward the command tent, he saw Paul Rubenstein already coming out of it. Rourke quickened his pace, joining Paul just outside. "Nothing inside but a tech with a bump on his head. He's gagged and bound, hand and foot, with duct tape."

"Duct tape?"

"Like they carry on aircraft."

John Rourke nodded to his friend, then looked toward the aircraft. "Any other personnel?"

"Two sentries, gone. What's going on?"

"I don't know. Get your men." Rourke then called across the open expanse of snow field toward the two German commandos, his voice a loud stage whisper. "Get our people. Hurry it up. Then the two of you position yourselves on the west end of the camp." Rourke looked back to Paul Rubenstein. "Put two of your men on the eastern boundary. The rest of us are attacking that force moving up on the aircraft." Rourke glanced at the mission clock. "Still better than two minutes before Commander Washington's men are going to go into action."

John secured the suppressor-fitted pistol and unslung the HK-91 rifle.

# Chapter Thirty-One

Annie ordered, "Hold your fire until they fire. Remember, we're a lot bigger target."

"I don't understand it, Mrs. Rubenstein," the pilot said, crouched beside her. "They've got those damned armored half-tracks that whiz over the snow like a bat out of hell, but they're advancing on foot. It's like they don't know what the hell they're doing."

"I know that, but whatever they've got planned, they didn't tell us. They could be holding those armored half-tracks in reserve," she told him, which of course didn't make any sense tactically. She'd never been to a war college, nor studied tactics, but she knew stupidity when she saw it. Armor would come first, softening up the target for the infantry, which would close for the kill. The reverse was suicidal ...

Michael Rourke's hands balled into fists on the twin operating handles of the energy cannon. Although the foot soldiers approaching could easily have surrounded them, the only activity he could see was coming from the direction of the Nazi encampment. About three dozen men were moving into an assault formation. The formation itself was absurd. With armor available—the half-tracks which were like the old Arctic Cats his father had spoken of—were armored and could easily have been used to spearhead an assault. The vehicles were armed with energy cannons and were fitted with firing ports for conventional small arms. And, of course, the actual Nazi headquarters was within a few miles of here, not more than fifty, certainly.

Why this type of attack?

Natalia, beside him, cheeked her M-16. "They're coming, Michael. This is insane."

"I know," was all he could say ...

After setting out more guards to watch the site of the encampment, John Rourke had six men remaining, including Paul. The seven of them removed the guards at the motorpool—two men who surrendered without any resistance—and used flex cuffs to bind the men. Then, Rourke, Paul and the others—SEALs and Long Range

Mountain Patrol commandos—each selected a vehicle. The vehicles were half-tracked armored Arctic Cats, each of them equipped with energy cannons which could be targeted and fired by the vehicle operator.

John Rourke sat at the controls, very similar to those of an ordinary vehicle. The transmission was automatic, but could be manually operated as well. Tracks and wheels each had independent drivers. Field of view was extraordinarily good, through video monitors, which covered the four cardinal directions as relevant to the vehicle's orientation, and through two additional cameras which covered the air space above. All six cameras were constantly displayed and the vehicle operator could select the field of view that he wished displayed on the main screen directly in front of the controls. Whichever field of view was chosen, the energy cannon's targeting computer was instantly on line.

John Rourke was reminded of the old expression concerning shooting fish in a barrel. This would be that. Whatever Deitrich Zimmer's plan was—and John Rourke was certain that there was one—it gave no sympathy to the Nazi personnel who would die in these predawn hours in what was once Northwestern Canada. Foot soldiers would be no match for these vehicles.

The engines—twin synth diesels—hummed, and the environmental controls were functioning perfectly. Parkas off, the sleeves of his black sweater and the black knit shirt beneath it pushed up to just below his elbow, John Rourke started the armored half-track from the motorpool area and across the encampment. The other six vehicles fell in, flanking him.

"This is Rourke," he said into the radio. There was always the chance that communications would be picked up by the enemy troops, but it was too late for them. If the Nazi headquarters picked up—which he doubted—there was no other choice now. The immediate danger was from the personnel attacking the aircraft.

"In less than thirty seconds, Commander Washington's frontal assault will begin. I'm assuming he's aware of the situation with the aircraft and will act accordingly. Needless to say, watch out for friendly faces. Let's get all the rest," John Rourke added.

He spun the wheel into a tight right and turned out directly behind the three dozen Nazis comprising the assault force, the six other vehicles still flanking him. It was time for these men to die, and he doubted that they were doing anything else but following incomprehensible orders.

Rourke started his vehicle forward, his main vidscreen on forward, the target computer already acquiring. "Spread out. Paul, to the far left. Lieutenant Johnson, to my far right. Crescent-shaped formation, each vehicle fifty yards apart."

Rourke, at the very center of the crescent, cut back on his speed, the two men directly flanking him doing the same, Rourke cutting back still further, while the half-tracks on the far sides of the crescent increased speed proportionately.

The attack on the aircraft was beginning, the

flashes of energy rifles lighting the night sky, but the only heavy energy weapons coming from the aircraft itself. The bulk of enemy fire seemed to be concentrated on the wings of the V-Stol cargo lifter, as if to disable the craft were the ultimate objective. Why?

Three men, a fire team, were beneath his bull's-eye array on the target computer and Rourke actuated the weapon, firing a series of energy bursts at the center of the target mass, all but vaporizing the three men. "God help us, this is wrong," John Rourke said into the radio, but there was no choice, because if he had stopped the half-track, gotten onto the PA and demanded surrender, there would have been no reply but incoming fire.

These men had orders.

There was no choice.

Six men, coming obliquely toward the aircraft cargo bay. John Rourke fired. Six men dead. He kept to his vector, the crescent formation encompassing the entire field now. The enemy personnel were helpless to stop them ...

Annie Rourke Rubenstein kept firing, despite the tears that wanted to come, to cloud her vision. This was not battle, but murder.

# Chapter Thirty-Two

"Even as we speak, gentlemen, a battle rages many miles north and west of here, in an attempt by Deitrich Zimmer to consummate his greatest goal—to obtain the help of John Rourke in the conquest of Earth."

"I don't understand, Colonel," James Darkwood said flatly. It was very pleasant sitting here, really, sipping fine brandy, smoking as good a cigar as could be obtained at any price. Manfred Kohl sipped brandy, but didn't smoke. "How could Dr. Zimmer hope to get Dr. Rourke to cooperate with him? That doesn't make any sense at all, Colonel."

Gruppenführer Croenberg leaned back into his easy chair, swirling his brandy in the glass he held at eye level. "There is a science to everything, gentlemen, whether it be war or race or the making of brandy."

James Darkwood couldn't resist speaking to Croenberg's remark. "Racial theory is a pile of shit, totally groundless. Sure, skin colors, some characteristics are different, but so what? There's nothing to suggest that one race is superior to another."

Croenberg slapped his knee and laughed aloud, leaning forward almost excitedly in his chair, his grey-blue eyes gleaming in the light from the lamp on the leather-covered wine table beside him. "Exactly! But race is a convenient excuse, is it not? You see, anyone of even modest intelligence realizes that all human beings are exactly alike in the most basic sense. Each human being is an individual in the broadest sense. There is no more difference between a black man and a white man, or a Jew or a Chinese than there is between two men of the same race."

"You are a Nazi, Herr Gruppenführer," Manfred Kohl said suddenly. "For you to admit that is heretical!"

"So?" And Croenberg leaned back and laughed. "Do not misunderstand me, my young friend," he said, leaning forward again, puffing on his cigar. "What I say to you here and what I say in order to achieve the ends I seek will be totally different. Deitrich Zimmer truly believes that his so-called Aryan race is superior. Do you know what the word Aryan really refers to?"

"A language group, right?" Darkwood opined.

"Exactly! Aryan peoples, if indeed they exist,

201

are those whose native language is Indo-Euro-pean. None of us remembers, of course, but in the days Before the Night of the War, there was far greater ethnic diversity. I believe there are a few actual persons possessed of Indian blood—from the Indian subcontinent—who still exist among the United States population. But, there were millions of them. Some were very light-skinned, some as dark as Africans. This is why the entire idea of Aryan racial conformity is so absurd, of course. These men and women, many of whom looked black, were just as Aryan as the Nordic stereotypes, the blond-haired and blue-eyed supermen Adolf Hitler so worshiped. Doubly curious, I have always thought, since Hitler himself was rather dark and somewhat swarthy. At any event, Deitrich Zimmer genuinely believes in his theories of race."

"What does he want with Doctor Rourke?"

"You must consider, Darkwood, that I am not your ally, merely Deitrich Zimmer's enemy. So, for a short while, we will be allies. Then, we will be enemies again."

"I know that," Darkwood said.

"Tell us, Herr Gruppenführer," Kohl persisted.

Croenberg's head, Croenberg leaning forward as he was, was clearly visible in the light. Beneath the skin, veins could indeed be seen. Except for the quite genuine-seeming smile on his face, the almost convivial glint in his eyes, the overall impression was grotesque. "Dr. Zimmer, as his supporters and enemies alike would agree, is a genius. He is, alas, quite insane. But that does not diminish the genius part of him. Dr. Zimmer wishes to be master of the Earth."

"And you don't?" Darkwood interrupted.

"I wish to be master of only a part of the Earth. I—as did Zimmer, in fact—realized some time ago that without an enemy, there is no means by which to exert power. There must be opposing forces, each perceived by the other as evil, but each perceived by itself as good. I wish to control one such force. Zimmer—and this is why he is so particularly dangerous to us all—wishes to control both good and evil. If he could, he would be master of Earth. If he is not stopped, that goal will be achieved, and John Rourke will help him."

"John Rourke might kill him," Darkwood volunteered.

"Only if given the chance. A question. Is Martin Zimmer dead?"

"I'm not—"

"At liberty to discuss that, Herr Darkwood? I intentionally left Martin Zimmer to die not long ago in Hawaii. I wanted him dead, because he is even worse than his 'father'; the desire for power is there, but not tempered by genius, only baser emotions. I thought that I had succeeded. I learned, through the efforts of a highly placed agent of my personal employ, that Martin Zimmer lives."

Manfred Kohl started to say something. James Darkwood extended his hand to his friend's thigh in order to preempt that. "What you're saying, Colonel. Is it relevant?"

"Oh, indeed! I see that Allied intelligence knows nothing about this. Fascinating."

"Nothing about what, Colonel?" Darkwood persisted.

Croenberg leaned back in his chair, puffed on his cigar. "Unlike my adversary, I am not insane. Nor do I wish to be God. He is, he does, Zimmer. He has perfected the process by which human beings can be replicated, cloned. He has also perfected the means by which the electromagnetic impulses of the human brain can be recorded and transferred from one brain to another. That means, gentlemen," Croenberg said, leaning very far forward, his lips drawn back in a smile, revealing even, white teeth, his eyes hard, "that he can copy whomsoever he chooses and use that person to his own will however he wishes. There would be no way to tell the difference. Fingerprints, retinal prints, DNA scans—they would all show that the subject was just who he or she claimed to be. You or I, your president or doctor—anyone could be duplicated, then controlled by Deitrich Zimmer.

"Picture what it would be like," Croenberg continued, "if the leaders of both sides were led by one man, served one intelligence, obeyed one will. That, my young friends, would be the ultimate power. The good Herr Dr. Zimmer wields such power, and that is precisely why I speak with you now.

"If there is God," Croenberg concluded, "such is His power alone. For a man to possess this is dangerous beyond understanding."

# Chapter Thirty-Three

His daughter's arms around his neck, his son's right hand in his, Natalia's eyes beaming toward him, John Rourke experienced an increasingly rare feeling of total peace. Kissing Annie, hugging Natalia, hugging his son, Annie back in Paul's arms, John Rourke leaned against the aircraft bulkhead, taking one of his thin, dark tobacco cigars from an inner pocket of his parka. He lit it in the blue yellow flame of his battered Zippo windlighter, the cigar's tip already guillotined. "This is a setup of some kind, and I'm not sure what."

"I uncovered some data you need to see, Dad," Michael told him. "Total force strength reports for Zimmer's headquarters, and a report on cloning and the recording of the human mind."

John Rourke smiled bitterly. "Wolfgang Mann was with us, as you may recall. But it wasn't Wolf, just a clone, preprogrammed to obey Dr. Zimmer, bearing explosives inside its body—probably in the large intestine—and ready to self-destruct in order to do Zimmer's bidding. What you're saying, Michael, only confirms our own suspicions. And, the fact that you got this data— from a field computer?"

"Yes," Michael said, nodding.

Rourke inhaled on his cigar, felt the smoke deep in his lungs, watched as he exhaled it through his nostrils. "That only means that Zimmer wants us to know what he's doing, is offering us an irresistible invitation. He knows what we're thinking, that if Wolf Mann could be cloned, so could your mother. He wants all of us inside his headquarters complex."

"We're going then," Natalia said.

"Yes," he told her. Her eyes were on him, their incredible, surreal blueness cutting through him. Yet, for some reason which John Thomas Rourke did not understand, he thought of Emma Shaw. "We're going. All of us. And I think it would be stupid to bring any of Commander Washington's men or any of the men from the commando units Paul and I brought with us. Whatever's going to happen is going to happen. Zimmer wants us all together, in his lair, alive and well—at least to begin with, hence this self-destructive military operation, all the data he's kindly provided us. I think it would be awfully rude of us not to accept such an invitation. And, anyway, it seems like that will be the only way we can find out about your mother, Michael, Annie.

"No one has to go, though," John Rourke told his family. "This might be the end, the last of everything. You all know me well enough to know that I've got a bit of an ego," Rourke said, smiling. "I always like to think I can outsmart our opponents. I think that this time, however, we're up against someone who's at least a little smarter than any of us. So far, he's gotten us to do exactly what he wants, and probably just on schedule. Before I came in, I stood outside for a long time, just watching the sky, trying to fathom what it is that Deitrich Zimmer has in mind. I can't think it out. Anyone who thinks he or she has an inkling of what's in store for us, speak now."

There was only one response, from Paul. "You know we're with you wherever you go, John. It's always been that way, and it'll be that way as long as we live. And, I agree. We don't know what it is Zimmer has in store, but we don't have any choice but to walk right into his trap."

John Rourke rolled back the cuff of his sweater, tapped ashes from his cigar into the ashtray built into the table beside him in the main compartment of the fuselage. "I suggest we make whatever preparations necessary, then strike out for Zimmer's assumed headquarters. We'll leave the commandos outside, to watch our backs, so all we'll have to worry about is inside the complex itself."

"What is it like, John?" Natalia asked.

"The structure is built partially within, partially atop a mountain of jagged grey granite, snow-splotched here and there, great sheets of ice within the crevasses dotting the mountain face. Within, the complex bespeaks solidness, only the best materials, only the best construction. Marble, granite, brass. In many ways, it's what you'd expect. I only saw the main level, not the ones above or the ones below. I don't know what the layout is, nor do I know the defense system. I'm sure we'll get inside easily enough, perhaps find Sarah just as easily, and maybe Wolfgang Mann, too. It's getting out that worries me. He knows the plan, and we don't. He's the one in charge and all we can do is play it out until we know his game. I'll admit it, guys, I'm outclassed."

Natalia came up to him, put her arms around him and very gently kissed his cheek. "You could never be outclassed, John. He may have the plan, he may have us following it because we have no choice, but he could never surpass you. You may not understand that as well as we do, but it's true. We've been with you since this started, and we will be with you until it ends. No matter what Deitrich Zimmer did, he could never match what you have done. He might win, and I am not denying that. I think we all try to look at things realistically. But he could never best you. I have read your Bible. Lucifer and his dark angels could never best the forces of light. Even if you die, John, a man like Zimmer would not win."

John Rourke hugged Natalia, his eyes flashing

toward Michael, who only smiled. John Rourke said nothing, only touched his lips to her hair.

As she stepped away, Rourke took his cigar from the ashtray and inhaled, exhaled, looked in turn at these men and women who were the only people—except for Sarah and his father and mother—whom he had ever loved. And then he thought of Emma Shaw. "I have no idea what I ever did to deserve a family like I have. No man could ask for better friends, for a finer son or daughter than I have." He looked at Natalia. "I know that someday you and Michael will bring me grandchildren, and that's magnificent beyond belief." He looked at his daughter. "And you and Paul, too." He closed his eyes, opened them, looked at the glowing tip of his cigar.

"Soon," John Rourke told them, "if we survive these days, my wife will be restored to me, in one way or the other. But I don't believe that things will ever be the way they could have been, should have been. And I'm sorry for that, sorry beyond measure. All we can do now is try to do our best, and hope that our best will be good enough."

# Chapter Thirty-Four

There were blackout drapes over the windows, but Croenberg separated them and stared out into the night. These two young men from Trans-Global Alliance Intelligence were really rather decent chaps. He was glad that he was not lying to them. The city, beyond the blackout drapes, was a shadow box of silhouetted shapes, punctuated by the glowing embers of fires which had burned in the aftermath of the Allied attack.

He inhaled the smoke from his cigar, tried to feel the warmth of his brandy. But, the warmth was gone. Without looking at Darkwood or Kohl, Croenberg said, "You see, there are degrees of evil, just as there are degrees of good, my young friends. Few things are one or the other. The enlightened man must choose.

"The course of action," Croenberg went on, "which Dietrich Zimmer wishes to follow might well result in his goal being achieved. However, should it fail, the world will be plunged into a war from which it might never recover. The Jew, Einstein, when asked what the weapons of World War III would be, responded that he did not know, but that the weapons of the next war after that, would be rocks and clubs. He was off by only a single war. Not bad, really. If this war is fought now, civilization will be in ruins. Who wishes to rule over that? I do not. Zimmer, on the other hand, is willing to risk that eventuality. He must be stopped. I had hoped to stop him myself. I discovered that such a dream was impossible from within alone. You see, Deitrich Zimmer has outguessed us all. Even the vile son whom I had thought was dead was never even in the slightest danger. The Martin Rourke Zimmer whom I left to die, whom Dr. Rourke thinks that he killed, was never even there. Merely a clone."

"A clone?" Manfred Kohl repeated.

"Zimmer's new scientific abilities—new to me, at any event—were the determining factor which dictated that this temporary alliance was necessary. If there is God, Zimmer has taken to himself God's powers. Zimmer can create life, endow that life however he chooses. There is a report, most secret until now. I understand that Zimmer is using this report as the means by which he will entrap the entire Rourke family. When I learned of the report, I realized that if Zimmer triumphed, and the world survived that triumph, he would be master of the world for all eternity."

James Darkwood's cigar had burned out. He looked at it, then at Croenberg, Croenberg watching his eyes. "Colonel, I'm not following you. I mean, I did all right in my science classes at the United States Naval Academy at Mid-Wake, but I trained for the Navy, not the laboratory."

Croenberg turned back to the draped windows, staring through the crack he'd made into the night. "Picture it this way, gentlemen. Deitrich Zimmer has perfected the means by which he can duplicate human beings, and also the means by which he can record the human mind. He can then transfer the data in such a recording to a new mind. Undoubtedly, Deitrich Zimmer has cloned himself many times over. By use of cryogenic sleep, Zimmer can have a fresh body waiting for him whenever he needs it, either for spare parts or as a replacement for the whole.

"Ever since man first began to contemplate his own mortality he has contemplated somehow being able to defeat it, to be immortal. Deitrich Zimmer has made himself immortal. The report touched only at the procedures.

"But, I know Deitrich Zimmer as few men do," Croenberg told them. "With his new abilities, he will live forever unless he is stopped now, his work totally destroyed. This is how it would work for him, gentlemen. Suppose that Zimmer has a series of alternate bodies awaiting his use. If he needed a heart or liver transplant, these bodies would be his donors, the perfect tissue match. Were he seriously injured, so gravely damaged that his body was beyond repair, the new body would be awaiting his requirements.

"The Herr Doctor is a quite methodical man, gentlemen. With his abilities to record the human mind, I would venture to say that, as a safety precaution, he would have new bodies waiting which had already been impressed with his memories, in the event that some accident should befall him and there were no time to record prior to death, or a bank of such recordings preexisting, which is more likely the case.

"This could be accomplished quite easily. I understand, from the data my own spies have brought to me, that the recording process is painless, requiring only that the subject be awake. Once each week or even once each day, should Zimmer desire, he could record the contents of his mind, leaving instructions for their use should disaster befall him. For that, he has Martin Zimmer. Martin, of course, would be given similar treatment. Together, they would rule the world for all eternity, until the very planet ceased to exist as a cradle for life.

"Imagine, if you will, gentlemen," Croenberg said, turning away from the window, letting the curtain drop from his fingertips, his eyes riveting on both men, "how it would have been if Alexander, or Napoleon, or Hitler, or Stalin had possessed this ability. The power which one could accrue in centuries of control would be limitless. With a mind as brilliant as Deitrich Zimmer's, no secret of the universe would remain unknown to him. He would bring about a new age, but only to serve his own needs. The processes by which he is capable of these miracles have been known to him for several decades."

And now, Croenberg returned to his chair, taking a swallow of his brandy before continuing to speak. "I imagine, gentlemen, that you are both still quite distrustful of me, as well you should be. But, in this particular situation, I will prove your most faithful ally. And, now I will tell you why.

"I am known as a merciless man," Croenberg told them. "But there was one person for whom I craved mercy—my wife, gentlemen. And when she was taken gravely ill, I went to my comrade, Deitrich Zimmer, and Zimmer examined her. Her illness, however, was impossible to treat. As a conventional doctor, Zimmer did what he could. But the technology existed, even then, that—had he wished—for his most loyal man all these years—he could have recorded my wife's mind before her death, cultured from her body the genetic material required to duplicate her, excised from this material the defective gene which brought about her untimely demise. She was twenty-eight years old, and we were married for seven years. Now, gentlemen, with mankind's life span expanded, I look forward, should I survive, to another half century without her, when in another decade, had Zimmer used his Godlike powers to save her and me, she would have been with me again."

"So, you want revenge for the death of your wife."

"Not for her death, but for her not being allowed to be reborn to me. Do you understand, Darkwood?"

"I understand," James Darkwood said.

"Then we have an arrangement?" Croenberg asked, leaning forward and offering his hand.

He was almost surprised that the American agent took it.

# Chapter Thirty-Five

The makeup technician tried powdering his cheeks, but Tim Shaw gently shoved her hand away. "No offense, ma'am, but I'm not into that stuff."

"Just to kill any shine, Inspector; that's all," she said, smiling.

"No thanks. If I'm too shiny, people can just close their eyes."

The makeup technician—cute looking, about five feet six, dark, wavy hair, a nice, even chocolate brown complexion—shot him a smile, then whispered, "You look great without it."

"Thanks, kid," Shaw told her, giving her a wink.

"Sixty seconds," the floor manager advised.

A sound technician checked the wireless lavolier microphone that was clipped to Shaw's tie. The interviewer, Tiffany Coggins, seated herself on the other side of the little table between the two chairs, leaned forward, smiled, said, "Nothing to worry about, Inspector. Except after you leave here, I guess. This is hot stuff."

"So are you," he told her. And, she was, tall, blond, long-legged and gorgeous.

She laughed. "This'll be on tape, so if anything goes wrong, there's no big trick to starting over."

"Yes, ma'am."

"You really intend to challenge the leader of this group of Nazi infiltrators to going one on one?"

"Not basketball, ma'am, but that's correct."

"Roll tape," someone shouted.

The floor manager said, "Camera one, move in a little closer on Inspector Shaw. Let's try it in ten . . . nine . . . eight . . ."

Shaw watched the floor manager's hand as he ticked off the seconds, then nodded. Tiffany Coggins began talking. "I'm here this morning with Inspector Timothy Shaw, head of the Honolulu TAC Squad. Welcome to 'Dateline Honolulu,' Inspector," and she leaned forward and they pressed the flesh.

"It's good to be here, ma'am."

"Please, call me Tiffany, Inspector Shaw."

"Only if you call me Tim," Shaw smiled.

"Tim. You asked for this interview and, as a part of 'Dateline Honolulu's' continuing involvement in community affairs, we agreed, but I won't say happily. I understand that you will be placing yourself in considerable danger."

"That's not exactly true, Tiffany," Shaw said. Tiffany Coggins leaned forward, lips glistening, a smile plastered to her pretty face. "I'm throwing out a challenge to the scumbag who caused the deaths of those kids at Sebastian's Reef Country Day School, the same piece of excrement who was behind the attack on my daughter's home, the one who was behind the assault on the missile shipment, who was too chicken himself to come after me just a few hours ago. Now that all his guys or most of 'em are dead, maybe he'll stop stayin' at home and come after me himself."

"Then you want to make this a personal thing, Tim."

"It's already personal, Tiffany. He's a Nazi scumbag and I'm a cop; that's as personal as it has to be. But, if you're asking if I want to see if he's got the guts to try for me himself, you're on the money. Personally, a lot of the guys have been betting that he probably stays hid out all the time, just—you'll pardon the expression on television—just jerkin' himself off every time he hears of some innocent person getting axed by his boys.

"Me, personally," Shaw went on, "I think this guy's probably the kind who couldn't jerk himself off at all. Anyway, if he's got the balls to come after me, I'm gonna be up in the mountains near my daughter's place. He knows how to find it. His slimes tried gettin' to me through her, but she was too good for 'em. She's a Navy pilot, you know, and we're all proud of her."

"And I understand, Inspector, that you're planning on waiting for this Nazi terrorist all by yourself? Why?"

"Well, that's right, Tiffany, and the reason for that is that this guy's too chicken to come after me any other way. If he thought I had a housecat with me, he'd probably use it as an excuse—afraid he'd get scratched. I'll be up, just toolin' around in the boonies havin' a good time. If he wants me, all he needs is the balls to try, you'll pardon the expression."

Tiffany Coggins was almost laughing when she asked him, "Do you have a description of this man, Tim?"

"How funny that you should ask, Tiffany," Shaw told her, starting to laugh himself. "Well, we figure he's about five feet one or shorter. That's so he can hide under rocks real good. His pants are always stained brown, if you know what I mean, and the tops of his shoes are always yellow."

"No, seriously, Tim!"

Shaw laughed. "No, Tiffany. All we know is that this guy lets his people do all his fighting, which is why nobody has a solid description. Tell you what, Tiffany; I'd like to ask a favor."

She was obviously taken aback a little, but responded immediately, saying, "If I can, Tim."

"After I polish off this guy, will you have me back on the air so I can give your viewers first-hand details on how a slimy Nazi coward died? I think it would be enlightening for them."

"You're that confident, Tim?"

Tim Shaw couldn't resist it. "Well, a kiss for luck wouldn't hurt any," Tim Shaw told her . . .

"No, Wilhelm! It would start a fire!"

Wilhelm Doring didn't care, the upraised chair he held crashing downward into the television screen, smashing it, sparks flying everywhere. Marie screamed, running to the wall and throwing the power coupling control, isolating the video monitor from the power supply. Wilhelm Doring dropped the chair. He sat down cross-legged on the floor. The smell from the screen was like that of a bad cigar.

Wearing only her slip, Marie dropped to her knees, hands moving tentatively toward him. He shoved her away and she fell backwards to the floor. "Leave me alone!"

"He does not know you, this awful man, does not know that you are brave and—"

"He is responsible, this man, for the deaths of all the men in my command. I can never go home again, Marie. Do you understand that? I could not live with the shame he has brought me."

"We do not have to do this, Wilhelm. We both speak English; we could hide here and no one would ever—"

"What is it you say!"

"I can work, Wilhelm," Marie told him, pleading. "I can work and you can—"

220

"What will you do? Sell your body in the street? That is all that you are suited for. And I? Should I begin to rob banks? I am a soldier. I will die as a soldier if I cannot live as a soldier. You may do what you will. A woman knows nothing of honor or duty. A woman only finds a man, then becomes a parasite. It does not matter what you do, Marie."

"I love you—"

"That is your misfortune," Wilhelm Doring told her.

She was crying, so he slapped her down to the floor again as he stood up. She lay there, whimpering, sniveling. If it would not require the waste of a bullet, to have put this wretched thing out of her misery would have been merciful, Doring thought.

"I will help you, then?" Marie Dreissling begged.

"You will help me if you fall over dead. Only dead will you no longer be a burden to me."

"Wilhelm!"

"Die, hm? I wish that you would die so that I could get about my business and kill this damned policeman, woman!"

Marie got up to her knees, looked up at him. Doring turned his face away. "You do not mean—"

"What use are you to me? Or, to yourself? You are no use to anyone or anything, and most certainly of no help to the cause. Do as you wish, but the only way you could be of any value would be if you died." He went over to the table, took a swallow from the bottle of vodka there, then lit a cigarette.

He heard the bathroom door close.

Women always ran off to cry their silly eyes out, escaping like children when things did not go their way. She said that she loved him. Her love was useless to him. He spit loose tobacco from the end of the cigarette, looked toward the bathroom door.

The toilet flushed. "Probably frightened her," he laughed.

He would go to the mountains, find this Inspector Shaw, personally kill Shaw and find some way of making an example of the policeman. What if he dumped the body at the police headquarters? Or the offices of "Dateline Honolulu," right at the feet of this bitch, Tiffany Coggins.

That was the only thing a woman was truly good for, try as women might to be useful. They made adequate servants, but men were even better at that.

Doring took another swallow from the bottle. He would shave, shower, prepare himself and his weapons, then hunt down this animal, this policeman, killing him like the dog that Shaw was. "Marie!"

There was no answer.

"Get out of the bathroom! I need to clean up, to get dressed."

There was no answer.

"Stupid woman! Cry someplace else. I need the bathroom."

There was no answer.

Doring took another swallow of vodka, put the cigarette into the corner of his mouth, walked across the room to the bathroom door and turned the knob. The door was locked. "Open the door!"

There was no answer.

"Stupid woman, open the door!"

There was no answer.

Wilhelm Doring threw his shoulder against the door. The door would not budge. Shaking his head, he went to the bed they shared, his things laid out already for him. There was the little wallet there which contained his lockpicking tools. He took it, opened it, withdrew a pry and a pick, then returned to the bathroom door. "I am becoming very angry with you, Marie."

There was no answer.

The cigarette was burned down so low by now that he could feel its heat on his lips. He dropped it to the floor and stepped on it. He bent over the lock, trying the tools. He almost had the lock, but the pry slipped.

Doring dropped to his knees before the lock-plate, starting to work the tools again. Then he noticed that his knees were wet.

He looked down.

He stood up.

The tools fell from his fingers.

Running out beneath the door was a growing puddle.

He backed away from it.

The puddle was not water, but blood.

# Chapter Thirty-Six

Anton Gabler merely awaited the word now.

That final word would be given by Herr Dr. Zimmer personally to him by radio.

He sat at his desk, watched the receiver, waiting for the buzz that would come from it. He would pick it up on the very first buzz, answering, "This is Dr. Gabler."

Then there would be the code phrase.

He would respond.

Then Herr Dr. Zimmer would say, "On my mark," and give the word.

Gabler would rise from his desk, walk across the room to the access control center and enter. The mission clock which Gabler would instantly set as the word was given would be counting down. When he reached the controls, he would adjust their mission clock to match his own, then begin the countdown, commencing final arming procedures.

Once he pushed the red button, his moment in history would be over.

That was a very sobering thought.

Gabler leafed through a report, too excited to pay it close attention. He set down the printout and turned to his computer terminal. He would bury himself in work until the buzzer sounded and his mission began. He summoned the file index, then acquired the file concerning his work in the salvage of nuclear material. He reread the earlier work in the field, eminently pleased with his thesis, sure of its potential success.

He stopped, listened for the buzz. It did not come.

Merely thinking about it, though, brought back the pleasant, warm stirring in his pants.

No one had wielded such power for six hundred and twenty-five years. Except him.

True, Herr Dr. Zimmer was giving the actual order, but without his own efforts, the device would not exist, nor could it be employed. Herr Dr. Zimmer would have the credit, of course, but that was the way with history. One remembered the names Hitler, Goebbels, Goring, but what of the men who did the actual work? Their names were known to a precious few, but some of the names were lost forever.

Gabler.

That name would be known. Anton Gabler was certain of that. Herr Dr. Zimmer had promised as much, really, telling him, "As my chief science advisor, you will be at the very pinnacle of the new world order, Anton. It will be you who will decide what is appropriate scientific research and what is not, you who will have the final word."

But, wasn't the final word being given by Herr Dr. Zimmer himself, when that buzzer sounded?

Anton Gabler returned to his work, trying not to consider that. This was important, would assure the survival of National Socialism, bring about that new world order. And the inferior races would be subjugated, eventually eliminated when their slave labor was no longer necessary. He would have charge of that, too, and was already devising the means by which the plan would be accomplished.

The problem with mass extermination was the manpower required to carry it out. If those who were about to be exterminated could provide this manpower, what a savings there would be. And, he had such a plan, where portable crematoriums would—

The buzz came.

Anton Gabler twisted round in his chair and reached for the receiver as the second buzz started. "Doctor Gabler here."

"It is a fine day to begin the future."

"Although we must never forget the past."

"Firestorm."

"Yes, Herr Doctor." Gabler hung up, activating the mission clock in the same instant.

He stood up from his desk, walked across the room. He called to his subordinates, "The center is sealed. The countdown has begun! To your stations!"

Men and those few women who were capable of the work moved quickly to their posts.

Anton Gabler began the admission sequence into the transparently walled room at the far end of the laboratory, retinal and palm identification sequences under way as his fingers punched the buttons in secret to activate the master locking device.

With an operation like this, nothing could be left to chance.

"Firestorm," Anton Gabler repeated. And, when he said the word, the feeling stirred within him again.

# Chapter Thirty-Seven

By a different car, this one driven by Croenberg's personal chauffeur, James Darkwood and Manfred Kohl traveled to the same spot where they had arrived. The aircraft would be waiting, as planned. Darkwood was beginning to have considerable faith in this arrangement with Croenberg. After all, simple revenge was easy to understand.

The sun was up. Darkwood would have preferred to leave, as they had arrived, in darkness.

That was impossible. Their discussions had consumed the night and to have waited, losing another twelve hours, would have been unconscionable.

Croenberg's chauffeur interrupted Darkwood's thoughts. "Gentlemen, forgive me, but we are being followed I think."

James Darkwood twisted round in the car seat. The rear window defroster had been at maximum capacity, but from the center it cleared and on the highway behind them there were two cars. The cars drove abreast, and were closing fast.

"Your Gruppenführer may have been found out," Manfred Kohl told the chauffeur.

"I hardly think so, sir. These will be agents in the Gestapo, who work independently. They monitor everyone. They will approach our vehicle and, if they feel that there is something amiss, they will ask to see papers."

"Will our papers pass?"

"It would be better for the Gruppenführer if these men were not allowed to file a report."

"Understood," Darkwood nodded, press checking the slide of his .45. It was the same Lancer copy of the Colt Government Model he carried whenever the mission allowed.

Kohl's pistol was more modern, but Darkwood was wedded to the older design and the big bullet it threw.

"May I suggest, gentlemen," the chauffeur began, "that the situation would best be served if I were to stop the car after the two of you were already out of the vehicle? The pursuit cars have not launched remote video probes yet and there might be a chance. I believe that there is a curve just ahead. I could stop the car and then go on for another few hundred meters."

"Just be careful yourself," Darkwood advised. But the plan sounded viable, all right, however hackneyed. The highway along which they drove was somewhat elevated over the surrounding terrain. If Croenberg's driver stopped for just a second or two, he and Manfred Kohl could be out, flip over the highway guard rail and hide along the embankment while the Gestapo vehicles passed. "Do what you think is best, Unterscharführer."

"Yes sir."

They were starting into the curve, Croenberg's driver speeding up as they entered it, leaving the two Gestapo cars well behind.

As they rounded the curve, the chauffeur warned, "I will stop now!" Darkwood and Kohl braced themselves, the car making a hard panic stop. Manfred Kohl threw open the door and was out, Darkwood after him into the brisk morning air. Manfred jumped the railing, Darkwood right behind him, but flipping it instead, going into a roll down the embankment, the sound of Croenberg's limousine already disappearing.

A second later there were the sounds of two cars speeding past on the road above.

Darkwood lay perfectly still, catching his breath. "James?"

"Fine, Manfred. You?"

"Ready?"

"Yes," Darkwood answered, nodding. Darkwood pushed himself to his feet, swinging his left hand across his trousers to loosen the decayed leaves and pine needles and snow, then moving in a crouch up toward the guard rail.

About three hundred yards further down the

road, Croenberg's limousine was stopped in the middle of the road with a Gestapo car in front of it and one behind, these parked at an oblique angle, preventing the car at the center from moving in either direction.

Unless there were more men in the cars, he and Kohl would have six Gestapo personnel to deal with. Their cars were equipped with video, of course, but the video was not broadcast to headquarters as a matter of course. So, with any luck, killing the men and destroying the video-disks would leave things in such a manner that no finger would point at Croenberg.

Darkwood thumbed back the hammer on the .45, upping the safety, his right thumb beneath the safety as he worked his way along the guard railing. Manfred's whisper was a harsh rasp as he said, "I will cross over to the other side."

"No, because if they see you prematurely then neither one of us will be in position. That Unterscharführer who's driving's no imbecile. He's got a gun ready, too. I figure he can take the one approaching the car door, and we get the other five."

"Who placed you in charge, James?"

"Nobody, but I've been in more shooting situations than you have."

"Agreed."

The driver's side front door of the limousine opened and Croenberg's chauffeur stepped out. There was the sound of a shot, then another and another. The Gestapo agent nearest the Unterscharführer went down.

Darkwood thumbed down the safety and fired from where he was, double tapping, putting down the man nearest to Croenberg's driver.

Manfred ran into the road, dropping to one knee, firing.

The four remaining Gestapo agents were moving, one of them running for the nearest of the cars, the other three aiming their weapons. Manfred fired again. One of the three went down.

Darkwood flipped over the guard rail and ran into the road, firing again, missing. Bullets tore into the pavement. Darkwood dove behind the nearest of the Gestapo cars. There was gunfire everywhere now, Darkwood losing track of whose. He edged along the side of the car, threw open the rear passenger door near him, looked inside. Nobody. But, indeed, the windshield video mount was humming.

Darkwood threw open the front door, slid across the front seat and threw the car into drive, stomping the gas pedal.

Another of the Gestapo agents went down. Manfred and the chauffeur were chasing after the last man as he went over the guard rail and tried to flee.

The other car was starting into motion.

Darkwood stomped the accelerator to the floorboard and rammed it, throwing himself down across the front seat just in the last second, striking the other car in the left front fender and the driver's side front door.

Darkwood crawled out, half falling to the pavement.

As he looked up, the man who'd run for the car, been driving when Darkwood crashed into it, was out, running up the road.

There was no sense shouting to the man to surrender. If the man had any brains, he knew that this was the sort of gunfight where losers wouldn't be allowed to live.

Darkwood thumbed down the safety of his .45 again. Lying prone, supporting his shooting hand with his cocked left elbow, James Darkwood fired once. The Gestapo agent's left hand clasped to the small of his back, a gun flying from his right hand.

The man stumbled forward. Darkwood fired again, the Gestapo agent's body rolling right, sprawling across the highway.

James Darkwood got to his feet, changing magazines for his pistol as he advanced.

From the woods below the highway, he heard shots and the sound of a man screaming.

Darkwood kicked the man he'd just shot. No movement. That was good, because if the fellow had been alive, that problem would have needed to be resolved. Hopefully, they were all dead.

Darkwood started back to the cars, looking down over the guard rail as he did. Their guns at their sides, Manfred Kohl and Croenberg's chauffeur were returning.

James Darkwood slid behind the wheel of the car he'd driven and began sabotaging the video disk.

# Chapter Thirty-Eight

There was a certain feeling of refreshment after the experience, a cleansing of self like nothing Deitrich Zimmer had ever imagined possible.

Drained, emotionally and physically, he sat in the silence of his command center, eyes closed, reveling in the feeling of peace.

In a moment, he would open his eyes, give the appropriate orders to his pilot and the command center would be airborne over the battlefield, but only briefly. Anton Gabler's device would be launched in only moments, taking precisely sixteen minutes and forty-three seconds to reach the target.

The aircraft would be into atmospheric insertion flight by then as assurance against Electro-Magnetic Pulse effect harming the instruments.

Zimmer wondered, absently, what would be the effect if an EMP event were to take place while one were recording the mind? The idea was worthy of exploration at some time in the future.

Zimmer opened his eyes now.

He turned back the protective covering on the panel in his lap and flipped the toggle switch beneath it. The diode reader above the keypad cleared to zeros and Zimmer tapped in the proper alpha-numeric sequence, then opened the second protective cover. He depressed the button beneath it and leaned back.

The recording he had just made was now being transmitted via one of the Trans-Global Alliance's own communications satellites, to the redoubt in what had once been the Himalaya Mountains, its location known only to himself and to Martin.

Now, if anything were to go wrong, he would survive, even if this body were to be reduced totally to atoms.

It was magnificent to be immortal, to know that death held no dominion.

He reset the controls, the transmission complete, setting aside the transmitter and standing. He walked forward, opened the door and stepped into the aircraft's main compartment. He told the copilot, "We are to be airborne at once. There is a flight plan marked 'Fireflight'; this is the plan that will be used. See that it is done."

"Yes, Herr Doctor!" the copilot responded, his body already in motion toward the cockpit.

Deitrich Zimmer returned to his command center, seating himself. He powered the microwave transmitter and spoke into the microphone. "This is Deitrich Zimmer. The hopes of the Aryan peoples of past, present and future go with you. Attack. The word is 'Firehunt.' Attack! Acknowledge all commanders."

He sat back, listening to the litany of their voices.

As soon as his forces moved, the Trans-Global Alliance forces would move to interdict.

There had already been the warnings that such people as the leaders of these weak-willed nations liked to give, to withdraw, to fall back, to step down from attack posture. He had done none of this, but enjoyed the fact that they had been foolish enough to try. While they tried, they built their forces, ready to counter him, little realizing that they were sealing their own doom. Had he acted at once, invaded this community within the mountain, fewer of the Trans-Global Alliance forces would have perished.

"Such fools," Zimmer said to no one but himself.

He could feel his plane going airborne.

He looked at the mission clock on the wall . . .


Gabler could do nothing but sit, and was too embarrassed to stand. The erection which had begun even before the call came through from Dr. Zimmer was stronger than ever. When he actually depressed the launch button, he'd thought for a moment that he would explode.

Instead, the experience was like nothing he'd ever known. Women could get orgasm after orgasm, he knew, but men did not. Yet, the sensation did not leave him as his eyes followed the course of the missile on the computerized plotting screen.

Perhaps, in the instant that the missile's warheads detonated, he would come. Alone in the transparently walled room, no one would see, no one would know.

Meanwhile, the exquisite feeling remained with him . . .


Emma Shaw had slept fitfully, getting six hours in all, and not the sort of sleep that really did any good. John was off in the middle of nowhere maybe getting killed, her father and her brother were fighting saboteurs in Hawaii and all she was doing was munching snacks and watching videos. This was insanity.

Only about a half dozen pilots remained awake in the ready room.

Except for her, they talked or played cards.

She had read a book, played three different types of solitaire, consumed half a bag of pretzels, even considered scrounging around to see if any of the other women among the group had any crocheting materials.

She sat down in front of the large vidscreen

and watched MTV. All of the videos were ones she had seen before. "Hey, guys? Anybody mind if I change channels?"

Nobody answered, so Emma Shaw took the remote from its nest on the wall beneath the screen and began flipping. The base had direct satellite downlink, which meant that programs from everywhere there was any broadcasting going on were possible. she found Eden's channel 1, the official government station and was about to flip past when she saw a face she had thought she would never see again.

The face was all but identical to John's face, and the face of his son, Michael. But it was Martin Zimmer's face. "Few of you know me by sight, but you know my image. I am Martin Zimmer, descendant of John Rourke, adopted son of Deitrich Zimmer. Citizens of Eden, I make this rare appearance before you today in response to the unprovoked aggression of the air pirates of the Trans-Global Alliance against our city. Thousands of you, my citizens, cannot hear my voice because you gave your lives for our nation.

"But, in these next few moments, revenge against the Trans-Global Alliance will be ours, due to the resourcefulness of our National Socialist allies under the leadership of my adoptive father, Dr. Deitrich Zimmer. At the precise moment that this prerecorded message to you ends, a new age will dawn and the combined forces of National Socialism will strike a death blow to our enemies.

"I speak, my citizens, of the power of the unleashed at our command."

"Oh, my God," Emma Shaw murmured. Then she shouted, "Everybody! Listen up to this!"

Martin Zimmer was still speaking: ". . . patiently, hoping against hope that our enemies would submit to reason. Yet, they have remained intransigent, forcing us to act before they can slaughter our peoples. Intelligence data have confirmed the fact that agents for the Trans-Global Alliance have been attempting to infiltrate Eden City with suitcase-sized weapons of mass destruction. Each one of these agents has been caught, and has admitted his or her crimes against the peaceful citizens of Eden and our gallant National Socialist Allies.

"Yet, the specter of holocaust could not be so easily dismissed as the unscrupulous plotters of death and destruction could be captured. It became necessary for Eden and the Nazi forces under the command of my adoptive father to launch a preemptive strike against the numerically superior forces of the enemy, as a means of preventing your deaths and the deaths of your children.

"It is, therefore, my reluctant duty to warn the enemies of National Socialism that their armies of death will be reduced to ashes. And, they have none other than themselves to blame. This message will end in a moment, as will the lives of vast numbers of the enemies of National Socialism. Be brave—"

"Guys! Listen!" Emma Shaw shouted. "Eden's going nuclear!"

Already, words like "madman" and "insane" and "global suicide" were in the air around her.

She couldn't hear Martin Zimmer's final words, but as the message dissolved into the Eden flag, the screen's image crackled and the lights in the ready room flickered, died.

Panic lights clicked and went on.

Someone—it sounded like a man—began to cry.

Emma Shaw got to her feet. "We're getting everything we've got airborne in case he's striking here! A lot of the ground stuff isn't hardened against EMP so this is gonna be a fly-it-your-selfer! Let's go!"

Emma Shaw grabbed her helmet and other gear. Running for the double doors which were already open, the single thought that kept going through her head frightened her. The lights could have gone out for a wide range of reasons, but one of those reasons was an Electromagnetic Pulse, which meant that the nuclear device was very high yield, atmospheric rather than ground, almost certainly, and maybe quite close.

She nearly stopped running, dropped her helmet, someone's foot kicking it as the other pilots ran past her, her hands grabbing her abdomen.

Emma Shaw knew the target. This was a trap, all along a trap. Deitrich Zimmer's forces weren't interested in the closed Aryan supremacy cult living inside a mountain in upstate New York.

Zimmer wanted Trans-Global Alliance forces

240

arrayed around him so that he could strike them down.

That was where the nuclear weapon was detonated.

She found her helmet, grabbed it and ran, holding back the tears. A lot of her friends would be dead by now, and a lot more were already dying.

# Chapter Thirty-Nine

The time was still early, the morning young here, the sun in these northern latitudes at this time of the year always low. The horizon was grey, the sun a dull yellow orb. But as John Rourke looked toward the east where the Nazi headquarters lay within and atop a mountain of living granite, there was a sudden brightness greater than that of the sun, as if the sun were multiplied or reflected many times over.

Rourke threw down the glasses and shouted to his family, "Get down and cover yourselves! Nuclear strike!"

Depending on the distance between the detonation and the plateau on which they had stood just a second ago, he might be blinded, and so might anyone else who had been looking. His eyes were shut now, the image of the second sun still in them.

Rourke counted seconds.

There was no blast effect, neither shock wave nor wind, nor was there any sound.

He looked up, the bright floaters in his eyes all but gone; although permanent retinal damage was still a possibility, it was unlikely.

Rourke got to his knees. His binoculars lay in the snow and he picked them up. The brightness was gone. He trained his binoculars toward the east. The artificial suns were gone. "The momentary danger is passed," John Rourke told his family, his voice almost a whisper.

Natalia was beside him. "Nuclear?"

"Yes."

"Multiple independently targeted reentry vehicles or a single blast, do you think?"

"Multiple. I saw several suns on the horizon. My guess would be ten one-megaton warheads air bursting."

"The usual pattern," Natalia agreed.

Paul suggested, "We're west of it, thankfully. The wind currents are easterly."

"Daddy?"

John Rourke looked away from Paul and Natalia, to where his son and daughter stood, arms around each other. Suddenly, they were children again, and only he and Natalia and Paul, who had been adults during the period of nuclear tension Before the Night of the War had any of the right questions or answers. "For a long time," John Rourke began, "we all lived under the threat of nuclear weapons. Then it looked as if everything would work out, that each side wanted seriously to disarm. Then the Night of the War came. This was an air blast, which is substantially lighter on radiation. From what little I saw, it might have been as far away as the other end of the continent. We're in no immediate danger. But I'd venture to say that the Trans-Global Alliance forces arrayed in which used to be upstate New York have been annihilated. There was probably a very powerful Electromagnetic Pulse.

"Today's aircraft are shielded against the effect as much as they can be," Rourke went on, "so depending on where a particular aircraft was and its particular electronics, some made it, some didn't. If the Nazis were the ones who used the weapon, then quite soon one of the Allied nations will use such a weapon in response, unless Zimmer can be neutralized, and perhaps even then.

"What has happened doesn't alter our mission. We still have to get your mother and Wolfgang Mann out of there, if indeed they're in there, then back to the plane. We'll still call in the support forces, but I don't think they'll respond. Emma Shaw was going to lead the two squadrons coming when we gave the signal. The base out of which they operated might have been close enough to be heavily damaged, so air support may not be coming. And the aircraft that's been waiting for us to call in for the equipment drop, might have been destroyed. Its mission was to stay airborne and refuel as needed. A multiplicity of things could have gone wrong."

Michael said, "Dad, if we find Deitrich Zimmer we have to kill him."

"I know."

"Regardless of what that means for Mom."

"I know."

"I'm sorry, Dad."

"I know," John Rourke responded again.

Annie came to him, put her arms around him. "Is this the end of everything, Daddy?"

"It might be," John Rourke told his daughter, holding her tight, loving her.

"Then we should do like we did before," Paul said, his voice strong, filled with the spirit of determination John Rourke had come to respect, admire. "We do what's right, and go on doing that until we can't do it anymore."

"Amen," Michael said, nodding.

Natalia, her voice strained, as if she were holding back tears, said, "I hope all of you are right, you know, that there is a God and all. Because we will need Him on our side if we are to do any good. And I have to say something I should have said a very long time ago."

John Rourke, still holding his daughter, turned his face toward Natalia, looked at her.

Natalia, her voice, sounding even more strained than before, said, "Without loving you, John, I would never have become the person that I am. I've often felt guilty for falling in love with Michael. As guilty, perhaps, as you felt for falling in love with me so long ago. You've read Shakespearean tragedy, I know. And each of the characters who was central to one or another play, had his fatal flaw. Yours is your perfection. If we walk into Zimmer's headquarters and rescue Sarah, give her up.

"Each of us here has someone not only to love, but to be loved by," Natalia went on. "Wolfgang Mann took the Sleep for one reason only. You taught me, John, taught all of us, that fidelity was the ultimate virtue, and also that it could be the ultimate sadness." Rourke let go of his daughter, stepped back from them. "I'm going to finish, John. Emma Shaw loves you. If you both survive, be with her. She loves you like I did, perhaps more. Sarah would be happier without you, John. That's as plain to those of us who love you—it is so abundantly clear that neither of you is meant for the other, but you still refuse to believe it. You love the ideal of Sarah, but she isn't that ideal. It is very hard to be worshipped from afar, and very lonely."

John Rourke turned away, not wanting to hear this. And he was disgusted, not by Natalia's words but by his own refusal to believe them. The one thing which had kept him going wasn't there.

People thought of him as a hero; he knew that. He did not consider himself to be that. All he had ever been was a man devoted to his family. And that was all about to slip through his fingers, after a lifetime of trying.

"We need to get out of here and be about what we came here to do," John Rourke whispered. He picked up his pack and his rifle and started walking.

# Chapter Forty

Emma Shaw knew which aircraft to avoid as she got the fighter airborne, wishing all the while that she had another Blackbird like the one she'd lost after hitting Eden Plant 234. They were unmatched for speed and had state-of-the-art electronics.

The V-Stol fighter she flew, an F-200, was armored against Electromagnetic Pulse, but only so far as laboratory tests could manage that. So far, however, so good. The cargo craft not designed for use in battle zones were another matter, however, their electronics more closely matching those of the fighter aircraft utilized Before the Night of the War.

One of the contributing factors to the Soviet Union's success in the wake of that horrible night of destruction was the more "primitive" electrical systems in their aircraft. U.S. and allied planes utilized printed circuitry, while Soviet aircraft generally possessed vacuum tube technology. After an EMP incident, the Soviets could change the tubes and be airborne again. U.S. planes needed to replace entire circuitry panels.

Current state-of-the-art employed shielded circuitry, in theory at least, proof against EMP. Emma Shaw hoped.

Her two fighter wings were scrambled, most of the individual aircraft off the ground. Meanwhile, there were air crashes dotting the field, the cargo ships out of battle zone were suddenly without any electrical power and falling from the sky like enormous rocks, their flight crews never having a chance. The normal radio channels were all gone, and only ship to ship was working. She spoke into the microphone built into her helmet. "This is bulldog leader to bulldog pups. Standard defensive formation at following grid coordinates." She read off the longitude and latitude from the screen of her navigation computer. "Until told otherwise, our mission is to interdict any incoming enemy ordnance until we run out of fuel. Stay on maximum fuel economy mode until ordered otherwise or in case of emergency. I don't have to tell you guys we may be staying up here until we're running on vapor, so watch yourselves. Nothing fancy. Let's have a moment of silent prayer, for the crews of the downed aircraft and our forces in Operation Snowbird." Operation Snowbird was the code name for the Trans-Global Alliance force deployment in upstate New York, most of which would surely be lost to the nuclear strike. "This is bulldog leader, out."

They could stay airborne for quite a long time in maximum fuel economy mode, but what about John Rourke and the family? The purpose of her two squadrons being assembled in the first place was to support John's efforts at Nazi headquarters. Now, however, that would have to wait. No other fighter squadrons were airborne, and there was no telling how soon they would be. The fuel trucks which serviced the aircraft were not armored against EMP, and normal communications were totally disrupted. Computers wouldn't be capable of running, their circuitry fried.

There was nothing to do but take up station in defense of the base and hope for word on how soon other fighter aircraft could get airborne to replace them, so they could get refueled and fly west. It was possible that the ground wouldn't even be able to reach them.

"Shit," Emma Shaw murmured. Then she bit her lower lip . . .


John Rourke dug in his poles and moved forward toward the edge of the ridge line. Below him stretched only virgin snow field, and beyond that a river valley, on the other side of which rose the mountain that was the Nazi headquarters.

Human forms would not be detected on sensing equipment at this distance, so they could move with relative impunity. It would only be when they reached the mountain itself that electronic security might be a problem. But Deitrich Zimmer didn't want them kept out; of that, John Rourke was certain.

He was also certain of something else: what Natalia had said to him was true.

Rourke signaled the others, then pushed off and down onto the slope, Natalia the best skier among them, keeping pace with him quite easily. They were the only two who, Before the Night of the War, had ever skied for sport. Under normal circumstances, whatever they were, this slope would have been challenging, but pleasant. Equipped as they were, with packs and weapons, however, the slope was at once more difficult to navigate and more dangerous should they fall. A back could snap, a leg fracture. Whether the injury were complex or simple, a fall could result in death here.

Rourke kept moving, guiding his skis into what seemed the natural contour of the mountain slope, Natalia staying slightly behind him now, Paul, Michael and Annie strung out further back still.

It was true that Wolfgang Mann was in love with Sarah. It was true that Sarah would be better off without a husband who had never been very good at being there when he was needed, always off doing something, anything but what he should have been doing. The philosophical differences which had existed between them had melted away in the aftermath of the Night of the War. She had learned that he was right to live for tomorrow by being prepared, but he had learned that she was right to live for today because tomorrow is uncertainty.

It was true that Sarah would be better off with Wolfgang Mann.

It was his fault, of course, that their marriage had worked out so poorly, despite the fact that they loved each other at first and still did love each other. A marriage was like anything else; in order to succeed, it had to be worked at. He hadn't worked at it, even though Before the Night of the War he had always been able to convince himself that he was trying his best to play by rules that he didn't understand.

The family. He had done everything that he did, for the family, his joy and his obligation. And the family was slipping away from him. His son and his daughter were grown, would be making families of their own, Annie already married, Michael soon to be.

And, he would be alone, because he would lose Sarah if he were able to save her. Alone, except perhaps for a wonderfully crazy woman who was as passionate as he was dispassionate.

John Rourke felt the corners of his mouth turning down into a grimace of determination. He would not give up. If he saved Sarah only so she could be with Wolfgang Mann, then so be it. It was her happiness that he wanted, not his own. Emma Shaw would not find happiness with him, either; a relationship with him would be totally illogical for any woman.

And, he was very tired very suddenly, tired of standing back and watching life instead of being in it.

# Chapter Forty-One

The old fedora had once been pearl grey, but its lustre disappeared quickly. When he retired it from day-to-day use and devolved to what was his standard headgear—a black fedora—he had kept the hat anyway, just because it fit right. It became his "sport" hat. He wore it on those rare occasions that he was able to get away and do some deep-sea fishing, wore it when he got out trap or skeet shooting, wore it when he just knocked around in the woods. He wore it very little, which was why after ten years of being retired from daily use it really didn't look much worse than it had before.

The vest which Tim Shaw wore was another matter entirely. Constructed to look like a photographer's vest, with pockets all over it which zipped and Velcroed closed, it was constructed of the latest bullet-resistant material and, when closed at the front, featured an extra fold-under panel which could stop a slow-moving rifle bullet and almost any handgun bullet. Blunt trauma was another question, of course, and nothing was proof against that except the best of ceramics, and then only to a degree. But a bruise, perhaps even some internal injuries—hairline fractures and the like—anything was generally better than springing a leak.

He carried nothing special in the way of armament as he left his daughter's little house behind and started up along the trail deeper into the mountains. In addition to his .45 automatic and his snubby .38 Special revolver, he carried one of the two rifles he owned. The one still at home was a nice little .22; he'd taught Eddie and Emma how to shoot on it, then moved them quickly into centerfire handguns. The rifle he carried with him was identical to the one John Rourke used, a Lancer replica of the HK-91 in .308, what used to be called 7.62mm NATO Before the Night of the War, when there was a North Atlantic Treaty Organization. In a musette bag hanging at his left side, Shaw carried spare magazines for the pistol and the rifle, and spare speedloaders for the revolver. In a teardrop-shaped daypack on his back, he carried some food, a first-aid kit and other little necessities, a sleeping bag rolled up beneath the pack and suspended there on straps.

With any luck, the man he wanted would come after him quickly enough and they'd settle the thing. While he—Tim Shaw—was tramping around in the boonies, the city of Honolulu was in big trouble. Evacuees from the eruption of Kilauea were coming in by the planeload, other Nazi groups were engaged in various types of sabotage and the entire Trans-Global Alliance was getting ready for war. The war would either start with or early on include an attack on the Hawaiian Islands in order to destroy the naval facilities at Pearl Harbor.

As Tim Shaw walked along, he whistled a happy little tune from his childhood, hoping that someone was out there to hear it, to target him, to get this thing going and done with. He didn't delude himself with any ideas of being truly bulletproof, but there was no other way to get the man he sought, the Nazi saboteur who killed schoolkids and their teachers, who didn't have any sense of good or evil, who was just a wild animal gone bad and living only for mindless destruction.

Tim Shaw wanted only one thing: he wanted to see the man dead. The one thing Tim Shaw didn't bother to bring along was a pair of handcuffs.

# Chapter Forty-Two

For once in his life, had he played the odds, John Rourke would not have been able to plan ahead. But, he did not play odds, and he always planned ahead.

Resting within a cave at the base of the slope before they attempted the river crossing, John Rourke said as much to Paul and Annie, Michael and Natalia. "Deitrich Zimmer has calculated our options in advance and arranged for us to be right where we are now, ready to penetrate his headquarters complex. He's probably assumed that we'd leave whatever other forces were wth us behind in favor of a soft penetration made by just the five of us. And, he's right. However, he expects certain behaviors, and it's our obligation, if we are to survive, to do what he doesn't expect."

"Commander Washington's force and the SEALs and Germans you brought, won't be more than ten minutes away once they're in position, but that can be a very long time," Michael said.

Rourke nodded agreement. "Indeed. A very long time. Zimmer has anticipated every move we make, simply because he's laid out an irresistible opportunity for us, and left the only courses of action that would be logical as viable. He expects us to know by now that this is an elaborate trap, but he knows we'll walk right into it anyway.

"Which is exactly what we have to do, but hopefully from a slightly different direction," Rourke went on. "The printout from the battlefield computer which you obtained, Michael, pretty much points the way we should go." And Rourke opened a notebook from within one of the musette bags beside him on the cave floor and took the pencil with it, beginning to draw a rough diagram of the Nazi mountain headquarters. "We're faced with three means of entry. The first is the front entrance, which is heavily guarded. The second is the service entrance, which, as the force-strength printout indicated, is lightly guarded and has less for us to worry about in terms of electronic countermeasures. The third way is the mountain side itself. To climb the mountain would be close to suicidal. Therefore, Deitrich Zimmer anticipates that we'll come in through the service entrance or attempt the impossible, to climb the mountain itself.

"But he's wrong on both counts," Rourke said, tapping at the crude drawing he'd made with the point of his pencil. "Zimmer is not expecting us to come in through the front, because that would have been too obvious for him to hope for. So, chances are, it's normally guarded. And, Zimmer has to take into account the fact that whatever backup forces we have will be waiting to strike as soon as called or from a definite time schedule. The backup forces would logically come in from a different direction, not the same one we used. Since the mountain face is near to impossible for even a small force, and we would probably use the service entrance, that means that the main entrance would be the one to be assaulted by our backup forces.

"We are going to reverse that, however," Rourke told them. "We're coming in the front and Commander Washington's force will come in at the service entrance when it's time. If we still have any air cover, after the nuclear blasts we detected, that air cover will strike against the mountain face. That means we have all three approaches—which are also the only three means of exit—covered."

"How do we get in the front, Daddy?" Annie asked him.

"Yeah, 'Daddy,' how?" Paul echoed.

John Rourke felt himself smiling in spite of the situation. "Funny that you should ask," he retorted. "All kidding aside, I considered the obvious things, knowing that Zimmer would consider them, too, and I felt that deviousness could best be combated by simplicity and openness."

"We just go up to the gates and knock," Natalia said, laughing.

John Rourke had seen such reactions before, where people in extreme danger, virtual no-win situations, resorted to levity as a means of denying the reality of their imminent demise. Yet, the laughter, the positiveness of it, seemed to renew courage and will. And, it was infectious. "No, we're not going to knock on the gates. We won't have to."

"I don't understand," Michael said.

"All right," John Rourke told his family. "Look at what we know. Deitrich Zimmer evidently has access to every detail of our backgrounds, as much as is known, at least, by the Trans-Global Alliance, the United States, and the government of Eden. He's a skilled research scientist, and he's utilizing the same procedures with us that he'd utilize in the laboratory. We're the rats, and we're sitting right now in an anteroom to the side of the maze we've been moving through ever since this started. He thinks he knows us so well that he can predict behaviors. And, up until now, he's been right. He's even, I'm sure, predicted a conversation such as this. The one thing he cannot predict is that we would do something which is totally illogical. That wouldn't fit at all. Look at Natalia's KGB background, my background—we both have a long track record of such operations and we know what doesn't work, so we'd never try it."

Rourke looked at Paul. "Paul, your background in publishing, and with computers—it's the same thing. And Michael, Annie, he's counting on the fact that the two of you have become so involved in the scheme of the things we do, that those procedures are inculcated in you both.

"Deitrich Zimmer," Rourke continued, "knows that I could no more ignore the option of potentially rescuing my wife than I could ignore the evil of his philosophy of National Socialism and racial superiority. He knows that we have to do just what he wants us to do. But he could not anticipate a totally illogical response."

"So, then we do knock on the front gates," Natalia said.

"Only figuratively, Natalia. Only figuratively."

"What will we do then?" Annie asked.

"The classic ways in which one gets inside an enemy castle—which is basically the situation with which we are confronted—are these: one either storms the gates in force, surreptitiously goes over the walls, finds some sort of secret entrance, disguises oneself as friendly force members or disguises oneself as some sort of harmless innocent."

"Those are the only ways, aren't they?" Michael asked. "I mean, what's left?"

"There's nothing left, which is why if we don't use one of the prescribed methods, Deitrich Zimmer will be unable to counter us and we'll slip past his trap because he won't know we're inside it."

"How, Dad?" Michael persisted.

"By not going in at all, in a sense, at least not until the garrison leaves."

Michael blinked his eyes, said, "What's going to make the garrison abandon the headquarters?"

"This should do it." John Rourke announced, taking from one pocket of his backpack a small box. "And the others like it." There was a combination lock set into the box. Rourke punched in the code, the box lid swung open. The box's interior was of heavy foam padding, as was the lining of the lid. Notched into the interior was a cutout, and nested there was a glass vial, inside the vial a pale green liquid. "Deitrich Zimmer, because he is so brilliant, is also somewhat cocky. And, as all of you now would be too polite to agree, if anyone should be capable of recognizing overwhelming ego, it would be me." Rourke allowed himself a smile. "Zimmer's ego, however, is the machine of his defeat and of our victory."

"What's in the vial, Daddy?"

"Annie, inside this vial is a serum. My backpack, which I left at the aircraft and retrieved after we knocked out Zimmer's forces there, contains little else but hypodermic syringes. Each of you knows how to use a syringe and each of you will be called upon to do so."

# Chapter Forty-Three

The exhaustion came upon her so quickly that she was barely able to sit down. And now, after less than an hour as she judged it, Almost-Sarah could barely keep her eyes open, and when she did, she saw two of Wolfgang Mann in the bunk opposite her. He had remained immobile for some time now, his chest rising and falling regularly enough—the real Sarah had been a nurse and Almost-Sarah supposed that was why she was able to view what was happening so clinically.

The thing about him that was extremely odd was that his right arm had extended toward his head, but never quite made it. And, it just stayed there, as if floating in the air, almost imperceptibly sinking toward his chest.

At the back of her mind—one of the real

Sarah's memories, no doubt—she remembered this as a symptom of some horrible disease.

But, she couldn't remember which disease, because her head ached so badly.

The guards should have come with the midday meal, but no one had opened their door for a very long time now.

Her joints hurt badly whenever she tried to move, and she would nod off, and when she awakened and tried to move, shooting pains ran through her arms and legs.

Her mouth was dry.

When she awakened this last time—and it was very difficult for her to know what was actual wakefulness and what was sleep anymore—she found that her right hand was moving, as if she were drawing a sketch of something. How long ago was it that she had actually drawn anything? She used to draw for children's books. But, that was the real Sarah who did that.

Wolfgang Mann was getting up, but he was still in his cot. There were two of him. "You are not the real Sarah, and you are evil!" Wolf told her.

She kept up the lie, "I am—" But her mouth was so dry that she couldn't talk without her throat closing and with coughing racking her body. And that made her ache so badly that the sleep came again.

And, she dreamed that she was with John and Michael and Annie and they were in a beautiful valley. But there was something odd about John. He wasn't carrying his guns. In fact, he didn't have a single gun on his body. She could see that perfectly clearly and she asked him, "Why aren't you armed, John?"

"Because everything is peaceful now and I don't need to be armed at all."

She did not understand this, because things were not peaceful at all. Behind him, sneaking up on them, was this horrible man with piercing eyes and she was holding her baby son and her body ached almost as badly as it did now and the man leveled the gun at her head and pulled the trigger and, although she knew it was impossible, she could see the bullet coming right at her head and feel it as it struck her head and feel her baby falling from her arms. But she had to hold the baby very tightly so he wouldn't be hurt, because he was perfect and he looked just like Michael had looked, and that was just like John, and the baby was so special to her.

Tears. Pain. Sleep.

# Chapter Forty-Four

"What have you done, John?" Natalia asked John Rourke, suddenly more grateful than she had ever realized she could be, that she was the woman of a man who was only a man and not so far beyond the abilities of other men.

"I planned ahead for Zimmer bringing me to his lair," John Rourke told her, told them all.

Natalia listened, waiting. She realized that her breathing was very rapid and she was suddenly very uncomfortable. "And?" Natalia grasped for Michael's hand, sliding her hand beneath his. He held her hand tightly.

"Between 1917 and 1929," John told them, "there was a disease which baffled scientists nearly as much as did the AIDS epidemic." John Rourke paused, then closed his eyes. "The disease was called encephalitis lethargica, and at first it was improperly diagnosed, because so many of the symptoms were identical to those of the influenza outbreak which followed the Great War and claimed so many lives. The earliest cataloging of the disease was by Constantin von Economo of Vienna, a professor of psychiatry and neurology at that city's university—not from someone actually within the classic medical community. Cases were found most prevalent during the winter months. In 1924, at its height, it was a severe public health threat, but within five years the disease had all but disappeared, leaving little behind but victims.

"Keep in mind, of course, that there were fifteen million people who died between 1917 and 1919 from the influenza outbreak. That was a tragedy of biblical proportions, a plague in every sense of the word, but a plague which could have been eradicated with some of the simplest of drugs that were commonplace in the days Before the Night of the War. The disease, which is not to be confused with similar symptoms which resulted from the bite of the tsetse fly, was commonly referred to as sleeping sickness. Some sufferers experienced such marked symptoms that they fell into comas and, in some cases, survived in this manner for years, even decades, never coming out of their sleep. Encephalitis lethargica's cause, although it is definitely known to be a viral disorder, remains unknown. However, it can be duplicated and redesigned."

266

"My God," Natalia whispered, believing the name as she said it.

"*Schlafkrankheit*, the identical disease, perhaps, or a quite similar strain, struck Germany in the eighteenth century. Some cases of what could be interpreted as encephalitis lethargica were reported in England prior to the general outbreak at the beginning of the twentieth century. The same diseases reoccurred among the population of New Germany during the period in which we last took the Sleep. Involuntary muscle spasms, rapid breathing, muscle aches, headache, and a wealth of other symptoms, besides the obvious one of profound sleep, were exhibited. The one conclusive symptom which evinced itself was double vision, uncommon in influenza, and, this peculiarity led to the discovery of the disease.

"I anticipated, when Deitrich Zimmer contacted us to set up the initial meeting, to exchange Martin—whom I'm sure now, he knew even then, was dead, if indeed the man I killed was Martin and not a clone—I anticipated that Zimmer would, because of his ego, invite me to see his facility, allow me to view Sarah. And, it only seemed logical to assume that something wasn't right, that the trade would never be accomplished, and that if I had the chance to be inside the enemy headquarters, I had to capitalize on the opportunity, effect whatever positive value from the episode that could be had. So, I considered my options and arrived at what I found to be the only viable solution, disease.

"Of course, I had to select the proper disease, so that it would strike quickly and profoundly, but be susceptible to a cure. I had no desire to be a mass murderer, nor certainly to cause the death of Sarah or Wolfgang Mann.

"There was little chance," John Rourke said, taking one of his thin, dark tobacco cigars from his parka, then lighting it in the blue-yellow flame of his battered Zippo, "that any true military solution was possible, and since Zimmer was possessed of such great intelligence, there was little chance of using guile to obtain the inevitable end we would seek. So, I went to the finest medical library in Hawaii.

"I discovered," he went on, "that encephalitis lethargica had occurred in New Germany about fifty years ago and, although many were stricken, modern medical technology was able to effect a cure through a vaccine, which would prevent the disease among those persons not already infected. I consulted with Intelligence in New Germany in order to find the medical authority most conversant with the disease. I explained my potential problem and she assisted in developing—very quickly, because we had precious little time—both a vectoring method and the other details required.

"Another reason for selecting encephalitis lethargica was that it had occurred, at about the same time, in Hawaii. Medical personnel from New Germany shared their technology and specimens of the viral agent as it existed in Hawaii. It was perfect.

"But, I had to think of a way of distributing the virus in such a manner that it would actually grip the majority of the population within the Nazi headquarters.

"For that," John explained, "I required an innocuous method of disseminating the virus." He looked at Paul. "Do you recall my having a delivery made from Lancer Firearms just before our aircraft left for Canada?"

"Yeah. I don't understand what that has—"

"I had a magazine for a German MP-40 sent to me, pulled the follower and the spring, placed the follower in the top of the magazine in such a manner that it would pivot, and used the magazine as the container for the aerosol—nothing harmful to the ozone, of course—but used the magazine to contain my vectoring device. The spare magazine was stuffed in the waistband of my trousers when I borrowed your Schmiesser as a close-range weapon when I went to visit Deitrich Zimmer's headquarters. As I moved through the building, I merely tapped the single cartridge I'd glued to the follower of the trick magazine. This released a small amount of the contents of the container secreted within the magazine. I spread the virus throughout every area of the compound through which I was brought."

"That's incredible," Michael said.

Natalia said nothing.

John said, "But, of course, I'd already had myself vaccinated and had the clothing I wore treated with a compound which prevents viral contamination. So, I did what I came for and left, leaving behind enough viral agent to incapacitate thousands of people, and very quickly, within approximately forty-eight hours, dependent of course upon the general state of the individual's health. And, I had enough vaccine produced—that was another criterion, which fortunately the disease allowed, that vaccine could be produced within hours using modern technology—but I had enough produced that I could safely be able to vaccinate three times the number of infected persons.

"By now," John said, glancing almost perfunctorily at the Rolex on his wrist, "the entire headquarters complex will be stricken. We can walk in. And, of course, anyone who left the facility—such as Dr. Zimmer—will require the vaccine as well."

"Couldn't this start an epidemic?"

"Not really," John told them. "The virus doesn't survive in extreme cold temperatures, and Deitrich Zimmer's army will remain as an integral unit. As soon as our business here is done, for humanitarian reasons Zimmer's forces will be notified and whatever quantity of vaccine might be required will be supplied.

"After administration of the vaccine, symptoms disappear in less than a few hours. It was totally luck, but it's our ticket in and out alive with Sarah and Wolfgang," John told them, exhaling smoke through his nostrils. "Now, let's everyone roll up his or her sleeve and we'll get started."

Natalia was speechless.

270

# Chapter Forty-Five

Deitrich Zimmer recognized the symptoms as soon as they occurred, and even before ordering that necessary countermeasures should be taken and quantities of appropriate vaccine prepared, he considered the fact that John Rourke had out-smarted him, would evade the trap he had set because no personnel would be well enough to bring it off.

And, despite the pain in his head, the muscle spasms, the feeling of lethargy, Deitrich Zimmer laughed and shouted, "Bravo!" Here, indeed, was the worthiest adversary he could encounter.

Immediately, he ordered his pilot, who was beginning to experience symptoms, to land at the nearest available Eden base where a small quantity of vaccine, prepared to his order, would

271

be in progress of preparation—if they could land while the pilot or copilot was still able.

Assuming they made a safe landing, in only a few hours after the vaccine's administration, Zimmer would be fit enough to travel again. The work done in New Germany fifty years ago in order to counter an outbreak of encephalitis lethargica had been so expert that use of the disease in biological warfare would be grossly impractical, except in such a limited application as John Rourke had chosen as his means of overpowering the headquarters garrison. It was not even necessary for Deitrich Zimmer to bother contacting his commander there. The use of encephalitis lethargica was so patently and unexpectedly brilliant that it could not possibly have been countered by anyone but a trained medical professional, and even at that, not in time to preclude wholesale inability for duty.

Dr. John Thomas Rourke displayed true genius. Rourke had obviously disseminated the viral agent during the time he spent at the headquarters in what had been northwestern Canada, before the Night of the War, visiting there at Zimmer's own invitation. Rourke would have known full well that the strain of encephalitis lethargica he utilized, the same strain which had caused the outbreak in New Germany, would take forty-eight hours or slightly more, depending on the health of the victim, in order to manifest itself. Once symptoms appeared, however, the disease took hold with lightning quickness.

Deitrich Zimmer had only a slight worry, that

272

the double vision he was beginning to experience would be experienced by his air crew as well, and precipitate a crash. Yet, if this form in which he lived died, this body perished, Martin had strict instructions on exactly how to bring one of the waiting clones out of cryogenic Sleep and program its brain with Zimmer's memories. Right down to using the last recording which Zimmer had transmitted only a short while ago.

If they did not make it to the ground, he would carry on, just as he had. If someone believed in the soul, of course, then death was inevitable.

Had Zimmer believed in that concept, however, his life would have been totally different. Fortunately for him, he did not. It was obvious that John Rourke did.

Deitrich Zimmer logged these thoughts in a conventional way, by speaking into a disk recorder. In all but the most severe of situations which could result from the craft going down, the disk would survive.

Deitrich Zimmer would survive, regardless of how severe it might be . . .


By the time they were across the river and nearing the Nazi headquarters, which was probably one of several such facilities dotted around the globe, John had told them, it would be dark. Some of the defenders of the complex might still be able to act with limited capacity, and therefore it would be necessary for them to approach with stealth.

The immediate problem was the construction of a simple rope bridge over the raging torrent sweeping through the gorge before them. The river separated the plateau snow field and the slopes from the mountain beyond. They traveled this circuitous route because John was still wary that if they were detected too early, enough of the personnel inside the complex might be able to act that some contingency plan or another would be carried out against Sarah's and Wolfgang's lives. So close to nearly certain success, there was no sense in taking chances.

During the construction of such a bridge—an interlacing of ropes strung over an obstacle, but requiring someone to string it—it was fortunate indeed to be a woman, Natalia Anastasia Tiemerovna thought. She could have built such a bridge as well as any man and better than most, but she didn't object to being pampered under the circumstances, being left to watch the gear on the side of the fast-running watercourse, with Annie to keep her company while John, Paul and Michael did the wet, cold work.

"I feel like a shit just sitting here," Annie told her as she came to sit beside her.

"Don't, Annie. Men feel themselves better-suited to such work and they feel better about themselves sparing us any involvement. It's a male bonding thing. I've always found it odd, you know," Natalia mused, lighting a cigarette, "that certain things are too physically demanding for us. I remember the time that Vladmir and I posed as an American couple. It was a true education. I would go to the supermarket wearing some nice little pair of slacks and a sweater or something, and have my list, and coupons and all of that. It amazed me, when I watched people, that a man who wouldn't think of going through a door ahead of a woman, and would blanch—"

"Your English is beautiful."

"I've just been reading a great deal in all my spare time," Natalia laughed, winking. "But a man who wouldn't think of letting a woman do anything which might be physically exerting saw nothing odd in the idea of a woman carrying two sacks of groceries while she had a baby in her arms who was kicking and wiggling and screaming."

Annie smiled, looked out over the river. "They're making progress. And, they almost look like they're having fun, in a weird sort of way. You were right."

Natalia was looking in the same direction. John was into the water, waist deep, Michael leaning precariously over a rock, Paul stringing rope. "They are having fun. It's very much like a group of women all cooking together or making a quilt," Natalia observed. "Or, watching children." She looked at the glowing tip of her cigarette and stubbed it out. When she married Michael, and he made her pregnant, she wouldn't smoke at all until after the baby was born.

# Chapter Forty-Six

He was baiting the Nazi, not attempting to commit suicide. So, when Tim Shaw reached the high valley above Emma's little house, he kept to its perimeter, the going a little slower there because the ground was less even, the tree cover—mostly snow-laden pines—more dense. But, it was safer as far as a sniper shooting him would be concerned.

Unless Eddie had gone back on his word, there wouldn't be any police personnel for miles, leaving things wide open for the man Tim Shaw hoped was stalking him even now. If this idea failed, then Shaw's nameless adversary would go right on killing innocents . . .

* * *

Camouflage stick across his cheekbones, over the bridge of his nose, across his chest in a lightning bolt pattern, along his arms, too—he would show the American policeman the true nature of war and the warrior, show him before the fellow died what would hopefully be a lingering and miserable death.

For some reason, perhaps the uncomfortable similarities between camouflage stick and makeup, Wilhelm Doring thought of the woman, Marie Dreissling, dead in her own blood, body slumping limply from the toilet into the sink, her face white, the color drained from her along with the blood through the artery she cut in her thigh. It was all the inane creature was good for, and possibly the first sensible thing she had ever done, as well as the last.

The little training Marie had been given before accompanying them on their disastrous mission to Hawaii had included close-range killing techniques. She had used such a technique on herself. Wilhelm Doring doubted she would have had the courage or ability to use the technique, or any other, on the enemy.

Excess baggage, he was glad to be rid of her, even if it meant that he could never again return to the apartment. There had been nothing to do with the body, and even if there had been, her blood was everywhere, spurted all over the bathroom walls and floor and saturated along the carpet in the room beyond.

And, the apartment might be an academic issue at any event. This policeman, however stupid the breed, was clever. Perhaps neither of them would ever leave these mountains and the policeman, Tim Shaw, would also be victorious. If so, then so be it.

One less enemy for National Socialism.

And one less man who had shamed the Reich through his ineptitudes.

Perhaps there was a poetry to justice after all.

All along, Wilhelm Doring had underestimated his enemy, until now, he had believed what his training officers had told him, that Americans were soft, easily terrified, prone to defeatism because once their pretty lives were disrupted they would not know how to react except in panic. That had not proven true at all. It seemed that the average policeman here, certainly if a member of some elite SWAT unit, was a highly motivated fighting man. What he might lack in finesse, he made up for in energy.

When Doring left the apartment, he took with him only those items which were essential equipment for combat. The knife which was lashed in an inverted carry to his web gear over his heart, a Fairbairn-Sykes pattern, had its edges sharpened to where he could wisk the blade over his arm and the hair would fly away. At his right thigh he carried an energy pistol, the latest and best made in Eden. His rifle was the official countersniper weapon, the G-70S, selective fire, firing the 5.62mm caseless armor-piercing T-56 cartridge. Additionally, he carried a weapon under the muzzle of which he thought Inspector Tim Shaw of Honolulu's Tactical Squad might appreciate dying. It was a Lancer copy of the Remington 870 police shotgun, the design dating from Before the Night of the War . . .


It wasn't that age was catching up to him—although he suspected that he was old enough to be his adversary's father—but it seemed prudent to take a break. Shaw found a convenient niche in the rocks a few yards above the perimeter of the valley above which he walked and plunked his gear down and his body beside it.

Before doing anything, he set out a device called Perimeter Guardsman. It was a low-scan microwave detection and ranging system which, when set properly, would alert him if anything anywhere near the size of a man were approaching within two hundred yards. For a sniper, two hundred yards was close. But, the niche protected Shaw somewhat from that contingency at any event.

He debated whether or not to smoke. Cigarette smoke might betray his position, but so would sharp eyes. "Fuck it," Shaw muttered to himself, but he'd light up later, anyway.

A more modern man than himself would have taken a nourishing trail mix from his gear. Tim Shaw preferred candy, milk chocolate from New Germany. It wasn't the expensive kind sold in the exclusive shops, but the type which was found in convenience stores and supermarkets. None of that mattered, since he liked the taste of it.

If the opportunity presented itself, he would

like to get the name of his adversary; why, Shaw really didn't know, except perhaps that the fellow had his. Fair was fair.

He felt strangely out of touch, no radio, no pager, nothing that would facilitate contact with the outside world. He had intentionally done it that way, because contact with the outside would be a crutch and, if he were to fall back on it, might cost him his quarry.

The day was crisp and cool, the perfect day for the out-of-doors.

Shaw finished half the candy bar, then closed the foil around the remainder, saving it for later. He'd stopped at Ziggy's Deli and gotten Ziggy to vacuum pack a half dozen sandwiches for him, just in case. And this seemed like a just-in-case situation. it didn't matter which one he picked, because all the sandwiches were the same. Hot pastrami on white, which made a lot of people cringe. The pastrami would taste better on something besides white bread, everyone always told him. Shaw always shrugged it off. After a bite of his sandwich, he took a bite of the kosher pickle.

Guys who were Jew-haters like these Nazis were nuts, he thought. Not to mention all the ordinary, normal things Jewish people did, but where would the world be without real delicatessens?

# Chapter Forty-Seven

They approached the wall from five different directions under cover of darkness. With the sun gone, the cold was numbing and the wind more biting than it had been throughout the long day.

Paul Rubenstein's left hand was on the Schmiesser's pistol grip, his right on the pistol grip of his M-16. He could not see the others—his wife, his brother-in-law and his two friends, John and Natalia—but that was basically the idea, that they come at the fortress's main gate in such a manner that if one of them were spotted the others wouldn't be. So far, however, there had been no signs of activity within the Nazi headquarters, nor on the walls.

From a distance, the structure had appeared

quite modern—which it was, of course—and formidable. It was formidable, to be sure, but the architecture of the place more resembled that of a castle than that of a present-day military installation. The place looked medieval, with its vaulted turrets and its rugged grey stone.

But the walls looked black now.

A moon periodically bathed the snow field before it in pale blue-white light, but there were so many high clouds scudding on the wind that it was only necessary, during these periods of brightness, to drop to the nearest position of concealment and wait a moment or so, then continue on.

The snow field, under normal conditions with a garrison capable of fighting back, would have been an ideal killing ground, barren of any true cover.

But within two hundred yards of the immense front gates—these an even darker black, so dark that they were like night—there had yet to be any sign of resistance. Even possessed of the knowledge of John's bio-warfare attack on the facility, Paul Rubenstein was still nervous.

As he neared what he judged to be about seventy-five yards from the main gates, he saw Natalia, running along beside the south wall, keeping so close to its blackness that she was more shadow than substance.

He kept going.

John and Michael would be using a plumbline firing device to launch ropes to the top of the wall, then scale the wall from opposite ends, reach the summit and come toward the main gates.

Paul Rubenstein spied his wife, moving flush along the northern stretch of the wall which flanked the gates.

For the last several minutes, he had been paralleling a roadway which connected the headquarters to a single airstrip, this apparently for landing and take-off of cargo lifters without vertical take-off and landing capabilities. There was a landing pad atop the portion of the structure which was at the height of the mountain, this apparently for the V-Stols and helicopter traffic.

The headquarters could not have been as immense as it appeared, because the gates at the mountain's base were close to two thousand feet below the summit. John had been taken in by aircraft and had left the same way, never reaching the base of the mountain. If it were somehow sealed away from the upper level, it was possible, however remotely, that there were still operational forces at this level.

That was a scary thought.

He stopped some fifteen feet from the gates and waited as Natalia and Annie worked their way toward him.

And he waited, too, for the gates to open . . .


John Rourke rolled over the wall and dropped into a crouch in the shadow beyond, the Crain LS-X knife tight in his right fist.

283

The complex was as still as death.

And John Rourke was suddenly afraid, that he had somehow miscalculated and that the strain of encephalitis lethargica he had utilized had somehow taken hold more quickly and that the vaccine which he carried with him would not save the lives of the people within—and not just the lives of his wife and Wolfgang Mann. If he had miscalculated, he would be a mass murderer. To kill in combat was one thing, but to kill this way would be beyond excuse.

He started moving, listening for any sounds which might provide a clue as to the condition of the garrison. He saw nothing, no lights, and periodically, he had to stop to reorient himself because the darkness was so total.

When the moon shone, he stopped, concealing himself within a niche at the height of a downward-descending stairwell. Beyond this wall on which he waited, there was no parade ground, in fact there was very little open area at all. There were several structures—blockhouses—likely associated with command and control functions for entry security. There were two bombproof doors leading into the mountain itself, and what lay beyond these was anyone's guess. He theorized, however, that there were powerful and very fast turbo elevators, toward the height of the mountain.

Rourke continued on as clouds obscured the moon again. On the wall, as he'd climbed, the wind had cut through him, despite his state-of-the-art arctic wear. But part of the sensation of cold was nerves, he knew. What was about to transpire would determine the future course of his life, and to a large degree the lives of his son and daughter. If he could successfully rescue Sarah—and assuming that she was, indeed, recovering from an operation which had brought her out of a near-death coma—and if he could save Wolfgang Mann, he was sealing his own fate as surely as if he were a Japanese warrior about to commit ritual suicide.

There would be no turning back from this.

Wolfgang Mann was honorable, and had circumstances been different, and something between Wolfgang and Sarah even started to develop, Wolf would have come to him. The same, obviously, went for Sarah. But John Rourke was not blind to the affinity each had for the other.

If Sarah's happiness would best be served by her leaving him—

The thought was something he rejected. He would think about this when the time came that decisions had to be made. Now, he was intent on saving the lives of two people, one of whom was a friend, one of whom was the woman he'd vowed to love forever.

# Chapter Forty-Eight

In exactly seventy-two minutes, according to the continuous fuel expenditure summary from her onboard computers, she would have to order her twin squadrons down out of their patrolling formation—which was a violation of a general order in the event of nuclear attack—or watch as her comrades and she herself started falling from the sky when vapor would no longer keep them flying.

Emma Shaw muttered one of her father's favorite words beginning with the letter *f* as her eyes alternated between video and what she could see with the naked eye. Some few fighter planes and V-Stol cargo jobs were getting airborne, but there was still no radio signal from the base, or at least none that her own equipment or that aboard any of the other members of her squadron could receive. She made a decision, which would only shorten her own fuel supply and not that of the others and, if she were careful, and stayed out of the patrolling formation, she could more or less make up the fuel she'd expend.

She started into a long, slow sweep of the tower, another practice which was severely frowned upon, although "buzzing the tower" was regularly done at higher speeds. Emma Shaw did not have the fuel to waste.

Unlike aboard the Blackbird she'd flown in the attack on Plant 234, there was no sexy-voiced computer companion to keep her company, and she missed "Gorgeous," fully intending—if she could take care of the little matter of living long enough—to wangle things so that the next time she flew a Blackbird she'd have the same program. Gorgeous was a little spineless, but okay in a pinch.

As it was, however, her own eyes and warning buzzers were her only means of keeping track of what was going on in all directions around her, her only means of preventing herself from crashing into something taking off.

She wanted level flight when she passed the tower, and as little speed as possible so that she might be able at least to catch some glimpse of what was going on inside.

Way below the minimum altitude over the hard deck, she started making the pass.

It was then that she noticed something at the

far edge of the field which had been too small for her to notice from her operational altitude: a man, arms extended, in his hands—flags. Semaphore signals. Semaphore signaling was still taught, but rarely taken seriously past a test or two at the Naval Academy, because so much of Naval aviation these days was from submersible carriers, and semaphores were impossible.

"Oh, shit," Emma Shaw muttered under her breath.

She slowed her approach to so close to stall speed that her palms started sweating inside her gloves.

Semaphore signaling was logical under the circumstances, of course, but this was maddening, trying to remember something she hadn't studied, hadn't even thought of in more years than she wanted to count.

The first five letters spelled "B-O-R-N-E." Then, "E-N-E-M-Y A-T-T-A-C-K I-M-M-" And, she was past him.

But Emma Shaw didn't have to catch the rest of the words. The message was "airborne. Enemy attack imminent."

She wished she had some flags, so she could wig-wag back, "How?"

Emma Shaw pulled up her nose and started to climb . . .


Wilhelm Doring's eyes ached from maintaining the level of concentration he had for nearly an hour, blinking only occasionally, never turning his head away from the narrow V-wedge of rock through which, he knew, the policeman would pass.

Sooner or later, whether Inspector Tim Shaw were eating another one of his sandwiches, smoking a cigarette or having intercourse with a tree, the man Wilhelm Doring despised on such a truly personal level would have to pass through the wedge. Unless, of course, the man gave up and turned back in the direction from which he had come.

And Shaw would never do that, because Shaw wanted this meeting as much as he did, wanted their private war to come to a conclusion here in these mountains however it might conclude.

In a way which was beginning to bother Wilhelm Doring, he almost admired Shaw, the tenacity, the brutality when required, the perseverance. Shaw would have made a marvelous commando leader, because he had daring. Unfortunately for Shaw, however, the policeman overestimated his own abilities. He would never come out of his hoped-for encounter alive.

Darkness was beginning to fall, the sky to the west more incredibly beautiful in its purple light than anything Wilhelm Doring had ever witnessed.

This was the perfect place for death.

As if Death were a god who had heard his thoughts, Tim Shaw started through the V-wedge of rock, into the killing ground.

"Not so smart after all, my friend." And Doring's own nearly verbalized thought disturbed him.

Respect for the enemy was something he had learned was a sign of weakness, and he could not afford to be weak now or ever.

As slowly, very slowly, Wilhelm Doring began to raise the sniper rifle to his shoulder, Inspector Shaw stopped, at the midpoint of the V-wedge of rock.

The policeman, Shaw, turned around and went back, disappearing.

"No!" Wilhelm Doring almost said aloud. This could not be. There was no way in which the man could have known that he was waiting precisely there. And, if Shaw had known, wouldn't Shaw have opened fire?

Through the sniper rifle's night scope, Doring could see nothing at first, then he detected a wisp of grey in the wind. "A cigarette! A damned cigarette!"

And, despite his anger and frustration, Wilhelm Doring almost laughed.

In the days prior to the advent of noncarcinogenic tobacco, he recalled, there had been warnings on cigarette labels, proclaiming that cigarette smoke—for a variety of reasons—was hazardous to the health.

Cigarette smoking had saved Inspector Tim Shaw's life for another few moments. Doring rested his rifle, rested his eyes for an instant.

Soon, Inspector Shaw's cigarette would be burned down, and so would Shaw's life . . .

\* \* \*

When he was a rookie cop, about a quarter century ago, he had been amazed that even in a firearms-intensive society such as the post-War United States, where firearms ownership and practice were encouraged as much as possible—there were men and women who joined the force who had never mastered any firearm at all. But then, he recalled an experience from his youth. As a Scout—he made Eagle, an honor and achievement of which he was still quite proud—he was equally dumbfounded when there were boys and girls of his own age who, it seemed, had never developed any understanding of the woods.

Just as shooting was a natural part of his life, so had been trekking in the woods when he was only a lad. Only with a lot of age and a little wisdom, as Shaw saw it, had he realized that one couldn't go through life expecting everybody to be motivated to learn. Timothy Shaw was a city boy, and wouldn't have changed that for the world. Concrete was better than grass, fluorescents at least as fascinating as starlight.

But, learning was learning. Tim Shaw's father had loved the woods, taking every chance he could to get away for a weekend and spend some time in what he called "the great outdoors." Although boys were always supposed to like that sort of thing, Tim Shaw preferred the city—everything from the baseball park to the beach. Yet, he never resisted learning about the out-of-doors and developing an appreciation for it.

He had learned, for example, that wild things were not particularly fond of the presence of man. Albeit that there were fewer wild species since the Night of the War—essentially, almost exclusively, those which had been returned to the wild—nature was still abundant, especially here in the islands.

Why was it, then, that the birds and insects which would normally have been active at twilight were silent tonight? Why, for example, had the deer whose trail Shaw had been following more as something to alleviate boredom for the last half hour, suddenly veered off almost at a right angle when approaching the notch in the rocks through which Tim Shaw had just been about to walk?

What if, Shaw asked himself, there were a man on the other side?

Granted, Shaw told himself, he was becoming a little paranoid after almost a full day of this, even wondering if the Nazi had taken up the challenge and come after him. Yet—and it was the city-slicker cop reacting now—he somehow knew somebody was out there, waiting. There were some experienced firemen who could tell if flames lay on the other side of a closed door without touching the door in order to see if it were hot. Touching the door was merely confirmation of a fact already known.

There were some experienced cops who could tell if, instead of fire, a man with a gun or knife and the burning passion to use it lay on the other side of a door.

Tim Shaw knew little about fires, but a lot about being a cop—or, at least, he hoped so.

He had taken a single—long—drag on the cigarette, then left the cigarette sitting on the edge of a rock. As silently as he could, he began climbing the big old magnolia tree, hoping it would branch out close enough to the next tree, so that he could work his way around the V-wedge of rock.

And that, birds and insects aside, was the other thing which made him step back, light a cigarette change his line of travel. The V-wedge was the only way through the area unless one kept to the trees.

This, as killing grounds went, was perfect.

# Chapter Forty-Nine

Men lay everywhere—the Nazis used females for only the most menial tasks, sexist as well as racist John Rourke thought. As they would pass a fallen guard, the man burning with fever, obviously in physical torment, many of the guards or other personnel with limbs half-suspended at odd angles, some of them jabbering in delirium, one of them would always stop and administer a shot of the vaccine, then a second shot—this was sedation.

Although he had not planned to do so quite so soon, John Rourke had already called in to Commander Washington, signaling the SEAL Team commander and his unit to follow them.

By the time John Rourke, Annie and Paul Rubenstein, Michael and Natalia reached the elevator shafts beyond the bombproof doors, Rourke was certain that his manufactured epidemic had not only struck, but conquered.

Although it was the only means by which he could ever have gained entry to the Nazi headquarters complex, he felt badly for having used it. Bio-warfare of any kind was supremely dishonorable, even in a good cause.

The elevator shafts were enormous tubes, the color of brass—once burnished, now tarnished from neglect. Up through the center of the mountain the tubes ran, disappearing from sight above. Two elevators, both of them large enough to handle freight the size of a tank, perhaps powerful enough for that, too.

There were no call buttons, but the elevator controls were apparent enough, controlled from a synth-glass enclosed booth mounted into the living rock, accessed by two metal ladders. It was like a control station for a ski lift.

Michael and Paul had already ascended the ladders, found the controllers down, injected them, then began to inspect the controls, calling out their progress as they went. "Think I figured it out, John. To be on the safe side, we should leave somebody down here, just in case there are no controls from above. Be a heck of a long walk down, assuming there are stairs."

"You and Annie stay, Michael."

"No! I want to see Momma and—"

"And what good will it do if we can't get your mother down? I'll bring her back to you, sweetheart," Rourke told his daughter, touching his left hand to her shoulder, touching his lips to her forehead. "You and Michael won't get cheated. I promise you that, darling."

Annie nodded, rose up on her toes, kissed her father's cheek.

"The three of us? You and Paul and I?"

"Yes," Rourke told Natalia. The three of us. Just like in the old days, Natalia."

"Just like in the old days, John," she nodded, smiling. "Paul, it's the three of us," Natalia sang out toward the control booth.

"On my way," Paul called out. He took the ladder easily, hands on the outer supports, feet along the sides, slowing his descent, never stopping it. As he jumped the last few feet, Paul turned toward them, went to Annie and took her in his arms. "We'll pull this off," he told her, then kissed her.

John Rourke called up to his son, "Michael! Get us an elevator. Keep a lid on things here."

"Be careful, Dad. Natalia—Paul—"

"Always," John Rourke told his son.

There was an exceedingly loud pneumatic hiss, a split second later the door was opening to the elevator on their right.

"Third floor, ladies' lingerie," Paul remarked as he stepped inside.

Natalia thwacked the fore-end of her M-16 with her left palm. "Let's go!" She looked up toward the control booth, toward Michael, then stepped inside.

Rourke followed them in. There was a complete control panel, several floors blocked off by card access, it appeared, not open to conventional access by using the buttons to program. Paul called up toward Michael, "Can you get us onto the floors requiring a key?"

"I don't know. Which one you want?"

John Rourke considered for a moment, then called to his son, "Try the third from the top. As best I could judge, that was where the hospital was."

"Right! Hold on; these suckers are fast, I bet," Michael shouted.

The doors thwacked shut as Annie called to them, "Be careful!"

There was a sudden lurch, the sensation of movement all too quick to be comfortable. John Rourke slung his HK-91 forward on its sling at his side.

Natalia whispered, "Like the old days, the three of us."

# Chapter Fifty

The idea, of course, would be to pop the guy while he lay in wait, if he lay in wait at all. As soon as Tim Shaw navigated the last limb—the trees here grew so densely that moving in them was almost easy—he would have a clear view of the other side of the V-wedge and know if there were someone waiting—just enough light still filled the sky in the west that all was not in perfect shadow yet.

Popping the guy, even if he was a Nazi, was not to Tim Shaw's liking. He'd killed men in the line of duty and likely would do so again, if he survived now. But he'd never walked up to somebody in cold blood and just blown the person away.

Under the circumstances, however, he doubted there would be any choice.

The limbs of the trees had creaked a bit under his weight, but that was all right, because the wind was picking up and all the tree limbs were creaking. There would be no way that his unnamed enemy would know the difference, could know it.

Shaw's hat was crushed and stuffed inside his multipocketed bullet-resistant vest, his rifle strapped tight across his back, muzzle down, as he prepared to make the transfer from the tree he was in to the next one, the limb looking more solid than the one he'd already navigated.

"Nice and easy," Shaw whispered to himself.

He moved his left food onto the limb of the new tree, exerting his weight to test it. So far, so good. His arms stretched out and he found a handhold, crouched and started to slip onto the new limb.

There was a crack, loud as a pistol shot in a whorehouse, and Tim Shaw was suddenly weightless, then just as suddenly he was falling. Involuntarily, Shaw snarled, "Shit!"

He fell through a series of branches, neverending, it seemed, but he knew that they would end. Twigs and leaves tore at his exposed skin, slapped him. He hit something very hard, his fall ceasing for a split second, then there was a second crack, louder than before—and this time it was a rifle shot.

A bullet whined past Shaw's face.

He looked down, seeing only blackness, trying to judge the angle from which the shot had originated. He could not. A second shot, this one grazing his left tricep. Pain consumed him and he shook his head to clear it, knowing what he had to do if he even hoped not to die. He faked a scream of pain—which wasn't hard because his left arm felt like it was on fire—and shouted, "Damn it!" Then he rolled out of the tree limb and let himself fall, trying to pull his legs under him so that he could hit the ground and roll, trying to gauge how great the distance was. He'd been up thirty feet or more to start with, had no idea how much distance remained between him and the ground.

He found out, impacting before he got his legs under him, his right knee striking something hard and his entire right leg going numb with pain. He was able to roll, his hands hitting the ground a microsecond before, his right wrist nearly breaking. But he pushed himself right so that he'd spread the impact.

He slammed up against something in the dark and just lay there, trying to grab a breath, realizing he had grossly miscalculated and was about to pay for it.

And he heard a voice above him with an undisguised German accent, but the English otherwise perfect. "I want you to know, policeman, who it is who has taken your life."

Shaw's left arm, despite the gunshot wound and the impact, moved okay and he was already snaking his hand toward the .45 that he could still feel there tucked inside the waistband of his trousers. His back ached terrifically and he thought that it might be broken, but never having broken his back before, he had nothing with which to compare the feeling.

The rifle strapped across his back was perhaps what had caused it when he hit.

Yet, he could wiggle his toes and somewhere he remembered reading or hearing that the ability to do that might be a good sign.

The wind was heightening dramatically now, the rustle of trees everywhere about him like a chorus of voices. His left fist closed on the butt of the .45. But he realized all along that the Nazi would be looking for a play like that, be ready for it. So, at the same time, he had begun moving his right hand. In his vest pocket on the right side he had the little Smith & Wesson revolver.

The Nazi stood over him now and Shaw looked up at the biggest knife blade he'd ever seen, realizing anything that was about to cut into you looked big, even a little switchblade. "So, what's your name, motherfucker?"

The Nazi stooped over him with the knife and started to speak. Tim Shaw drew the .45, knowing it was too obvious, too slow, the Nazi rearing back, kicking, the man's foot impacting Shaw's left wrist, sending the .45 flying as Shaw's fingers went totally numb.

And the Nazi laughed. "I had expected better, policeman." Then he bent forward, bringing the knife down toward Tim Shaw's throat.

Tim Shaw twisted the little enclosed hammer

revolver in his pocket. Only the shell of the vest was bullet-resistant, the sewn-on pockets ordinary cloth. Shaw asked, "Then how's this, buddy?" as Shaw pulled the revolver's trigger, the gun still in the pocket.

The Nazi's body lurched upward, as he staggered back. Shaw shook his little gun free of the pocket, pointed it. The Nazi was three or four feet away, Shaw fired a second shot, like the first one aimed for the throat and face. The Nazi's knife flew from his hands, his hands went groping to his face. There was a shriek like no human sound Tim Shaw had ever heard before.

Shaw fired a third shot and the Nazi's body was flung back into the darkness.

Tim Shaw's right arm sagged to the ground, no longer able to support the weight of his gun and his hand, and his eyes started closing. If the guy was still alive, things would be very bad.

As Shaw's eyes finally closed because the pain was too intense to keep them open, he wiggled his toes one more time, mumbled the words, "So far, so good," and then just lay his head back, listening to the murmuring voices of the trees and feeling the coolness of the night wind.

# Chapter Fifty-One

Rourke, Rubenstein and Natalia stepped from the elevator. Rourke had guessed right. This was the same floor Rourke remembered, where he had seen Sarah. Bodies lay strewn about the floor, slumped over the charge desk. While Rourke and Natalia waited at the elevator—John Rourke barely able to make himself do the sensible thing and wait—Paul found a chair, then wedged the chair in the elevator door, to keep the elevator from closing.

They still might require a fast means of escape.

"Washington's men should be out front in another seven or eight minutes," Natalia announced after a glance at the diminutive ladies' Rolex on her wrist. Their arctic outerwear had been left on the lower level, and Natalia was dressed as she so frequently was over the course of the time they had known one another—a black, close-fitting jumpsuit, a shoulder holster over it with her suppressor-fitted Walther PPK/S hanging inverted from it. Her double full-flap holster rig nested above her hips with the twin stainless steel Metalife Custom L-Frame Smith & Wessons with the flatted barrels—engraved into the barrel flats were American eagles. In an all but unnoticeable pouch at her right thigh, the pouch a pocket within the jumpsuit, was her WeeHawk bladed Bali-Song knife. Held tight in her tiny right fist was the pistol grip of her M-16, the gun slung cross-body, left to right.

Paul, like John Rourke, wore black rip-stop BDU pants and a black knit shirt. His two mismatched Browning High Powers were carried in a double shoulder-rig of suede-lined black ballistic nylon. The German MP-40 submachine-gun was suspended at his left side, an M-16 at his right, their slings crisscrossed over his upper body.

Rourke held his HK-91 at high port as they walked along the corridor, the twin stainless Detonics CombatMasters in their double Alessi shoulder rig under his armpits, the two ScoreMasters this time in full-flap holsters at his hips, the Crain LS-X knife suspended from the same belt. Inside the waistband of his BDU pants was the little A.G. Russell Sting IA Black Chrome and the hip-gripped Smith & Wesson Centennial. Each of them carried across their bodies a military-issue gas-mask bag.

Periodically, as they passed a body, they would

check for signs of life. So far, no one had been found dead as a result of an infection with the strain of encephalitis lethargica. And, John Rourke hoped that would remain the case, enemy personnel or not.

Commander Washington's men had enough of the vaccine with them to cover the entire population of the garrison. Each of the personnel already vaccinated at ground level was tagged to guard against redundant injection.

By the time the personnel here were able to move about, heads aching, dehydrated from fever—if all went well, the Nazi headquarters complex would be in Trans-Global Alliance hands, the Nazis prisoners and this facility a much-needed base in northwestern North America, all without a shot being fired. If their luck held.

But, John Rourke's plan wasn't to wait for that. He would get Sarah and Wolfgang to the lower level, hold that position until the facility was entirely secured. He hoped.

The elevators were located at the central portion of the floor, the rooms and corridors surrounding them.

As they reached the end of one corridor, having found nothing but hospital rooms, only two of them with patients, and three nurses collapsed at their stations, they turned into the next corridor.

At its far end were double doors which looked too sturdily built for an entryway to just another ordinary wing of the hospital or an operating complex.

John Rourke quickened his pace to a jogging run, Natalia and Paul flanking him.

Paul was making a radio check with Michael and Annie below. "Reception's poor, but we can make each other out. No problems, so far. Word from Commander Washington is that he'll be delayed another five minutes. Some kind of mechanical problems. Puts him here in about twelve minutes."

"Not a disaster, I hope," Rourke observed.

They reached the doors, Natalia rapping the butt of her rifle against them. They didn't budge, nor was there any sign of electrical activity. She dropped into a crouch before them, inspecting the locks at the center in minute detail. "I'd say we should pick them. It won't take more than a minute. If we use explosives, no telling what damage we'll do on the other side."

"Agreed," Rourke nodded. "Paul, keep in constant touch with Michael and keep an eye on the main corridor and the elevators. Natalia'll shout when she's ready. While Natalia's taking care of the locks, I'll start administering injections to the personnel we've found." And Rourke set off at a trot for the nearest of the stricken Nazis . . .

Annie felt uncomfortable sitting, still wearing the BDU pants climactic necessity had forced upon her. She stood up, pacing the elevator control booth. There were video surveillance monitors running constant pictures of the headquarters complex's ground-level exterior.

306

And there were similar views from above. Nothing but darkness and some stars. "You're into astronomy, Michael. What's that constellation? The one in the screen showing the north view."

Michael said something into the radio to Paul, then stood up and walked over to stand beside her at the bank of monitors. "What constellation, Sis?"

"That." And Annie pointed toward the upper right hand portion of the screen. But the shape of the constellation had already changed, and the stars within it seemed to have grown. Before Michael could speak, Annie whispered, "Holy smoke—is that—"

"Helicopters. And Trans-Global Alliance doesn't have helicopters in this theater of operation. Get on the radio and tell Paul we've got company coming in." Annie ran to the other side of the room, picked up the handset. Michael shouted at her. "Make it an ETA of about two minutes. They'll know there's something wrong. Shit!"

Annie pressed the push to talk button, saying, "Come in Paul. There's trouble. Do you read me?"

"What kind of trouble, sweetheart?"

"Helicopter squadron coming from the north." She looked over her shoulder. "How many, Michael?"

"Six, I think. Yeah—six. They gotta get outa there and down the elevators."

"Paul. Michael counts six helicopters coming in. They'll know there's something wrong. You

307

and Natalia and Daddy—get down here, right away. Over."

"Still working on finding Sarah and Wolf. Natalia's picking the locks. You get a transmission out to Commander Washington's SEAL force and tell 'em what's going on. Have Michael check and see if he can screw up the other elevator so the one we've got blocked is the only one that'll work. Let me know. Out."

Annie called to her brother. "You hear Paul?"

"I'm on my way," Michael was starting through the doorway and down the ladder.

Annie's eyes scanned the control panels. The controls were probably redundant with those up top. "Shit," she hissed through her teeth. She picked up the other handset and started contacting Commander Washington, but her eyes went to the north-pointing video monitor. The six helicopters were closing fast on the mountain-top landing pad . . .


Natalia had the locks, stood, calling out over her shoulder, "I've got the doors, John, Paul."

Paul was shouting something as he ran down the corridor toward her. "Trouble. Six choppers coming in up top. Have to be Nazi."

John was coming out of one of the patient rooms.

Natalia shrugged her shoulders, pushed her M-16 forward on its sling and took a step back. "We can't wait. Back me up, Paul." Natalia wheeled half right and snapped her left foot outward with all the force she could muster, kicking at the point where the two doors met. If anyone were standing behind them waiting, he'd be in for a headache.

The doors flung back as Natalia suggested, "I go right?"

"Fine," Paul responded, Natalia crossing from left to right as she went through the doorway, Paul right to left.

As she entered, she mule-kicked the door into the wall, in case someone might be standing behind it.

There was no one, at least no one awake.

At a simple desk about three meters inside the doorway, a guard lay slumped over his desk. Another man was propped up against the wall, moaning in delirium.

Paul crossed the foyer to the corridor beyond. There was a series of doors on either side, all of them secure. "Cells," Paul noted.

Natalia was already going through the desk, looking for entry cards as John ran in from the corridor beyond.

Natalia found entry cards in the center drawer of the desk, having to move the unconscious man in order to do so. "You and Paul check the cells. I'll take care of injecting these men."

She handed John the entry cards and he nodded and was gone.

Natalia shrugged out of the little day pack she wore, took a hypodermic from inside and set to work rolling up the man's left sleeve.

# Chapter Fifty-Two

Paul was filling him in on the radio transmission from Michael and Annie as they entered the third cell. This one, the door locked, seemed promising.

Beyond the door was what John Rourke sought, but for an instant he didn't move. Sarah lay half out of her bunk, so still she could have been dead, a bandage across her forehead, her face pale as death.

At the far edge of his peripheral vision, Rourke saw Wolfgang Mann, lying perfectly flat on his back.

Rourke crossed the room to his wife, telling Paul, "Check Wolfgang."

The cell was about the size of two large bathrooms. At the center of the back wall was an enclosure which Rourke assumed housed whatever bathroom facilities there were. Other than that and the two cots, the cell—extremely well lit—was bare.

Rourke dropped to his knees beside his wife's inert form, touching his hands to her neck and wrist. There was a pulse, but it was very faint.

"Wolfgang's alive," Paul called out.

"Sarah, too," Rourke told his friend. "Call Michael and Annie after you give Wolf the injection. Tell them everything's okay and we'll be starting down. Check the status on our visitors."

"Right," Paul answered.

John Rourke paused for a second as he prepared to give his wife the injection of vaccine. And he touched his lips to her cheek . . .

As best Annie could tell, judging from the fact that her brother was still working on the second elevator itself and judging by the systems diagram panel, Michael's attempt to disable the second elevator wasn't working. They could always use explosives, but if they damaged the first elevator, then it would be impossible for her father, her husband and Natalia to come back, impossible for them to get her mother and Wolfgang Mann to safety.

They were stuck. As the radio message came in from Paul, Annie said as much. "We've got six choppers on the landing pad up above. A communication just came through from the landing pad, demanding to know what was happening and why the personnel in the control booth and the control tower were unconscious or delirious. Over."

"You try warning them away because of a medical emergency? Over."

"I told them we thought it might be plague, but they either didn't buy it or didn't care—or maybe they were just too dumb to know they were in danger. The monitor for the landing pad area got shot out. I think they're coming all the way down. And Commander Washington's people are still a couple of minutes away at least. Get down here. Over."

"You and Michael get to a position of cover. I'll signal as soon as we're into the elevator, get us going, then get outa there and be ready to cover us. Love you. Be careful. Out."

She loved him, all of them.

"Michael! Get outa there. We've got to hurry!" Her right hand was poised over the elevator control, ready to bring them down the moment she got the signal . . .


John Rourke carried his wife in his arms. She moaned softly, her body trembling slightly in her delirium. The vaccine, when administered in time—there should have been at least a twenty-four hour margin of safety remaining—would prevent any permanent damage, if it behaved as it was supposed to. He hoped, he prayed, that he had not tragically miscalculated.

Wolfgang was slung over Paul's shoulder in a

fireman's carry. Natalia sprinted ahead of them, securing the area near the elevators.

Annie's voice was coming through on Paul's radio, the earpiece pulled so they all could hear. "As far as I can tell from the control panel, they've given up on trying to control your elevator, and—wait a minute—the second elevator is being activated. They can control that. Hope to God they can't override your elevator."

"Tell her to be ready and then get out of there, Annie and Michael both," John Rourke ordered.

Paul spoke into the handset. "We'll be in the elevator in about another thirty seconds. I'll give the signal, start us down and get out. Make sure those front gates are guarded. If whoever it is up top is smart, he'll send a couple of those choppers down to ground level. Stay with me."

They reached the elevator, Natalia flicking the chair out from between the doors, wedging the door open with her body. John Rourke stepped inside. Paul followed him, setting Wolfgang down on the floor in the corner farthest away from the other elevator shaft. John Rourke lay Sarah there, too, then crouched before them.

As Natalia jumped into the elevator, Paul shouted into the handset, "Bring us down and get to cover! Now, babes!"

The elevator doors slammed shut. There was a violent lurch and the car started downward. But, in the same instant, there was a roar from above them. The second car was moving in the shaft beside them.

There was a thudding sound on the roof of

313

their car, then another and another and the access door in the elevator's roof was thrown open and back. A man in SS winter camouflage jumped through.

Simultaneously, John Rourke, Natalia and Paul Rubenstein shot him dead and the man fell to the floor.

An object was thrown down through the opening, Rourke shouting, "Masks! Now!" Rourke let his rifle fall across his knees on its sling, tearing open the gas-mask bag at his left side, the elevator car already starting to fill with what he hoped was only tear gas. Rourke popped the seals at the cheeks of the mask as first one, then another, then another SS commando jumped down into the car. There was no time to shoot, Rourke vaulting up and hurling his body into the three men.

Rourke's left fist snapped outward, hammering into the face of the man nearest him. A knife flashed, sliced downward toward him. The butt of an M-16 blocked it, Paul stepping in, arcing the muzzle of his rifle down across the side of the man's face.

In the blur as Rourke was spun around and slammed into the wall by the other two SS men, Rourke spotted at least two more men, maybe three, coming down from the top of the car. Their commander had planned ahead well, ordering men onto the roof of the car, ordering them to be ready to jump if they encountered the second elevator car, then get inside and seize control.

Rourke's left fist slammed forward into the gut of the man nearest him, Rourke's right knee smashing upward into the man's crotch. As the man doubled forward, Rourke's right moved in a tight uppercut to the tip of the SS man's jaw and Rourke's body twisted left as he laced his left fist into the man's right temple.

A fist hammered toward Rourke and Rourke dodged his head, catching only a part of the blow's force, against his right ear.

There was a familiar—and very welcome— sound, a click-click-click, and Natalia was into the fray, her knife moving as though it had a will of its own, opening the carotid of one man, stabbing into the chest of another.

Two more SS commandos jumped down into the car. Rourke took a step forward, the man who'd struck him along the ear clinging to Rourke's right arm now. Rourke wheeled right, bracing himself against one opponent's body as he sidekicked into the right knee, then the abdomen of one of the new arrivals.

And Rourke felt his balance going, pulled down as two men swarmed over him.

Rourke's right knee smashed upward, finding flesh instead of bone, a rush of foul-smelling breath on Rourke's face, a scream of pain from the man he'd knee-smashed. Rourke's right hand caught hold of the other man, Rourke's thumb hooking in the left corner of the man's mouth, Rourke's fingers closing over the man's left ear. Rourke snapped his right arm outward, crashing the man's head into the elevator car's wall.

Paul's right foot flashed past Rourke, contacting the man—still on top of John Rourke—in the side of the head. The man rolled away. Rourke edged back. Paul's foot snapped out again, this time connecting at the SS man's right temple, the man's head cracking back into the wall.

Rourke was to his knees. The man whose head he had smashed into the wall had a knife. Rourke swung the butt of his rifle up, pivoting the sling on his shoulder, catching the man so hard at the base of the jaw that the gas mask the man wore was ripped away.

Rourke's left hand found the butt of one of the Detonics ScoreMasters and Rourke stabbed the pistol toward the man as he thumbed back the hammer, then fired point blank into the SS man's face.

Rourke was to his feet, back to the wall, a pistol in each hand now. And he fired, killing the man Paul had just thrown against the wall. Natalia's knife slashed across the throat of one man and, as she wheeled to finish a second man, Rourke fired both pistols, killing him.

Paul stood with his back to the doors, his submachine gun's bolt locking back. Natalia's rifle was on the floor, but one of the revolvers was in her left hand. A man started to dive down into the cloud of white fumes filling the elevator car, Rourke, Rubenstein and Natalia began opening fire simultaneously, his body falling limp, halfway through the opening.

In seconds, the elevator car would reach the ground, and only seconds after that the other car, in which more of the SS commandos would be waiting.

"Natalia? Can you take—"

"I can't carry Sarah and move as rapidly as you can. Paul, give me your M-16."

"All right," Rourke nodded. Cocked and locked—a carry he didn't particularly like—Rourke stuffed the two ScoreMasters into his belt, then swept Sarah up into his arms. She was coughing, eyes streaming tears.

Paul handed his rifle to Natalia and grabbed Wolfgang Mann's arms, hauling Mann, still unconscious, up into a standing position. Paul bent, catching Mann over his left shoulder, then raised to his full height. The German MP-40 submachine gun was back in Paul's right fist.

Rourke stood beside the doors, Paul behind him.

Natalia, one M-16 trained on the overhead, the other trained on the door, said, "You two run for it and I will be right behind you."

"Don't get killed on us," Paul cautioned.

"Why didn't I think of that?" she answered, smiling.

The elevator stopped.

The doors snapped open.

John Rourke went into a dead run the instant Natalia was out the doors, Paul Rubenstein right beside him.

Rourke was fewer than thirty feet from the

elevator when he heard the gunfire start, Natalia's M-16s on full auto firing in short, textbook-perfect three-round bursts.

From ahead of him, there was the sound of an explosion, then another and another. And small-arms fire, then, both cartridge and energy. Michael ran toward him, a pistol in his right hand. "I'll take Mom!"

Annie, an M-16 in her hands, dashed past, running back toward the elevators, to help Natalia.

Rourke handed off his wife to his son, then wheeled toward the elevators. Natalia, feet spread apart, perhaps twenty feet away from the elevator bank, fired out the last bursts from the M-16s in her hands, at least six men dead between her and the elevator door.

Annie's M-16 was opening up as Natalia drew her revolvers.

Running in a headlong assault through the open blast doors were another dozen of the SS commandos.

Rourke swung his HK-91 forward and fired. Paul, beside him, Wolfgang Mann over his shoulder still, started emptying the German MP-40 into their ranks.

Rourke's assault rifle empty, no time to change magazines, he let the weapon drop to his side on its sling and broke the two Detonics miniguns from their double shoulder rig, thumbs sweeping back the hammers.

Paul's submachine gun was still firing.

318

Kneeling beside them, his body shielding his mother, Michael kept his .44 Magnum revolver booming again and again.

The Nazi commandos were still coming.

Rourke had no choice but to advance, take the action away from his wife. His pistols at shoulder level, firing, Rourke marched forward, killing, shooting one of the SS men in the face, another in the thorax, still another in the chest.

As a man wheeled the muzzle of his assault rifle toward him, Rourke shot the man in the left eye.

Firing, killing, both pistols empty. Rourke smashed the butt of the gun in his right hand across the forehead of one of the commandos.

Slides locked back, Rourke stuffed the twin stainless Detonics miniguns into his belt, drawing the partially spent ScoreMasters.

As he got ready to fire, there was another explosion from beyond the blast doors, and through the inrushing smoke ran gas-masked Navy SEALs. Rourke heard Commander Washington shouting, "Hold your fire! Hold your fire!"

John Thomas Rourke held his fire, belting one of the pistols only.

He tore the mask from his face, blinked, looked around him.

Paul stood beside him, smoke still trailing from the muzzle of his submachine-gun, Wolfgang Mann still over his shoulder. Rourke looked back toward the elevator bank. Natalia leaned on Annie as the two of them walked over toward him. Natalia called out, "It's not even a bleeder, but it hurts!" and she gestured toward her left thigh.

Rourke looked at his son.

Michael, cradling his mother in his arms, looked back. He said, "Mom's gonna be okay."

John Rourke exhaled, closed his eyes and prayed that his son was right.

Rourke opened his eyes, stood there, as Commander Washington's SEAL personnel came swarming through the opening now, German Long Range Mountain Patrol Commandos with them.

Rourke walked over to stand beside his son and his wife, then dropped to one knee. Sarah's eyelids fluttered and opened. She looked up at him.

"John?"

There was nothing John Rourke could say, but he bowed his head and touched his lips to her cheek.

GREAT BOOKS

E-BOOKS

AUDIOBOOKS

& MORE

Visit us today

www.speakingvolumes.us

www.ingramcontent.com/pod-product-compliance
Lightning Source LLC
Chambersburg PA
CBHW050554260626
47157CB00002B/561